DEADLY BLACK PEARLS

JONNI RICH

Deadly Black Pearls

Copyright © 2020 by Jonni Rich.

ISBN 10: 1888141-38-7
ISBN 13: 978-1-888141-38-2

Published by:
Southeast Media Productions
Carlisle, PA
U.S.A.
www.semediapro.com

CHAPTER 1

South Pacific Ocean
International Waters

The Zephyr, the thirty-eight-foot sailing yacht Carol Powell and her father, Charlie Powell, co-owned, plowed through heavy seas. The Zephyr no longer followed the trade wind's path. Sailing outside national jurisdiction upon the high seas under the flag-state—United States of America, she chugged ahead, her engines struggling.

Waves city blocks high sprayed Carol, now aboveboard, anxious and worried. How would this terrifying trip end?

Carol's fiancé, Gary West, a questionable navigator, insisted on remaining in charge. She had more sailing experience. He refused listening to her. She'd fallen in love with his assertiveness. Now he appeared stubborn, not assertive. Perhaps not stubborn, but driven. Driven by what? She wondered for the hundredth time.

Leaving Marina Del Ray, they'd headed for Maui and Maalaea Bay as planned. She and her father, Charlie, had sailed to Maui many times. Charlie questioned Gary's sailing ability, since his daughter and her fiancé would sail alone. Gary, the handsome surfer she loved, owned several trinket shops along the Marina Del Ray beach. He surfed with the best of them. His sailing time limited, at best.

She brushed seawater from her brow. *Stay calm. Don't panic. There are only the two of us aboard. We must depend on each other.*

She quickly learned - after leaving Marina Del Ray - Gary wasn't the navigator and sailor he'd led her to believe. Her dad warned her. Her father had been right. Blame the stars in her eyes.

They had radio trouble. Gary claimed the Marine VHF fixed set, voice-only radio failed—she believed differently. Nor was she allowed access to the radio. "I don't need you tinkering with it." Said before a full-blown tantrum. "Please Carol, trust me."

She mustn't allow Gary to sense her growing suspicions. She must keep up the girlfriend-boyfriend relationship, which now seemed more a charade.

She stood—her sea legs wobbly. The greasy bacon Gary prepared for breakfast threatened to spill. Why was she seasick? This wasn't her first rodeo. Had Gary put something into her food? His obsessive reliance on herbs and questionable supplements troubled her.

She dropped down on the foredeck's green Naugahyde® cushion—quickly looking away from the its muddy green—the color of sludge made her dizzier.

She should've suspected something the moment they reached Hawaii. Instead of sailing on to Maui and into Maalaea Bay as they'd planned, Gary had insisted on Oahu Island, and continuing down the coast before stopping at Pokai Bay just south of the big surfing park at Mahaka Beach.

The moment the Zephyr slid into a slip; Gary went ashore, vague about the exact time he'd return.

She stayed onboard to prepare lunch. As the afternoon wore on, she realized Gary wasn't coming—not in time for lunch, anyway. She ate alone—coconut shrimp—huge West Coast prawns. The expensive shrimp blew a big hole in their food budget. Nothing was too good for her man—her mantra back in Marina Del Ray when she had stowed food into the boat's freezers.

Late that afternoon, she walked ashore to the marina hotel. From the hotel lobby, she put in a call to her dad. Her father planned an extended trip on his Harley. He often took to the road on his bike when she was away. No answer on his landline or his cellular. She sent a satellite telegram telling him her location since it differed from their original itinerary. Her heart jarred as she typed, *everything fine. Beautiful weather. See you soon.*

Leaving the hotel, she wandered through the open-air markets. She bought fruit, mangos, kiwi, and thin-skinned oranges. Ukulele music sounded nearby, accompanied by streams of laughter. A private luau. A party. Peeved with Gary, she sat on a park bench and listened to the music for the longest time.

As breezy twilight filtered through the palm trees, she returned to the Zephyr. Onboard, she changed into shorts and a halter. Gary arrived a half-hour later. His goofy expression didn't fool her. She knew he'd had a hit. He was the one with the problem. He'd promised, no drugs on this trip. So much for promises. "Sorry I'm late, sweetheart. Couldn't be helped. Met some guys I know. Couldn't believe it. Who'd-a thought it, way out here?"

"Yeah, who?" Her voice sounded strained and anxious in her own ears, wishing she'd never sailed on this trip,

"You don't have to get testy about it," he scolded. It didn't get better after that.

The nausea again. Carol closed her eyes until it passed.

If she'd stood her ground at Mahaka Beach, called him out for changing their plans, none of what happened later would've occurred.

The next morning, he dropped the bombshell. 'We're not going on to Maui,' he said flatly.

Shocked, she cried. "Not stopping in Maalaea Bay like we planned?"

"That's right. Those friends. We're meeting them in Majuro."

"The Marshall Islands? I don't understand." The Marshall Islands, a country in Oceania, consisted of a string of volcanic and coral reef islands between Hawaii and the Philippines.

"A business deal, baby," continued Gary. "These guys have tons of merchandise I can use in my stores. At a price I can't resist," he added, gloating.

Gary's shops in Marina Del Ray carried surfboards, diving equipment and tourist trinkets.

Gary spread his hands. "Baby, if we get in trouble, you're a pro at this sailing rig."

"I've only assisted Dad navigating this far out," she reasoned. "You don't know the Pacific as I do. It can be treacherous."

"How about we think about it." He slipped his arm around her, drawing her close. He kissed the side of her face. Gary became the Gary she fell in love with. Later, after they made love, he took her dancing on the island. Leaving the little nightclub, they made love again on the Zephyr deck beneath the stars.

She fell asleep toward dawn. When she woke, they were in the open sea, many kilometers from Pokai Bay. He'd set sail to the Marshalls without further discussion. She stormed below. Gary was operating the radio.

"I thought the radio isn't working."

"Come on, don't look so glum. Give me a kiss."

She offered her cheek woodenly for his peck.

"Good thing the radio kicked in. Looks like Papeete___"

He clammed. From that moment on, he never left her alone with the radio. He spent hours tinkering with it.

They reached the Marshalls without mishap, pulling into port at Majuro mid-afternoon alongside a shabby ketch. Dozens of other sleek, expensive boats bobbed in port.

They went ashore. Gary rented a car, and they drove along the lagoon. *Beautiful,* she mused, the blue-sky overhead, puffy white clouds, and palm trees swaying in the breezes. She'd forgotten the beauty of this place. They visited a supermarket, a welcome sight. They bought a few snacks. Gary insisted on waiting until they left Majuro before restocking the Zephyr's pantry. Made sense to her. Later that night, they went to one of the island's few nightclubs and watched native dancers perform. A magical night, the island as bright as day under the tropical moon and Gary at his most charming.

At sea again, he sailed to The Islands of Tahiti, the islands of French Polynesia. The islands lay south of the equator sparkling and humid. Tahiti - she'd sailed there with her father on charter trips many times.

"What about the men you were to meet?" she'd asked, confused, "- in Majuro?"

"Stop bring a worrywart. I told you they'd be here."

Shortly after arriving, three rough looking men on the catamaran beside them hailed Gary.

Were these the men with the merchandise he wanted so badly?

"I've gotta haggle with these guys," he explained. "When I haggle, I'm not a nice guy." He motioned the men aboard the Zephyr.

She went below—tried the radio. Dead. Voices rose and fell topside. The on-deck haggling went on for a very long time. She started forward, eased up the hatch nearest Gary and listened from the stairs. Dark now, the moonlight aided her vision. Gary stood, his back to her, his arms crossed over his upper body. He didn't appear happy.

"You got the money," demanded the taller of the men.

Gary passed a duffel bag to him. She gasped as the man unzipped the bag and thumbed through bound packs of cash. Where had Gary obtained that much money—Gary, a small-time souvenir shop owner?

Apparently satisfied with the transaction, the man handed Gary a small bag with a drawstring top. Gary opened the bag. He appeared satisfied, as well. Souvenirs, she puzzled. Merchandise for his little shops? Not hardly.

The men left the Zephyr. A short time later, under the dark of night, the catamaran took the middle of the night wind and sailed out of the lagoon toward open sea. Gary stood on deck a long time, watching it sail away.

Carol waited on the metal steps too alarmed to move. Gary took a penknife from his windbreaker pocket and slit the underside of one of the foredeck's cushions. He stuffed the bag inside the slit in the cushion and turned the cushion over. He started toward the hatch. She hurried to the galley, trembling, as his footsteps clattered downward. She decided to hit him head-on with questions. Offense being the better defense. "What did those guys want?"

He grinned. "I bought some stuff for the shop."

"What stuff? Where is it?"

"I'll pick it up later. Don't worry."

Only, she did worry. However, the next morning her worries centered on other more desperate matters—the Zephyr's engine. Instead of sounding sluggish, the engine sputtered, and kept dying, the scent of wasted fuel polluting the air.

Gary cursed and kicked the wall. Hurrying topside, she left him with his temper tantrum. A short time later, he joined her. "I'm sorry I lost my temper," he pled. "Do you mind staying onboard while I go ashore and try to find some parts for the motor?"

She agreed. She worried he'd bought drugs from the men. Once he was gone, she turned the cushion over to see what he'd hidden there. She reached inside the slit cushion and retrieved a gray leather bag. Inside, lay the most beautiful pearls she'd ever seen, pearls as magnificent as those she and her dad often viewed in Tahiti at the Pearl Museum. Stolen! No one had to tell her these were stolen. She knew that without a doubt. She slipped the bag into her pocket. Somewhere in the back of her mind, that part of the brain that acts on instinct apart from logic, she wanted to keep Gary out of trouble. If he didn't have the pearls, he couldn't be accused of stealing them. Crazy reasoning, but she wasn't thinking clearly.

He returned later with some parts and a native man who claimed to be a boat mechanic. They tried to get the engine going. No luck.

She went below to the icebox and pulled out sandwich makings. "Let's go topside and eat," she suggested. "Let the guy work with the motor."

He shrugged, wiping his grease-covered hands along his denim cut-offs. "Sure, why not."

The following day, the motor still refused to start. It appeared they needed parts that had to be ordered, which meant a longer stay on the island. What if Gary got antsy about the pearls and decided to look at them? She couldn't risk that. She formed a hasty plan. "I've been thinking," she said. "Why don't I fly to New Orleans. I'm overdue to visit my grandmother." Too, she knew her father may likely ride the Harley to New Orleans. "Once you get the boat repaired, sail there. I'll meet you."

"Not a bad idea, Carol," agreed Gary at once. He seemed eager to be rid of her.

"My grandmother could be in Ville Nouvelle, a little town farther north along the Mississippi River," she added, aware of her grandmother's eccentric lifestyle. "Quaint as anything. Grandmother grew up there. There's a woman in Ville Nouvelle, Emmaline Beard. She'll know how to get in touch with me and grandmother."

Deadly Black Pearls

CHAPTER 2

Beard House, Ville Nouvelle, Louisiana

The Beard Mansion doorbell, Westminster chimes in the Key of E major, sounded at 6:50 a.m.—an unprecedented occurrence. No one in Ville Nouvelle, Louisiana rang that doorbell. No one used the massive Beard front door, period.

"Who on earth!" exclaimed Emmaline Beard sitting at the broad kitchen table, her hair in curlers, drinking her first cup of coffee of the morning. Maizie White, her housekeeper/companion stood at the sink. Both women were acutely aware that Beard mansion now stood in a changing neighborhood. The melodic chimes again. They exchanged anxious glances.

Maizie wiped her hands down the front of her apron. "Think it's a prankster?"

"Go armed," urged Emmaline.

Maizie grabbed the baseball bat behind the kitchen door—not that either woman had ever had occasion to use the bat—but it waited, in case. Emmaline followed Maizie along the hall as far as the dining room. She slipped inside the dining room door, leaving the door cracked enough for her to both hear and glimpse whoever stood outside. A young man stood on the threshold. A stranger oddly dressed, this blustery February morning. He wore white cutoffs and a vee-neck sleeveless tee-shirt. "Does Emmaline Beard live here?"

"Who wants to know?" asked Maizie.

"I'm Gary West. Tell her it's about Carol Powell, her niece … uh…. friend. It's a matter of life and death."

Maizie hesitated. "Uh... er, come in, I guess. Wait in here." Maizie directed the man across the hall to the library.

"Psst! Psst!" Emmaline gestured Maizie into the dining room. "Niece! I have no niece."

"I know that. But he said friend, too. And if it's life and death-"

"What's life and death?"

"I don't know," Maizie said, beginning to lose her starch.

"Carol Powell," Emmaline mused aloud.

"Carol Powell," Maizie repeated. "He said it was about her. Who's Carol Powell?"

"She's not my niece," Emmaline declared for the second time. However, the name Carol Powell rang a distant bell.

"Did you see his ponytail?"

"Yes, I saw the ponytail." It came to Emmaline then. Carol Powell was the granddaughter of an old friend, Josephine Powell. Josephine grew up in the parish years ago. Hadn't heard from her in ages. "I don't like this," Emmaline said.

"It's cold as the dickens in the library with them vents off." Maizie shuddered.

Emmaline cinched her velour robe closer. "I can't heat every room in this mausoleum." She raked her hand through her hair, forgetting she'd not removed the row of brush rollers. "A cold room is good enough for a stranger."

"You could slip through that secret door there by the fireplace and scare the stuffing out of him."

Papa Beard, Emmaline's eccentric father had secret passages and panels throughout the mansion. "And, the point would be-. Really, Maizie, you amaze me at times." Emmaline started across the hall to the library to learn what the stranger wanted. "Wait in the hall with the bat." She eased the library door open. The young man stood, his back to the door, peering out the huge windows onto the spacious lawns. He was of middle height, powerfully built, very muscular and deeply tanned. "You wished to see me?" she said, her voice gravelly and harsh.

He turned, advancing toward her hurriedly. She stepped back. Obviously, the boor didn't respect personal space.

"Are you Miss Beard?" His voice carried a note of panic.

"I'm Emmaline Beard." She spoke loudly for Maizie to hear - Maizie wielding the baseball bat.

"What a relief. It's about Carol." He looked around nervously. "Is she here? Please, tell me she's here. If anything went wrong, I'll kill myself."

Weirdo, Emmaline thought, not wearing enough clothes on a cold February morning, plus a West Coast accent, plus the dramatic killing himself statement. "I have no idea what you're talking about." She spoke overloud, "Who is Carol?"

He blinked. Then his words tumbled out in a torrent. "Carol Powell, Josephine Powell's granddaughter. She said if I missed her in New Orleans, I was to meet her here. She said to ask for Emmaline Beard. That you'd know-" His voice trailed - he smiled - showcasing a mouth-full of square, white teeth, brilliant against his deep tan. "I'm Gary West, Carol's fiancé." He shook his head in exasperation, the ponytail swinging. "I don't know where to start."

"Try the beginning," Emmaline said impatiently, her feet growing colder in her flimsy slippers. "Make it quick; I have an early appointment."

She hadn't the time this morning for distractions, unexpected or otherwise - today being the first day of the antebellum mansions' spring tour, and she, the hostess at LeFevre House."

His smiled again. Those teeth. "The beginning. Yeah, the beginning. We were sailing from the West Coast when our boat developed engine problems. Caught us in the middle of nowhere in the South Seas. Our radio went out.'

"Caught who in the middle of the South Sea?"

"Carol and me. We were sailing alone."

Emmaline dimly recalled hearing Carol and her father lived somewhere in southern California. Some bayside town. "Go on."

"Uh… We made it to Tahiti. I had to wait for engine parts I'd ordered. We decided Carol should fly to New Orleans to her grandmother's."

"That would be Josephine Powell," Emmaline interjected, some of his narrative making sense.

"Yes, yes. Josephine Powell. That's her. Only she wasn't home. The housekeeper didn't know where she'd gone or when she'd return. Carol had told me to come here. You'd know how to reach her and her grandmother." West paused, took a ragged breath, then continued. "The repairs took forever." He gestured helplessly.

Emmaline had never heard directly from Carol Powell in the girl's life. As a child Carol often visited Ville Nouvelle with her grandmother, Josephine. Her connection to Josephine, the odd Christmas card now and again. "I don't hear from Josephine regularly. I have no idea of either Carol or Josephine's whereabouts."

Gary West's expression crumbled. "I'm way too long getting into port. I had trouble finding you."

"I'm sorry for your dilemma," Emmaline said truthfully. "I suggest you go to the sheriff's department here in town and tell them your story. Sheriff Smith will put out an all-points for Carol. Now, if you'll excuse me-"

"I rushed up here," he blurted, all but clutching the front of Emmaline's robe. "I don't blame Carol if she's mad at me."

"I really can't help you. I wouldn't know where to start. Now, if you'll -"

He danced up on his toes. "Is it okay if I check back with you? I've gotta find Carol."

Emmaline suddenly didn't like this ill-dressed, frantic young man. "Of course, you may call me. Though I feel it will do you no good."

He ducked his head crestfallen. "Okay. Yes ma'am. I apologize for disturbing you. It's just Carol told me to ask for you." Grasping Emmaline's hand impulsively, he pumped it. "I'll see myself out." Pivoting, he rushed to the

14

door, the ponytail flipping from side to side. Wheeling back, his hand on the doorknob, he said over his broad shoulder. "I'll check back with you." He plunged out into the nippy February morning.

Maizie slipped from behind the potted palm where she waited with the baseball bat. She locked the door. "Ain't that the weirdest thing?" she said, cinching the deadbolt.

"For sure."

"He ain't nobody from around here. Could tell by the way he talked."

Emmaline shrugged. "I can't help him, regardless of what he thinks Carol Powell led him to believe."

"Ain't that the truth! You gotta get over to LeFevre House. You need any help gettin' in that costume rig?"

"I can manage."

"This ain't gettin' my kitchen work done, either." Maizie pattered down the hall.

* * *

Upstairs, Emmaline shucked off the warm robe and wriggled into the antebellum linen shift lying across the bed. The undergarment felt like ice against her skin. She wrapped the front-laced corset around her ample middle, spewing a few choice words as she attempted hooking the corset. Out of breath, she tackled the petticoats next, three of them, and at last, the green silk gown. She nixed the voluminous wig this morning and instead stuck on a perky velvet bonnet.

Outside, the bristling cold wind hit her on the way to the garage. She backed the Coupe de Ville out and waited for traffic to ease along her narrow street. Normally this section of Ville Nouvelle saw little traffic. Not this morning, however, nor any morning during the past week. Not with Dante Washington, the famous actor/comedian, in town organizing a protest march - the federal government was attempting to locate a nuclear waste dump along the Mississippi River. Ville Nouvelle citizenry were up in arms.

Dante Washington was a native of Ville Nouvelle. His parents lived in the area. Dante came from Hollywood to protest the proposed nuclear dump location. His stellar presence amped up scores of protesters flooding into the once-sleepy, little town.

Emmaline punched the car horn at a beer truck, while shooting out in front of the truck. The driver grimaced and spouted a few choice words. Men were so rude these days.

She drove on to LeFevre House, the mansion which once belonged to distant relatives on Emmaline's mother's side of the family.

She prayed for a decent first tour day. Ticket sales had virtually trickled in. Blame the bad economy. As the last heir, she'd donated the great house to the local historical society to avoid taxes and upkeep. The deal hit an official snag when the property on which the house stood was deemed to belong permanently to LeFevre heirs. Only the house itself could be donated. She could thank slick Baton Rouge lawyers for preserving her interest in the property. She could also thank them for her encumbrance in sharing part of the upkeep expense.

She couldn't blame them for her father's final marriage and divorce from the Houston woman. The divorce had practically put Emmaline and her father in the poor house. He'd sold some mineral rights to settle the greedy divorcee.

To defray her part of LeFevre House expenses, Emmaline held a theatrical each year after the antebellum house tour ended to supplement her coffers. Being the only theatrical maven in Ville Nouvelle and surrounding areas had its perks, extra money, and assurance LeFevre House wouldn't rot down to the land it rested upon - the land she owned.

She braked at a red light. Her next birthday, her fifty-fourth, troubled her. How long could a person keep on keeping on? I'm the oldest virgin in Louisiana, she thought.

The light changed. She drove on to South Dock Street, giving her time to wonder about the odd man seeking Carol Powell. In the maybe five or six minutes in his presence, he struck her as desperate. She'd also lodged a dislike for him. Not a charitable impression since he'd claimed engine trouble in open seas and separation from his fiancée.

Her cell phone pinged. Byrd Jeffcoat, her Houston scientist friend. A friend from childhood. A little shiver of excitement trailed up her spine as she yanked off the bonnet in order to press the phone closer to her ear. "Hello."

She pictured him in his Houston lab, starched white lab coat, curly, red hair, cut close—bustling and brawny—an honest-to-God morning person. "Great to hear from you - you're coming to Ville Nouvelle, aren't you?"

Byrd, a staunch supporter of his old hometown, visited every year during the antebellum mansion tour. He attended her theatrical and often stayed over for the local horse race.

"Couple days, three max." He made a sound in his throat like a half-laugh. "You know how Vi is when I'm away." Violet Causey, Byrd's only sibling and next-door neighbor, depended on him for emotional support after her husband's death, and any other need that crossed her scattered brain.

"Good. I'm looking forward to seeing you."

"What're you up to this morning?"

"First day of the spring tour. On my way to LeFevre House."

"Zero hour, huh? Good luck with the first day."

"I need all the luck I can get," she groused. "Worst ticket sales in years. So much for mail-out solicitations. We need a new publicist." Notes loomed on the business loan she'd secured for needed upgrades. Thus far, she nor the historical society qualified for a grant.

"Awwwh, the tour buses will roll in," he said cheerfully. "They always do. You said this year's theatrical is a Jack-the-Ripper play—that'll bring them in."

"It's a real thriller," she said. "Called *On Whitechapel Road*. Only, it's Jack-the-Ripper with an extra twist. I can't tell you who - I mean what. I promised someone. Good stuff, too."

"Betty is buzzing me." Betty, Byrd's long-time secretary, was an impatient woman. "See you when I get there." He punched off.

She banged the steering wheel with her flat palm. Byrd, Byrd, Byrd. If the stars had been properly aligned, they'd be a married couple now with married kids, and a couple of grandkids. Instead, the stars played havoc with them. After high school, Byrd's family had moved to Houston. He'd attended Rice University, and she, LSU Baton Rouge. He'd fallen in love with Sherry something or other. The young woman had died as the result of a car accident. She'd encountered car trouble on a lonely country road, exited her vehicle to inspect the source of the trouble when an eighteen-wheeler, rounding a sharp curve, struck her. She'd lived in a vegetative state for several years with the faithful Byrd at her side. How long could one man grieve? How long did loyalty to the dead continue? She refused to allow herself to believe *forever*.

The light changed. She turned the corner from South Dock onto Camellia Lane, the side street with the back entrance to LeFevre House. Parking and cutting the engine, she shifted the cumbersome hoops and petticoats to exit the car. A chilling breeze propelled her up the brick walkway to the house.

Once inside, she switched off the alarm system and minced down the hall to reset the thermostat, her high-top, button-boots clicking on the cypress flooring. LeFevre House, in its day the epitome of South Louisiana grandeur, wasn't particularly grand this frosty morning. Cold as a tomb.

As the gush of warm air swooshed through the vents, Emmaline, hoop skirts swinging, hurried to the staff's mini kitchen, located in a back section off the original butler's pantry. This section was off limits to the public. The white tile floor and stainless-steel appliances anything but eighteenth-century decor. She filled the coffeepot and set it to brew. Checking the fridge for the sandwiches Maizie brought the day before for staff, she found everything in place.

While the coffee brewed, she munched on a pimento-cheese sandwich and gazed out the side window to the gift shop and ticket booth - two white, clapboard buildings with deep green shutters. At that moment, Tom, the maintenance man and ticket booth employee, pulled onto the asphalt in his red Toyota Corolla. He spotted her at the window and waved. She gave him a thumbs up. The ticket booth's red *open* sign flicked on.

Coffee in hand, Emmaline made her way to the foyer. She opened the guest book on the carved mahogany credenza to the proper page and fished a white, feather-plumed pen from the credenza drawer. The pen, a cheap variety, often went missing.

The front door opened. Esther Marshall, her assistant, bustled into the hall, bronze taffeta skirts crackling. Esther, a forty something woman with stylish, red-tinted hair, square jaws, and dark eyes, rubbed her palms together. "Can you believe how cold it is this morning?" Not waiting for Emmaline's response, take-charge Esther started toward the mini kitchen. Emmaline trailed. "Coffee smells fantastic," Esther said. "I'll take a cup out to Tom?" Esther pulled down a large stainless-steel cup from the cabinet over the tiny sink, filled it with coffee, topping it with cream and sugar. "A tour bus followed me over the river bridge," she said. "They're on their way here."

"We can only pray." Emmaline, out of sorts and not optimistic, sniffed. Maybe her miserable mood related to the odd visit from the man claiming to be Carol Powell's fiancé. Or not. Maybe something she couldn't put her finger on. *I'm a paranoid old woman now,* she thought. *I don't want to be fifty-four. And single.*

Esther tugged her jacket closer. "The tour bus is here," she said excitedly, peering out the window. "Tourists are filing out and lining up. Looks like a real crowd. I'll run this coffee out to Tom. Back in a jiff."

Tom had his own coffee pot. Esther would flirt with a signpost. Emmaline checked the lectern, the old-fashioned stand with deep recessed shelves like a pulpit from bygone days, behind which she stood to give the house history. Her notes were there. Of course, she didn't need notes. She knew the house history by heart. She'd even improvised and re-written some of it.

Esther burst back inside. "Tom said over fifty tourists."

"Great!" Emmaline mentally computed sightseers to dollars. "We'll take fifteen people the first and second run, third and last group, twelve people each, unless some don't wish to be separated."

"We could have stragglers," Esther said. "Walk-ins."

"True. Not usually on the first day, though." God forbid there were small children, especially little boys with screwdrivers for fingers plundering among the antiques.

Usually, tour bus patrons purchased tickets through travel agents or online. However, not many this year. She blamed the unsettled economy.

At the stroke of ten, Tom punched tickets and directed guests to the house. Esther scurried to the front door. Competent woman, Esther. Somewhat pushy and brassy, but pleasant enough, directing patrons to the guest register, then leading them to the drawing room where Emmaline gave the house history. After the history, Emmaline led the visitors through the downstairs rooms. Then Esther shepherded the group outside across the wide back gallery to the cemetery, next on to the gift shop where Idabelle Beard, Emmaline's distant cousin, watched with hawk's eyes for sticky fingers and pushed as much Louisiana memorabilia as possible. Idabelle worked on commission.

Emmaline made her way to the lectern while the tourists lined up on the gallery. Minutes passed, her foreboding mood deepening. Her gynecologist had warned her about change of life, like hot flashes and mood swings. Lightheaded, she grabbed the lectern. Would she faint? She'd never fainted in her life. "Esther."

Esther poked her head around the door. "What is it?"

"I'm not feeling my best." Fresh air should help. "Take the first group and give the lecture. You know the house history as well as I do." She felt as if she'd suffocate if she didn't get outside into fresh air. "Take them through the house and I'll…"

Surprised, Esther's large dark eyes widened. "You're sick? Oh, my gosh! Don't worry. I'll take care of everything." Esther hurried to unlock the front door to the excited group of strangers while Emmaline fled down the hall to the back gallery. "And, don't let the plumed pens go walking," she hissed in a whisper. "Remember, no one goes upstairs."

"I know the rules," Esther lip-synched. The arriving tourists sounded like a tree full of chattering blue jays as Esther opened the door.

Emmaline hurried around the gallery to the section where the old porch made an ell facing Camellia Lane the side street. Esther's thick drawl came through the long windows. Out of sight, Emmaline could hear what was going on inside.

"Though LeFevre House is listed with our local historical society, it remains a private residence, as well." Esther intoned. "Miss Emmaline Beard, a direct descendant of the LeFevres, owns part of the property. She has refurbished the house. It's a labor of love for her," gushed Esther. "The house presently has twenty-eight rooms. Most furnishings are original to the house and were ordered from Europe, arriving upriver by boat from New Orleans.

"Here in the first glass case, you see Pierre LeFevre's original land grant from the king of France. Also, Pierre and Adelaide's marriage license in French, along with the gorgeous diamond ring and necklace he presented Adelaide on their wedding day. You'll notice," Esther said, "the diamond is a cabochon cut, popular at that time. It's a deep solitaire stone of over four carats, though not as wide and showy as faceted diamonds are cut today. The pendant is over twenty carats in smaller - but brilliant - stones."

Emmaline, feeling somewhat better, smirked. The diamonds in the glass case were paste - fakes - but skillful fakes. Esther continued. "These papers in the next showcase are notices for Ville Nouvelle citizens to build up the levees along their property. The individual colonists were responsible for levee upkeep and were heavily taxed if they didn't comply. Flooding was commonplace in those early days and detrimental to everyone, not just those with valuable crops."

Emmaline knew the next showcase held Native American memorabilia. ". . . The beautiful feather headdress you see in the smaller case is Red Shoe's, a Choctow chieftain, a wily cunning character."

The dining room next. Esther didn't disappoint. "Ladies and gentlemen, you're in sugar cane country where meals in those long-ago days were social events attended by family, extended family, and guests. The table is set as it was in Pierre and Adelaide's day. The china and silver you see displayed is the private property of Miss Emmaline Beard."

Muffled words from one of the tourists.

"No, you may not handle the china, it's very fragile and irreplaceable."

What foolish people, Emmaline thought. Why did they think the table was cordoned off with red velvet ropes? There was no accounting for gauche persons.

A white van circled Camellia Lane and stopped. Oh, no! Emmaline forgot she'd given permission to Reverend Nairn Lemuel from Lemuel's Boarding School for Troubled Youth, to bring a group of boys on the tour for a shot of culture. Only, she hadn't meant today—the first tour day.

Emmaline believed in supporting youths who'd tripped over some of society's rules and were young enough to rehabilitate as future, good citizens. Even Dante Washington, the famous comedian/actor, graduated from Pastor Lemuel's facility. Pastor stopped the van in front of the ticket booth house. Good - Tom would hold the boys at bay until the paying public went through the house.

The morning warmed. She lingered on the gallery out of sight as the sun rose higher in the bright blue sky. She should go inside and lower the thermostat. A penny saved was a penny earned. Too awkward to trail through the groups with Esther directing them. Emmaline braced herself against the old wood under the overhanging, upper gallery.

She thought about her play, *On Whitechapel Road*. It needed a great deal of work yet. Kimberley, the local sheriff's secretary, Emmaline's friend, and one of her most talented actresses, had stumbled over lines during the last rehearsal. As was her practice, Emmaline waited until the last minute to assign permanent parts to her slate of amateur actors. She knew they hated that. The small troupe never knew which role would fall to them. Thus, they learned every role. At each rehearsal, she had them read different parts until she decided who was best for what. This practice made them understand the production in a way they otherwise wouldn't, and covered bases if one or the other had to drop out at the last minute.

The one exception, Sheriff Rodney Smith, handsome and personable, always played the lead. He did a great job, ham that he was. He drew many patrons to the theatrical. Especially women. He'd grown quite proud of his leading man status. Too, his beautiful baritone singing voice never failed to cause a stir among the ladies. A true hunk who reveled in his hunkiness. Emmaline, uncomfortable in the tight costume, took an anxious breath. The costumes weren't ready, nor the scenery. Pastor Lemuel's boys painted the scenery. They hadn't finished. Three weeks max and then the theatrical. After that, the horse race.

Horse racing dominated Ville Nouvelle's sporting blood. The larger farms owned and sponsored their contenders. Competition ran deep. Ville Nouvelle enjoyed a lively spring.

Emmaline pressed nearer the wall as Esther led the first group of tourists out to the cemetery. She should go inside. However, Esther always locked the front door, keeping the next group of sightseers waiting on the front gallery until the first group were in the gift shop.

Too, it was pleasant if nippy outside, the garden resplendent with early jonquils and perky, colorful tulips. The row of tall camellias, early bloomers, paraded their lovely white, pink, and blood-red blossoms to perfection. Waxy broad leaves on the towering Magnolia trees glistened in the sun. Already, spring grass pushed up through brown patches of lawn.

Dozens of recently cleaned and painted birdhouses hung from the trees. Darting cardinals flashed brilliant red streaks through the greenery. She gazed beyond the garden to the back of the property, where a weathered board fence separated the mansion lawns from a local walking trail called the Black Path. The Black Path attracted walkers, joggers, and anyone enjoying the stands of ancient trees along the winding way that stretched for miles.

She turned to go inside, when approaching footsteps slapped the brick walkway beside the house. Someone running. Emmaline frowned as a young woman charged into view. The petite woman saw her and bounded onto the gallery. "Are you Miss Beard?"

"Yes, I'm Emmaline Beard."

"Thank God."

CHAPTER 3

The girl, blond, twentyish, dressed in ill-fitting white slacks and a pink tee, came abreast of Emmaline. She thrust a package the size of a paperback book, wrapped in brown paper, into Emmaline's hands. "I'm Carol Powell. This package is for my grandmother, Josephine Powell. She'll know what to do. Please let no one else have it. Tell her I'll be in touch." The girl paused, out of breath. Before Emmaline could respond the young woman whispered. "She mustn't try to find me. It's too dangerous. You will promise, won't you?" The girl thumped the package with her trembling index finger as she suppressed a cry. "No one else must have it."

"I don't know when I'll see Josephine," Emmaline began uncertainly.

"Please, I can't trust anyone else."

"Your fiancé was at my house this morning asking for you."

"No!" shrieked the girl.

"But -"

Before Emmaline could say more, the girl bolted toward the back gate, lifted the latch, and ran out into the street. Emmaline, encumbered by the heavy skirts and petticoats, followed. By the time she puffed to the gate, the street lay empty in both directions.

* * *

Once genteel, the Earlington Hotel in Hot Springs, Arkansas had gone to seed - but managed a faded dignity, and still catered to some of its original clientele who remembered the old days with white-gloved doormen, and red-coated waiters in the formal dining rooms. Josephine Powell, such a patron, sat at the window in her fourth-floor room, sipping root beer from a paper cup.

Not much to see now from the window except a few spindly pine trees surrounding the parking lot, and patches of grass punching through cracks in the concrete. A disgrace. Josephine remembered the hotel in its prime as society's crème de la crème when she and her deceased husband, James Powell, visited. Back then, a band played in the dining room throughout dinner. Later, there was dancing on the rooftop dance floor. The dancing went on until all hours.

Sighing, Josephine repeated a Bible verse. Something from the Psalms. *I will lift up mine eyes unto the hills. My help comes from the Lord.* She quoted it without joy. If only the majestic Ouachita Mountains in the distance could lift her spirits.

Polishing off the root beer, she crushed the paper cup and tossed it into the gray, plastic trashcan beneath the window.

She'd escaped New Orleans again. Barely in time, too. Outwitting the hospital staff proved easy—simple, really. Her exodus replayed in her mind. She chuckled recalling her daring caper. No piggyback on her IV meant no narcotics. She peeled back the IV adhesive, then slipped the needle from her arm. Dressing quickly, she walked past the nurses' station attracting no attention. Once out the hospital's main door, she jog-walked the block to the coffee shop on the corner. In a back booth, she took out her cell phone and put in a quick call to Earl, her handyman. Earl knew to follow directions. She entered the little park across from the coffee shop and waited for him. He arrived in record time, driving her black Lincoln. She no longer drove the vehicle.

Leaning back against the plush leather seats, she'd dozed while he sped up US 61 to Natchez, Mississippi, then US 425 to Monroe, Louisiana, and after other highway changes, arrived in Hot Springs on US 270, and at last the Earlington Hotel.

Earl told her the hospital had called her residence reaching Kim, her Vietnamese housekeeper. Kim, speaking very little English, repeated the garbled message to Earl.

"I told Kim I'd take care of it," Earl told Josephine.

Of course, he'd take care of it. Earl had helped her before. He knew who buttered his bread.

Tired of looking out the window, Josephine went to her bag and sifted her pills into her palm. She popped them into her mouth, then remembered she'd finished the root beer. Rushing to the bathroom, she filled a glass with tap water and swallowed the medication. Taking a deep breath, she sat down on the side of the bed and removed her shoes. What next, she wondered?

She'd never been good at planning her next moves. Something would turn up. It always did. She'd had no choice except to leave New Orleans. And, leave quickly. Charles, her wastrel son, had telephoned her at the hospital asking for more money. A loan, he'd said, giving her a ridiculous story about his daughter, Carol, as standing for part of the loan collateral. Something about their jointly owned boat, the Zephyr.

If only Charles had taken after her side of the family, the New Orleans Clarkes, things would be different. Instead, her only child was the fleshly incarnation of James, his spendthrift father. The thousands—no millions of dollars she'd squandered on both James and Charles's harebrained schemes made Josephine dizzy. When dizzy, she became confused, and when confused, she wanted to sleep. She smiled. The pills she'd taken ensured blessed sleep. But first, she should eat something. Yes, take care of her health. Josephine moved from the bed and unwrapped a fast food sandwich. She took a bite - chewed the tasteless burger - washed it down with tap water. It lay like lead in her stomach.

She needed a plan. Cousin Helen Condor, of course. Being a famous psychic, Cousin Helen could put her on the right path. Groggy from the medication, she telephoned her relative's unlisted number. "May I speak to Helen? This is her cousin, Josephine. This is an emergency."

"Miss Condor is away. Out of town."

"Where is she?" Josephine asked.

"I'm not certain. Is there a message?"

"No. No message. I'll call back."

Puzzling.

* * *

Next morning, Emmaline jerked awake. The bedside clock pointed to half past eight. She'd overslept again. After a quick shower, she dressed, then brushed her hair hurriedly. She slapped some base across her face and applied lipstick. No time for anything else. Rushing to the kitchen, she poured a cup of coffee. "Why didn't you wake me?" she complained to Maizie.

Maizie, at the sink slicing a fat tomato, looked up. "You said last night Miss Esther was helping again. I thought you wanted to sleep in."

She'd forgotten. She had told Maizie exactly that. Not her housekeeper's fault she'd overslept. Esther was in control at LeFevre House. "Is Miss Condor here?" Emmaline had invited Helen Condor, her old friend, the famous national psychic, to help with the *Whitechapel Road* theatrical.

"You mean Miss Helen?"

"Of course, I mean Miss Helen."

Slipping the tomatoes onto a blue serving dish, Maizie turned. "She got here real early, then she left about an hour ago with Mr. Etienne LeDeux. He's her kinfolk."

"I know he's her relative."

"I didn't," Maizie said innocently.

How could Helen leave without touching base with her hostess? Helen, far from orthodox in behavior, and like most famous persons marched to her own drummer, Emmaline couldn't understand why Helen chose sour-faced Etienne's company over hers. Still, Helen *knew On Whitechapel Road* needed more work and the curtain due to go up in three weeks. Emmaline hadn't made the major cast calls yet. She couldn't decide to cast by type - or against type. "Will Helen be here tonight?"

Maizie slipped the platter of tomatoes into the fridge. "She didn't say. She took a bag. Miss Helen is pretty peculiar, if I say so."

"Many brilliant people appear odd," Emmaline replied archly. "She's a psychic to the rich and famous, and her new Jack-the-Ripper book just hit the newsstands. It's a *New York Times* best seller."

"Is that a fact. And, Miss Helen come here to help you with your Jack-the-Ripper play? Ain't that the berries."

At times, Maizie's comments grated. "I invited her to Ville Nouvelle. That's all I'm saying."

"She's here all right. You want croutons on your salad tonight?"

"Please."

"Then, I gotta go to the store," Maizie announced, knowing Emmaline preferred homemade croutons. "My soul, it's raining," the housekeeper grumbled, peering out the window over the sink. "I left my umbrella at the apartment."

Maizie lived in the garage apartment, at the back of the property, that once functioned as a carriage house.

"You know you're welcome to anything here." Emmaline pulled a red and white golf umbrella, that had seen better days, from beside the door. She handed it to Maizie.

"Don't forget the meeting tonight," Maizie reminded her.

Emmaline frowned. "What meeting?"

"That atomic bomb meeting at Foursquare Christian Church. You said you'd come."

Emmaline had completely forgotten. "I don't know - and, it isn't an atomic bomb meeting. It's a protest gathering against the rumor that the government wants to put a nuclear dump site somewhere around here. That's why Dante Washington and his minions are in town."

"- clogging up the streets," Maizie said, talking over Emmaline. "Said they want to put that bomb stuff at the Washington farm. Their boy, Dante, is a big Hollywood star. He ain't gonna allow that."

"I'm aware of Dante's success," replied Emmaline. "No one knows the exact location of the nuclear site. I doubt even the federal government knows."

"Well, the bomb stuff *is* going out there. That's what I heard," Maizie insisted, eyes large. She stared at Emmaline. "I told everybody you'd be at the meeting. You can't go backing out now. It ain't Christian."

Emmaline rolled her eyes. The meeting held little enthusiasm for her, though she opposed the nuclear dump as vehemently as anyone in Ville Nouvelle. She knew Pastor Narin Lemuel planned to spearhead the protest at the Foursquare Christian Church. He was quite the activist. Too, he leaned toward riotous services at his own church, guitars, banjos, drums, and holiness shouting and holiness dancing. Services often lasting until the wee hours. Fired up about the protest, this meeting could last hours. She may be able to catch a few minutes of the protest if she hurried after the tour. "I'll try to come for a while," she said, "I can't risk Helen showing up here, and I'm not home."

"Looks like Miss Helen wants to run all over town instead of sitting here."

Emmaline gave Maizie her you're-out-of-line stare. Didn't faze the innocent.

"She knows I work the tour at LeFevre House," Emmaline said defensively. "And, Etienne is her relative. She likely feels an obligation." None of this was Maizie's business. But whenever did Maizie mind her own business? "What time does the protest meeting start?"

Maizie's blue eyes focused on her tiny watch dial as if it held the keys to the universe. "Eight-thirty," she said squinting. "That'll be way after dark. Now, don't you go driving fast and run off a rain slick road out there by the Washington place. You know you can't see to drive after dark."

"Really, Maizie!"

"You know it's the truth and you know you hate to wear your glasses."

Emmaline shook her head. The housekeeper's sunflower print tunic bespoke her river-bottom upbringing. "Plain folks," Maizie said when she came to work at Beard House before Emmaline's father died. "I'm from plain folks. I tell the truth, I don't steal, and I don't take no guff."

The drive to LeFevre House took longer than usual, due to the rain and the traffic. She'd alerted Esther earlier to lead the tours again. Crazy weather. Pouring rain one minute and the sun out the next. She arrived at the tour house, parked the car in the back, slipped inside, and eased down the passageway where she could observe the tour without being seen.

Esther had the first group of tourists in the dining room. The wind came up, a regular gale, rattling the old windows. They were in for heavy weather. "Oh, rats!" Emmaline realized she'd forgotten to inform Maizie the ranch boys were due later this afternoon at Beard House to work on props. She pulled out her cell phone and made a quick call to alert Maizie.

"Good thing you got me before I left for the store," Maizie said. "I'll make hot dogs for the boys."

Emmaline toyed with the idea of telephoning Helen. Then decided against it. Helen and Etienne were relatives. Awkward to summon Helen, and then run off to the nuclear waste meeting. She looked forward to seeing Dante Washington again. She'd always like him, even back when he was a strapping youth helping tend her flowerbeds.

Let Esther run the LeFevre House show. Emmaline slipped upstairs to the section of house forbidden to tourists. She stood at the window and watched the first group of tourists pop open umbrellas and go out through the cemetery. Esther looked like a mother duck leading the line of umbrellas behind her. She was doing a great job taking over. Hmmmh, she'd watch Esther in the future. Authority went to Esther's head.

The woman cheerfully took care of all the tourists while Emmaline sat upstairs and worked on the theatrical. The last group come and gone, and the house locked, Esther climbed upstairs. "You did an amazing job today." Congratulations never hurt anyone, not even pushy Esther.

"Thanks." Esther plopped down in a matching rocking chair. "You know I want to help every way I can."

"I appreciate it. By the way, are you going to the protest meeting tonight?"

"Darn tootin', I'll be there. Imagine the government shoving a nuclear waste dump on Ville Nouvelle." That was Esther for you.

Emmaline tucked her notebook into her oversize bag. "I can't decide whether to cast Sheriff Smith as the ripper or not. He expects it. It's the lead, of course."

"Who else would you consider?"

Emmaline deflected her assistant's question for the moment, though Esther had a point. "I could cast against type and cast someone totally different in the lead part—say Etienne LeDeux." Helen would like that—her relative in the lead part. Etienne had played supporting roles before. He sang, too. Mostly bass.

Esther laughed, "You aren't serious. You can't be. Not with all of Sheriff Rodney's groupies panting for him."

Emmaline smirked. "Let them pant."

Esther stood. "I'm going downstairs. Put everything in order for tomorrow."

After Esther departed downstairs, Emmaline, dreading the drive home in the rain, went to the window. Raindrops sluiced down the old wavy, window-glass, giving her a sense of comfort. A door banged somewhere in the house. The wind again. She stood and pressed closer to the window. She saw the problem. Not a banging door, but an upstairs shutter, had loosened and flopped in the wind. She made a note to have Tom see about it.

The rain began to slacken to a soft pattering. She opened the French doors and walked gingerly over the rain-swept gallery to look over at the gift shop. She wondered if Idabelle had gone for the day.

Her car was gone. The back parking lot resembled a lake. She leaned over, gripping the wooden railing. Something small and colorful lay below near the asphalt—something a tourist had dropped. Her hand lurched. She almost toppled over. What in the world? She saw the problem. A portion of the railing was missing. When had that happened? "My soul," she whispered, looking below. Something lay sprawled beneath the upper gallery. Something clad in white jeans and a darkened, pink tee-shirt.

Emmaline hurried across the slippery veranda floor to the garçonnière stairs, the outside set of stairs, originally enabling male members of the household to come and go unobserved at questionable hours. She rushed downward along the wet staircase.

A woman's body, twisted in a macabre position, lay in frozen stillness. The person was dead, no doubt about it. Emmaline knew the dead girl was Carol Powell. She put her hands over her mouth and screamed—but no sound came forth.

CHAPTER 4

Pastor Narin Lemuel Boys Ranch

Pastor Lemuel closed the door to his prayer closet and dashed outside, umbrella splayed against the downpour. He splashed through the muddy path to the gymnasium. "Blasted rain," he muttered.

And that telephone call! He shouldn't have answered. Sheriff Rodney Smith calling about a woman's body found at LeFevre House. Since the boys toured the house the day before, Smith wanted to talk to them. Specifically, the three boys who often worked for Miss Beard. The threesome, Scott Mason, Chad Ludlum and Jeremy Worms. The young men Miss Beard selected to help with her theatrical. Pastor Lemuel didn't approve of a serial killer's murderous theme for a play, but Miss Beard had odd taste, in his opinion. Came from having money. A person had to have money to live in that fancy Beard mansion. On the other hand, Miss Emmaline Beard heavily sponsored the Boy's Ranch. He couldn't fault her for anything. He could only pray for her.

Now, a dead body at LeFevre house, another of Miss Beard's properties; seemed like the Lord was trying to tell the woman something.

He'd delayed confronting the three boys about the young woman's unfortunate murder until he'd prayed about the matter. Prayer didn't provide immediate answers. However - his duty appeared immediately - speak to the boys before the sheriff questioned them.

If the woman's death wasn't enough, the postman delivered a barrage of hate mail earlier, condemning the pastor's stand against the Ville Nouvelle racetrack. Some months back, Pastor Lemuel had written a letter, published in the newspaper, declaring horse race betting a sin.

He suspected Etienne LeDeux spearheaded the hate mail. LeDeux could be a nasty person. Though a powerful man in the parish: Etienne LeDeux had as many enemies as friends.

The people who sent those hate letters were Godless and clueless about God calling him, Pastor Lemuel, to resist activities demoralizing the populace. He'd resist evil until his dying breath. He'd never hide his light beneath a bushel. The dead woman at LeFevre House likely had connections with the horse crowd, he thought with a superior snort. He'd told Sheriff Smith as much.

The parish may go to hell in a handbasket, but not before Pastor Lemuel's warnings against corruption registered loud and clear. The racetrack meant public drinking, open gambling, and further community decay. Yes, he thought with a sigh, the horses would continue to race, probably long after he was gone. Also, Miss Beard's bad taste in plays would continue to draw in patrons. He would resist sin where he saw it and in the Lord's way. Tonight, he'd speak at the nuclear protest meeting about the horror and sin of weapons of mass destruction.

Lemuel reached the recreation room door—the ante room leading into the gymnasium. The building was a gift from Dante Washington.

Excited youthful voices rang within. Whistles blew. Basketballs slammed across the floor and crashed against the backstops. Composing himself before he confronted the threesome, he stomped black, gumbo-mud from his thick boots onto a rush mat, shook the umbrella, and tossed it into the ceramic receptacle.

Ping-pong balls clicked across a game table as Scott and Chad volleyed expert returns. Both were promising boys who'd embraced the Christian gospel, and by all appearances had turned around their young, wayward lives.

The third youth, Jeremy, sat slouched against the far wall - limp, mouse-colored hair spilling over one eye, watching the basketball players. Jeremy, diabolically resourceful, managed to skip barber call for a couple of months. His hair trailed over his collar. Lemuel warned him. Skip the next call, and he'd do the honors himself. A buzz.

Jeremy's father, a wealthy Shreveport merchant with political pull, had managed to get his son's first offense drug dealing charges lowered to a minor offense. Special privileges and the bench's leniency made Jeremy even more

36

insolent. Lemuel carefully picked his battles with Jeremy, but by the God of all that was right, he'd cut that boy's hair or die in the attempt.

The pastor had sheared other boys in the past. His most famous haircut victim... Dante Washington, the famous Hollywood comedian and actor. The haircut hadn't caused Dante to rebel. Quite the opposite. He came to respect authority and respected Pastor Lemuel. A friendship flourished between them to this day. Dante made it big after leaving the ranch. The white van Pastor Lemuel drove was paid in full by Dante Washington. The state-of-the-art gymnasium - provided by Dante, as well.

Straightening his shoulders and forcing a pleasant expression on his face, Lemuel called to the three boys. "Chad, Scott, and Jeremy, I need to speak to you. Come to my office."

* * *

Los Angeles
One month earlier

Dante Washington crumpled the letter in his powerful fist. "We aren't taking this sitting down!"

"Baby, what's going on with your mama?" asked his fourth wife, Shemika. She'd seen the return address on the letter. She never opened Dante's mail.

"Read it yourself." He threw the letter to Shemika.

Shemika Washington smoothed the paper with long stroking motions. Masking her anxious expression, she read her mother-in-law's neat, round script. "I don't understand," she said, passing the letter back to her husband. "A nuclear waste site in her backyard? How can the government do that?"

"The Feds," Dante thundered, jumping up and slamming his palm against the wall, "can do any damn thing they want, and to anyone they want."

In the past, Dante's parents had farmed a small cotton plot west of Ville Nouvelle. After Dante made the big time, his parents' farming days were over. He'd built a comfortable Creole style house for them on their Ville Nouvelle land. Idella Washington, Dante's mother, refused to leave the home-place after her husband died, though Dante tried repeatedly to relocate her to Los Angeles.

"Mama Della can always move to California with us," Shemika offered, though she hadn't a clue how to indoctrinate the older woman into a Rodeo Drive lifestyle.

"That's not Mama's style," Dante sneered, his voice dripping contempt at his wife's suggestion.

Her expression innocent, Shemika tried not to overreact. Loving her lifestyle, and Dante, too, and determined to keep marital harmony intact, she endured a lot. Her husband's obsession with his mother made her uncomfortable… like a tight shoe worrying her foot. Another divorce would put him in the poor house, even with their pre-nup.

"If Mama Della won't come out here, I don't see there's much you can do to protect her land from the nuclear dump," said Shemika.

"Oh, you don't. Naw, you don't." Dante dropped down on the white, plush sofa, crossed his arms across his massive chest, and stared at Shemika. "All you want is to sit on your pampered ass and forget the fact I've got a mama . . . a good, Christian woman, who's the main reason I'm the person I am today."

"Baby, that's not what I mean at all -" Shemika's fears encompassed more than Dante's mother. For instance, the way Dante handled projects and problems - any project, or any problem. Being the type of man capable of managing only one large emotional battle at a time, Ville Nouvelle's nuclear waste problem would consume him. Consume them both before it was over.

He beat the couch with his fist, bursting a seam.

"Dante," she whispered. "What are you doing?"

He grabbed his cell phone.

"You calling Mama Della?" Her voice trailed, small and anxious. She hated it when she sounded frightened. Dante mustn't become angry. They had too much to lose. "Baby, if you get pushy on this nuclear business, the government might audit us again. That tax thing is hanging over our head."

Dante ignored her. "Pastor Lemuel," he boomed into the cell phone. "Man, it's good to hear your voice."

Shemika edged to her husband's side. He gestured her away.

"You're one of the few people I can talk to who doesn't have his hand out." Dante chuckled at something said on the other end of the line. "Man, I've got some questions about stuff going on in Ville Nouvelle."

Dante stood and stomped into the bedroom. He slammed the door in his wife's face.

* * *

LeFevre House

All afternoon and now evening, Sheriff Smith and Deputy Otis Fontenot, Smith's deputy, nick-named Saucer, for his wide, flat face, prowled around LeFevre House and grounds. Other deputies swarmed on the scene. A sheriff's department crime photographer took pictures. Finally, the coroner arrived. After his preliminary examination, the body was moved behind a makeshift tent.

Emmaline sat at the table in the LeFevre House mini kitchen under orders from Sheriff Smith. He'd instructed her to wait until he could speak with her. She'd never felt more alone in her life. She needed support. If only Byrd was here. She needed someone with a clearer head.

Esther had orders to stay for questioning, as well. Instead of sitting with Emmaline, Esther flitted around over the house, looking out windows, following the official's whereabouts. "They're measuring the back gallery," she announced, darting into the kitchen. She pulled out a chair and sat down across from Emmaline, her face a study in impatience. "How much longer are they gonna keep us here?"

Emmaline managed a weak smile. "I have no idea." As she spoke, footsteps sounded in the hall. Sheriff Smith and Saucer strode into the mini kitchen. Smith, dubbed Rod-the-Bod, by Ville Nouvelle's female population, didn't strike Emmaline as handsome at this moment. Dark circles pooled beneath his eyes, his mouth harsh at the corners. Before sitting down, he removed his broad-brim service hat and plopped it on the table. Saucer followed suit, red-faced and grim, his stomach spilling over his heavy service belt.

"You found the body," Smith said to Emmaline.

"Yes." She'd given this information three times before.

"Were you alone?"

"Others were at the house, Esther here, the tourists, but if you mean, was I was alone when I first saw the body -" She sounded defensive and she hated it. She had nothing to hide. Best to say nothing more.

"Would you step outside with me?" the sheriff said to Emmaline.

"Well... uh... yes, of course." She followed the sheriff to the sheet-tent housing the victim's remains. "Would you step inside and confirm this is the person you saw." He lifted the sheet, and Emmaline stepped inside the fabric barrier. "Her face. Her face is gone."

"Don't go hysterical on me, Miss Emmaline," warned the sheriff. "She was severely beaten around the face and head. "Do you identify her as the woman whom you saw at LeFevre House yesterday?"

"Yes, it's her. It's the girl calling herself Carol Powell. Her hair, her clothes, her petite frame. Yes, it's her."

"Thank you," said the sheriff, lifting a corner of the sheet and motioning Emmaline out. The coroner moved inside. A short time later an ambulance removed the body and drove away. The sheriff and Emmaline continued to the snack kitchen, where Esther and Saucer waited.

Sheriff Smith began interrogating Esther. "Miss Marshall, did you see the body as you were leading patrons out to the cemetery or to the gift shop?"

Esther's square face creased into an anxious smile. "I didn't see anything, not until Emmaline screamed."

40

The sheriff nodded to his deputy. "Saucer, take Ms. Marshall into another room and get her statement. You're free to go then," Smith said to Esther.

He turned to Emmaline. "How do you know no one saw the body before you did?"

"I don't," she said. "If anyone saw the body, wouldn't they make it known?"

"Not if they were the killer," Smith replied snidely. "You had a lot of people in the house. Since you said you were upstairs when you saw the victim, you can't vouch for anyone's whereabouts or what they saw." Smith, weariness about him, continued. "Start at the beginning. Tell me again how you found the body."

Emmaline repeated her story for the fourth time. As previously. she didn't think it relevant to explain her strange mood the past couple days. She doubted the sheriff would understand her need to escape upstairs when she didn't understand it herself. Nor could he relate to her change of life hot flashes, or the uncomfortable gown from hell. Or the fact she decided to allow Esther to earn her paycheck by putting her in charge of leading the tour. Personal problems were none of the sheriff's business. Facts, ma'am, just the facts. She'd heard that somewhere. She began woodenly. "I walked out on the upstairs gallery. First, I... uh... grabbed the railing for support - saw it broken. A spindle was missing. It was a fresh break. I'm sure the railing wasn't broken yesterday when we went through the house." Why offer that unreliable information? She couldn't swear the railing hadn't been broken earlier. "I looked down and saw the girl."

"Was she one of the tourists?"

"I told you before, I don't think so. Esther said she wasn't with any group going through the house."

Smith's frown alarmed her. "You identified the girl as Carol Powell. Was she a friend of yours?"

Why was he badgering her? She'd repeated her story time after time. "She told me her name was Carol Powell," Emmaline said wearily. "She isn't - wasn't a friend. I knew her as a child. Her grandmother often brought her to Ville Nouvelle."

"Go on."

"I knew the Powell girl's grandmother." Emmaline paused. "Years ago, Josephine and I were acquaintances. Friends from the old days. We aren't in regular contact now," she added.

"You associated the dead girl with her grandmother?"

Her voice trembled. "No, not at first. She told me Josephine was her grandmother. That was yesterday morning when she just uh - popped in on the tour. She hadn't bought a ticket or anything."

Smith frowned. "This young woman arrived at LeFevre House and told you she was Josephine Powell's granddaughter. The next day you find her murdered?" The sheriff sounded skeptical and irritated.

Emmaline brought her hand to her mouth. "Really, that's exactly what happened. I'm as incredulously surprised as you."

Emmaline's swollen feet threatened to push through the laced Victorian boots. A staple accidentally left in the gown's side-seam gouged her. She wanted to scream or cry. Perhaps both. "I've told you already that early yesterday morning before I left for the tour this young man claiming to be Carol Powell's fiancé, Gary West, came to Beard House asking for Carol. He said he'd been in New Orleans looking for Carol. He knew to go to his fiancée's grandmother, Josephine Powell. Carol wasn't at her grandmother's. I think Josephine was away, too." Emmaline, becoming confused, and aware of the sing-song quality of her voice, wished this interview over. Why allow Esther to leave and not her? Smith waited. He expected more. "I told this Gary person I had no idea of Carol or Josephine's whereabouts." Smith's penetrating expression made Emmaline feel guilty of something.

"Go on about the fiancé," he said.

"I never saw him before in my life. Cocky type. Wore a ponytail. He was dressed in short pants." Pausing to refocus her thoughts, Emmaline hated being on this end of the police questioning process. "He seemed truly worried about finding Carol Powell."

Smith scribbled in a notebook. "Any idea where I can find this fiancé?"

"I don't know. When he left, he said he'd be in touch, or something to that effect."

"If he gets in touch, contact us immediately."

"I will." She swallowed, exasperated.

Smith pocketed his notebook and reached for his hat. His demeanor more pleasant, he said, "I hear you have a famous person staying at your place." Apparently, he referred to Helen Condor, the psychic. News of visitors possessing the remotest celebrity status swept through the small community like a plague of locusts.

She frowned. She'd discussed inviting Helen to help with the theatrical, with the actors at one of the planning meetings. Smith, her leading man, knew this famous person's identity. Too tired to think, she managed. "Helen Condor, the psychic, is a longtime friend. She's agreed to help with the play."

Saucer chose that moment to rejoin them in the kitchen. "I heard what you said, Miss Emmaline. That's the same woman who writes them horoscopes for all them newspapers?"

"One and the same," replied Emmaline. Catching the sheriff's attention, she gestured around the breakroom. "What about tomorrow's tour?" She seriously needed the money.

"Correction," Smith said. "Today is the last tour day until further notice. This property is an active crime scene now. No one on the premises until our investigation is over. Can't say how long that will take. You know how things work here. Major crimes, we contact state."

"Yeah, nothing more major than murder." Saucer's input.

Dismally, she saw all her expensive promotion wasted. All profits gone. With over two tour weeks left, surely, she could salvage a few days. "You can't mean I'm to cancel them all."

"I'm sorry, Miss Beard, but that's exactly what I mean. You know we're a small municipality. Big crimes like this, we call in the State Police. After they finish their investigations, and if they aren't satisfied, the crime goes to the FBI. We aren't expecting it to go that far, but you never know. Hopefully, we'll wrap this up quickly and your tour can continue. But don't count on it. "About the dead woman," he added, "good thing you knew her identity. There was no identification on her body."

Smith's professional tone made Emmaline edgy. What really was on his mind?

He stared at her. "Tell me what you know or knew about Miss Powell in the past." He waited for her to elaborate.

Emmaline thought a moment. She certainly had nothing to hide. "Carol visited the area with Josephine, her grandmother, a few summers when she was a child of about ten or eleven years. That's all I know about her. A pretty little blond girl who had a pet rabbit."

"This Josephine Powell," continued Smith. "Where can I reach her?"

Emmaline turned the opal ring on her right hand, then made eye-contact with the sheriff. "She lives in New Orleans. I'm sure I have her address. I haven't heard from her in years. Josephine married young. We had little contact after that."

"Powell is Josephine's married name?"

"That's right. She was a Clarke before she married a naval man, James Powell. I'm afraid I know little about her after their marriage."

"Odd Carol Powell would look you up."

Emmaline thought so, too. She had no answer. "I'm as baffled as you, Sheriff," she said as obliquely as possible, wondering if he enjoyed seeing her uncomfortable.

"You stated she left through the back gate. The one to the side street, Camellia Lane. Left in a hurry."

"Exactly." Emmaline pictured Carol running away, leaving her standing, the package in her hand. *The package!* She'd forgotten it in the excitement. Where had she put it? Then she remembered. She'd hastily crammed it on one of the lectern shelves. Dare she mention it now? She couldn't. How would it look to suddenly remember something the fourth time Smith grilled her? She'd look a fool—or worse, appear she was hiding something. If only she'd thought about it earlier. Where was her brain? She swallowed a rising lump in her throat, rationalizing quickly. The girl brought a gift for her grandmother. Hadn't they visited exotic islands? Likely a trinket, a souvenir.

Smith was speaking. What had she missed? "...you're telling me that Carol Powell saw you on the veranda, approached you and asked if you were Emmaline Beard then ran out the back gate."

"Yes. That's exactly what happened."

"Her body was pushed from the gallery sometime during last night. Why would she come back to the house? There are no night tours."

"I can't explain any of that," Emmaline said firmly.

"You said Carol's fiancé was looking for her?"

"Yes. He told me he and Carol were sailing the South Seas. The boat needed repairs. Carol flew to New Orleans to wait for him. If she wasn't in New Orleans, Carol told him, to look me up. That is all I know, Sheriff Smith."

Smith stood abruptly. "Leave the house key with me. We'll want another look upstairs."

"Certainly." She fished the key from her bag.

"We'll be in touch," the sheriff said. Saucer pushed up from the chair, hitching up his pants.

The moment Sheriff Smith and Saucer started upstairs, Emmaline rushed to the lectern, retrieved the package, slipped it into her tote, and ran two red-lights on the way home to Beard House.

She let herself into the quiet house. Good, she needed alone time.

The Ranch boys weren't long gone, for the scent of fresh paint filled the air. Instead of checking the scenery they'd painted that afternoon, she flew to the kitchen and put on a kettle for tea. Her hands shook as she pulled down a cup and saucer.

Lights burned in Maizie's apartment windows. This was no time to tell Maizie about the disastrous interview. The teakettle whistled. She jumped. Her tea brewed, she hurried upstairs. She took a restorative sip of the comforting brew before yanking off the uncomfortable costume. Pulling on a caftan, she fished the package from her bag and stared at it. A plain, brown paper wrapped package with no address. Could be for anyone. Why give it to me? Curiosity seized her. Should she open it? Carol Powell instructed her to give it to her grandmother, Josephine. Carol Powell was dead. When, if ever, would she see Josephine Powell? The troublesome package beside her on the bed, she finished the tea. Next, she popped an aspirin.

Sighing, she dug through her desk for an old address book. Aha, she found Josephine's New Orleans address and telephone number. She put in a call. No answer. Emmaline sat a few minutes, her head throbbing. She tried to think. The phone number was a working number. That was something.

Should she contact the sheriff's department and declare the package? It could be evidence. Evidence she'd neglected to declare four times. Would Smith believe she'd innocently forgotten about the package? She must do something, she thought desperately. "I know," she said aloud, picking up the telephone.

She put in the call to the sheriff's department. "Kimberley," she said when Smith's secretary answered. "This is Emmaline Beard. I have information for the sheriff. She gave the secretary Josephine's address and telephone number. "He may be interested," she said.

Next, she telephoned her PR man about cancelling the LeFevre House tour until further notice.

She glanced at the clock. If she hurried, there was time to make part of the nuclear protest meeting at the Foursquare Church.

CHAPTER 5

Saturday, early in the day

The RV plowed over the rutted road to the thicket behind the Boy's Ranch property where Pastor Lemuel had prepared a secluded spot for Dante Washington to park an RV. The plan - keep Dante's wife, Shemika, out of sight should the nuclear protest march turn violent. Shemika loved the five-star hotel in Baton Rouge. She didn't buy this change in plans. Dante, excited about the response from the first protest meeting, tried to convince her that this new strategy was for her safety.

Shemika fumbled brewing coffee in the RV kitchen. She braced herself against the cupboard as the RV bounced from asphalt onto a dirt road.

"Rough spot," Dante called from the driver's seat.

Swearing under her breath, she mopped coffee stains from her white jeans. "I know."

"I told you to wait until we stop."

"I wanted my coffee."

Shrugging, he braked the vehicle, and waited until she poured their coffee and eased down beside him in the passenger's seat. "I hate you ruined your jeans."

"Yeah," she said. Brand new Rodeo Drive jeans. They cost a pretty penny. "Drink your coffee. I'm gonna change." She hurried to the back of the RV, shimmied out of the jeans, and pulled on a mini skirt.

"You have a washer and dryer in back," he reminded her when she rejoined him. He pounded the dashboard. "This baby is state-of-the-art."

"I came to the middle of nowhere to do laundry?" she hooted. "I don't think so." This trip meant trouble. She drove that point home to Dante every chance she got. He refused to listen because this proposed nuclear-waste site was too near his parents' home and land.

He reached over and rubbed her arm. "Get over it, your highness?"

"Yeah, your majesty." She glared out the window. He shifted gears and started forward.

"How deep you planning to drive in this wilderness?"

He didn't answer; his jaw set, his concentration millions of miles from her. She'd lost the Dante she loved and admired to this protest march and the hokey people in Ville Nouvelle. Only Dante would get himself mixed up in a mission like this protest. He bragged he had the power to sway the federal government's decision - his celebrity status. She suspected his motivation was the prime-time, camera cameos flashing his face across national media. His agent hadn't come up with much lately.

The motorhome bounced over a metal cattle-guard. Where was he taking her? "How much farther?"

He didn't answer.

She sucked in her bottom lip, worrying. They'd met no other vehicles for miles. The deep woods on either side of this pig-trail gave her the creeps. She shuddered. It seemed the end of the world to a Los Angeles girl. How could Dante expect her to stay stashed in this wilderness while he busied himself with the march? Taking a deep breath, she risked his temper. "You said it's too dangerous for me in town, but this place looks worse."

They'd fought over her wish to remain in Baton Rouge under the alias they used whenever they traveled stateside or left the country. She had the false ID with her. He'd refused. Too dangerous, he'd argued. His old friend, Pastor Lemuel, had offered this motorhome and the secluded spot to park it. If the march turned ugly, the pastor could shuttle Dante out here where he'd have all the conveniences of home.

A red flag dangled from a tree ahead. Dante grinned at her. "Home at last."

She shook her head and rolled her eyes.

He slowed the RV, turned in beside the flag, and stopped a few yards farther in a small clearing. Jumping out, he began the setup. Grabbing her sweater, she joined him. He popped out the living- area extension, put up the front awning. Stepping back, his hands on his hips, he admired his handiwork. "A five-star hotel, baby. You got a five-star hotel plus privacy. You get lonely, I'll get Mama Della out here to keep you company."

Shemika pulled her sweater tighter—uncertain about Dante's mother keeping her company. She had nothing in common with the elder Mrs. Washington. Too, the older woman remained good friends with Dante's first wife, a woman named Ivy, who lived in the area. Surely Dante didn't expect her to socialize with his first wife.

Edging nearer to him, she slipped her arm through his. Lately, it seemed everything she said came out wrong. She owed it to herself to make him realize how frightened she was in this wilderness. If he refused to listen to reason, she'd resort to playing him. "You can't be serious that you want me way out here. How am I gonna make it with you so far away in town?" She nipped his bicep with her teeth—play-biting. "You're so handsome, baby. Some other ole woman's gonna get her hooks in you. Lifting her mini-skirt, she flashed her goods."

Dante gave her arm an absent-minded squeeze, before turning away to adjust the sagging awning that dipped in the middle. "Looks straight now, huh, baby?"

She nodded. Dropping her gaze to her silver-manicured toes in jeweled, thong sandals, she wanted to cry. She was as out of place here as her inappropriate shoes, and Dante could care less.

He pulled out two lounge chairs, unfolding them under the awning. He must be crazy if he thought she'd venture outside the RV to sit in this jungle. Besides, it was too damn cold.

He stretched out on one of the chairs. "Baby, bring me another cup of that coffee."

She went inside, grateful the generator had the heating unit humming. She poured fresh coffee. While inside, she closed the blinds and curtains. This couldn't be happening to her - buried in this jungle. The Spanish moss he'd pointed out reminded her of veils of death. Gray death. She passed the coffee to him and eased down beside him.

"You really scared, baby?" he asked.

"Yeah. I'm not lying. I don't like it here. I'll be scared crazy by myself."

"Don't you worry, baby, I'll be back every evening." He didn't sound too convincing. His eyes narrowed; a muscle twitched in his jaw. He had other things on his mind than her. "Shemika," he said harshly. Startled, she looked up at him.

"I know you're not afraid of anything. I know what's got you riled. This trip isn't all about you. You're mostly pissed for yourself. You can't call no limos out here. You can't shop and party with your girlfriends. That's it. Ain't it? No Jimmy Choo shoe stores around the corner. That, and you don't think I can pull off this march and get the nuclear trash out of here. Tell, me girl, that's it, isn't it?" He gestured a wide sweep around the woods. "This is where I come from, baby. This is the real Dante."

She knew better than to push him too far when he got worked up. Instead, she leaned over and kissed the side of his face. "Baby, I'm not worried about the march. You could take on the world." She made her voice low and sultry - the way Dante liked it. Turning her chair around, she slipped her legs over his and started playing him—talking trash and running her tongue around his ear.

He pulled her onto his lap. His cup fell to the ground. "Pastor Lemuel won't be here for a couple of hours. That gives us time to catch up on some homework."

An uneasy feeling crushed Shemika as she followed him into the motor home. In the space of two hours, he'd be gone, and she'd be here - alone. What if this church meeting turned violent?

* * *

Late Evening

Emmaline arrived at Foursquare Church, the red brick and white clapboard structure, in a driving rain. Unnoticed, she slipped inside onto a back pew. Pastor Lemuel was speaking—his words lost in the rowdy crowd. She spotted Maizie on the front row. Dante Washington sat next to the podium. Practically everyone in the audience leapt to their feet shouting and talking over one another. Clearly out of control.

Pastor Lemuel, harried and red-in-the-face, tried to control the audience, though he should be accustomed to romping, stomping meetings, Emmaline thought. The pastor motioned to Dante Washington to stand. Everyone grew respectful and quiet. Celebrity and money evoke regard and even worship, observed Emmaline.

Dante's admirable voice carried like thunder. "Neighbors, friends, and kinfolks," he began, smiling. The congregation stood, giving him a standing ovation. Cheers and whistles rang the rafters. He waited for order. "It's wonderful you're here lending your support to this unholy project the federal government is trying to shove off on Ville Nouvelle citizens. I commend you all." More whistles and shouts of 'Amen brother' drowned out the comedian. When the uproar showed no sign of ending, he shouted information about a protest march for the following day. Most of the crowd was now chanting and singing.

Emmaline slipped out the back door. She arrived home shortly after eleven p.m. Retrieving the package from the armoire, she turned it in her hands. Flipping off her shoes, she eased down on the side of the bed. What was in the package? It could hold a clue to Carol's fate. Carol Powell had met a violent death. Had Carol realized her life was in danger?

Emmaline frowned. *Now, I'm implicated in her murder by not giving it to the authorities.*

No crime to open a package without an address, though. Was it? And, too, Carol *is* dead. She fetched a pair of sharp manicure scissors from her bureau drawer, snipped away the tape, and tore through the tightly wrapped paper. Inside lay a white box sealed with clear strapping tape. She sliced through the tape then lifted the lid. "My soul!" she exclaimed aloud. Black pearls.

A string of obscenely, large pearls carefully knotted around each orb, and as iridescent as the South Seas, lay in her lap. She lifted them. Heavy, too. In the antebellum tour business, and acquainted with antiques, Emmaline knew immediately the pearls were real and valuable. How valuable, she could only guess. Gently, she sifted them through her fingers. The final test—she drew them across her teeth as she'd seen her grandmamma do. Aha! Tiny, gritty imperfections. These were real.

Carol Powell died for these. A king's ransom in rare pearls. Had her fiancé wanted these pearls? That breezy, surfer-type guy who'd called at the house. Her heart lurched. Does he suspect I have the pearls now? Emmaline crammed them back into the box, slipped the box into a pair of fishnet pantyhose, and stashed them in the back of the armoire. She daren't tell Sheriff Smith. Not just yet.

Past midnight, she lay awake, wondering what to do, whom to contact. Byrd, of course. Her best friend in the world, Byrd Jeffcoat. He'd understand. He wouldn't like her not informing the authorities. Could she trust Byrd to keep quiet about the pearls until she checked them out and made the best decision of what to do with them? Even he must realize the awkward position she found herself in.

They were both amateur detectives, after all. Solving crimes made up her DNA. He, on the other hand, needed persuasion. They had one solved murder between them; a classmate believed drowned years before had been murdered by another classmate.

Maizie mustn't know about the pearls—for her safety. If the creepy fiancé called again, Maizie couldn't keep a secret. She'd blab everything she knew.

Byrd must help her. He'd grown up in Ville Nouvelle and visited often. He'd called her the day before. He planned to come for the theatrical. Ignoring the late hour, she seized the telephone and punched in his cellular number. No answer. She dialed his residence. No answer. Desperate, she telephoned Violet Causey, Byrd's widowed sister. Vi answered on the third ring.

"Violet, is Byrd there?"

"Is this you, Emmaline? Is something wrong? It's very late."

"I know, I apologize. I hope I didn't wake you."

"I wasn't asleep. What do you want with Byrd?"

Ignoring Vi's questions, Emmaline kept her voice at a normal level. "I'm trying to reach him. He doesn't answer his cellular or his landline." On the tip of blurting out she must speak to him about a matter of life or death, she stopped in time.

"He had dinner here tonight. I'm sure he's home."

Byrd had bought the house next to Violet after her husband died. Emmaline knew that Byrd's near location to his meddlesome sister meant she knew all his business. "If you talk to him in the morning, tell him I called."

"I know something is wrong," insisted Vi. "You sound in a panic."

"Uh . . . nothing major. A technicality." Was that ever an understatement?

The sound of a wildly barking dog bounced off Emmaline's ear. "Wait!" screeched Vi. "Chester's barking. Chester loathes Byrd." The phone rattled across a hard surface, likely a table. Muffled voices sounded in the background. Then Byrd's welcome voice. "Byrd, here. What's going on? You're not sick or anything?"

"God, I wish. I'm in a jam and I need your help. Can we speak privately . . . without the possibility of Vi listening."

He laughed. "I think she's occupied, but if it'll make you feel better, I'll call you on my cellular."

"Would you?" The moment they reconnected; Emmaline bypassed all pleasantries. "A girl was found murdered at LeFevre House. I discovered the body. The tour is cancelled. The house is a crime scene -"

"I don't see your problem," he interrupted. "You're not responsible for a dead woman no matter where she was found."

"There's more."

"Okay. Shoot."

She launched into rhetoric that sounded bizarre even to her own ears. "Early yesterday morning, a young man came to the house. He asked for Carol Powell.

53

He'd tried to see Josephine Powell in New Orleans—Carol Powell's grandmother. You remember Josephine. She was Josephine Clarke back in the day. Anyway, she was away. Josephine, not Carol."

"Slow down, I'm not following all this. Josephine Clarke, you say."

"What's this about Josephine Clarke?" Vi yelled in the background. "I know her. She was one of my best friends."

"Shut Vi's mouth."

"I'm trying to listen to Emmaline," Byrd said to his sister. "Okay, go on," he said to Emmaline.

"This man said his name was Gary West, claimed he and Carol are engaged. They were sailing somewhere—South Seas, he said, had trouble with his boat. Carol didn't wait around for boat repairs. She flew to New Orleans. Anyway, they were to meet in New Orleans. If that didn't work out, Carol gave him my name with instructions to come to Ville Nouvelle and see me if he couldn't reach Josephine."

"Josephine?" repeated Byrd. "Older than you and me. Frizzy auburn hair. Antsy."

"That's the person."

"Okay, she was one of Vi's friends."

"Is Josephine all right?" Vi blurted in the background.

"Is she?" Byrd asked.

Losing patience, Emmaline snapped. "How should I know? I haven't heard from her in years. I suspect she's this side of the grave since this guy was looking for her."

"She's okay," Byrd said to Vi.

"Vi has gone upstairs. What does all this have to do with me?"

"Just listen. You haven't heard the worst part. I got to the tour house and I didn't feel good that morning. I put Esther in charge. Nothing she likes better.

Anyway, I went out back to the gallery. This girl—this young woman rushed up—said she was Carol Powell. She gave me a package for Josephine. Before I could explain I hadn't seen Josephine in years, the girl ran out the back gate and into the street. I never saw her again until this morning when I found her found dead at LeFevre House. She'd been viciously beaten, especially her face."

He whistled. "Uh oh, the tour is cancelled and you're in the hot-seat?"

"Exactly. No tour until the police finish their investigation." She didn't go into detail about the State Police or the FBI possibly investigating. "Sheriff Smith questioned me all day yesterday. I don't like his tone."

"I can imagine."

"Byrd," she pled. "I'm desperate. I need you." She drummed her fingers. He couldn't refuse.

She heard his intake of breath, then exhale. "I'm tied up with an exploratory group from China. They're touring the lab." His small private laboratory catered to glue and all adhesives. "They're an adhesives group, wanting information about fusing high impact plastics. Seems they're not willing to pay the price for my franchise. Has me on eggshells. I play nicey-nice and at the same time don't give out any licensed information."

She realized he was busy. "I understand. But I need you here desperately. Smith is calling in state; I'll be grilled for days."

"No rubber hoses, though," he said.

"That isn't funny."

"No, it isn't. Forgive me."

"What was in the package?"

"How do you know I opened it?"

"I know you."

Gripping the phone tighter, Emmaline whispered. "Huge black pearls. I suspect they're valuable beyond my wildest estimates."

"The police think they're real?"

"That's the jam part. I didn't give the package to the police. I forgot about it. Insignificant, I thought. Carol brought her grandmother some trinket." Emmaline's heart hammered. "The sheriff questioned me four times—four times I forgot the package. You know how that looks. Like I was deliberately hiding it. I had no idea what was in it until tonight when I opened it. You understand why I need your help," she added desperately.

"Who knows about this package and the pearls?"

"No one. Except now you. I'm praying the killer doesn't know."

Byrd whistled. "What about the fiancé? You think he knows about the pearls?"

"I don't know. I haven't seen him since. I have no idea if he's still in town. I told Sheriff Smith about him." She paused a long moment. "Look Byrd, the package was entrusted to me. I take trust seriously. I intend to see that Josephine gets these pearls. In fact, it's more important now Carol is dead. These pearls are the last thing a loving granddaughter sent to her beloved grandmother." Loving and beloved stretched the truth—a fabrication, really, however, the terms soothed Emmaline's troubled conscience. Josephine had never been a loving person; more a high-strung, nervous wreck of a person.

"I don't know what I can do," Byrd hedged.

"I can't turn the pearls over to the sheriff until I find Josephine. I called her twice, finally got some foreign person, likely a maid. You know what to do. You have a P.I. license."

"Had a P.I. license," he corrected. "Back when I worked my way through college."

"You'd never let your license lapse. I know you."

He cleared his throat. "I told you, I'm tied up with the Chinese group. At best, I might be able to get away day after tomorrow."

"If that's the best you can do. . . I'll try to survive until then. You were coming for the theatrical and the horse race anyway."

He grunted something unintelligible. "You should take the pearls to a jeweler and have them appraised. They may be worthless."

She'd thought of that—the possible repercussions stopped her. "I know a little about pearls and estate jewelry. I'd bet my life these are genuine. Think killer, Byrd. Tipping my hand could cost my life. By the way, what are you doing at Vi's place so late?"

"She called me over, said she thought she heard something in the backyard."

They disconnected. First thing the following morning Emmaline put in a call to USNCB—point-of-contact for the U. S. Central Bureau of Interpol.

CHAPTER 6

Tuesday Evening

Three days later, just at twilight in a peppering rain, Byrd arrived at Beard House. A few lights burned inside the mansion. He killed the engine of his Lincoln Navigator and sat a few minutes admiring the old house. Beard House never failed to impress him. The massive structure dated back to the era of architectural excess and was even more imposing today.

He pulled his windbreaker tighter, grabbed his bag, alighted and dashed to the door off the kitchen. Locked. Tucking his neck lower into his jacket, he pounded the knocker.

Emmaline opened the door, a clutch of newspapers in her hand. "You're soaked. How long have you been standing there?"

"Long enough," he spluttered, rushing inside, shaking like a water-spaniel after a long swim. He peeled off his wet jacket and tossed it on the hall tree. "I need to change. Where's my room?"

"Papa's room, same as always."

Byrd climbed the stairs and pushed open the bedroom door. Dark mahogany paneling interspersed with family portraits ran the length of the walls. A lamp burned on the marble-topped bureau. Dropping his bag on the floor, he trekked into the adjoining bathroom—modern in stark contrast to the bedroom's period furnishings. Stripped, he stood in the shower, warm water sluicing over him until his body warmed. Once presentable, he joined Emmaline downstairs in the dining room as Maizie announced dinner.

Curious about the murder, he said. "About -"

Emmaline put her finger to her lips. He got the drift. *Don't talk about the murder or the pearls in Maizie's presence.* Okay, by him.

Instead, Emmaline said as she passed him the basket containing Maizie's famous yeast rolls, "Helen Condor is in town. Staying here at the house."

"The big-time psychic. Really?" The woman's face was plastered on all the grocery-store rags facing a person at check-out.

"You remember she grew up here."

He didn't remember but nodded anyway.

Throughout dinner, Emmaline sat like a leashed, birddog straining to hit the open field. She refused to speak in front of Maizie. Usually Maizie knew everything going on at Beard House.

After dessert, he stood. "I need to make some calls. We'll talk later."

"Your room or mine?" she whispered.

"Yours. Cozier."

Byrd trekked upstairs for privacy. He'd left his assistant, Dang, to deal with the Chinese people. Before he opened the door, loud moaning emitted from the bedroom directly across the hall from his bedroom. Surprised, he stopped. The door flew open and a woman trailed out. A woman in some sort of trance, wearing a flowing black robe-like garment. She either didn't see him or ignored him. Not acknowledging his presence, she continued moaning, gazing upward, holding something like a tuning fork over her head. "Magistrate," she cried. "Whitechapel Road will see another murder before dawn."

She blocked his path. Talk about invading personal space. "I beg your pardon," he said.

Blinking as if emerging from a fog, she darted a gaze at him. "Who are you?" She had a low, throaty voice.

"Byrd Jeffcoat," he said, "I could ask you the same thing."

Lowering the tuning fork instrument, she struck it against her palm. "What does it matter? You've ruined everything." Vibrations strummed from the tuning fork. Grasping it with both hands, she pushed it into her robe pocket, then strode into the bedroom from which she'd emerged. She slammed the door closed.

Helen Condor, he suspected. Emmaline's other houseguest. For the life, he didn't remember the woman. He forgot his calls to Houston, went on to Emmaline's bedroom and knocked. "I ran into your other guest," he said, gesturing down the hall.

Emmaline pushed the door closed. "Really, I thought Helen was out. She didn't come down to dinner. I'm very fortunate to have her here. She's a celebrity, you know, and she's advising me about my Jack-the-Ripper production. I wrote the dialogue," Emmaline said proudly.

"You told me."

"It'll likely flop," sighed Emmaline. "No tour. No theatrical."

"The two venues aren't connected," Byrd reminded her. "The old house tours bring in outsiders. Mostly folks around the area come to your theatricals. You'll have a great play, like always." He grinned. "Remember the year those boys from that nut's reform school threw lit firecrackers down on the stage."

She laughed. Truly laughed for the first time since she'd discovered Carol Powell's body. "Jesus, wasn't that awful."

"You pulled that off. You can pull anything off."

"I hope you're right."

"You know I'm right."

Grasping his hand, she longed to hug him. Instead, she pumped his grip like an insurance salesman. Their relationship wasn't a physical one, much to her chagrin. "Thanks for coming. I need you." The moment became awkward; the two of them standing in the middle of her bedroom not sure what to say next.

Emmaline broke the spell. "What am I thinking? Sit here in this chair." She rushed to the armoire and dug out the box of pearls. "You won't believe these." Opening the box, she poured the large pearls into his hands.

"Wow!" he exclaimed. "I'd stake my life these aren't fakes."

"Told you," she boasted.

"What have you found out about them?" He'd bet his last dollar she'd investigated the pearls on the QT.

She didn't answer at first. "Put them away. I can't stand looking at them. If only I could've helped Carol."

He pushed the pearls back into the box.

She spoke in a hushed whisper. "I think the killer wants these horrible pearls. I believe Carol was killed because of them."

He listened.

"I should've suspected something . . . Carol coming here," she said, "especially after that man claiming to be her fiancé showed up with his wild Pacific Ocean story. It all happened so fast I didn't put two and two together." Emmaline's bottom lip trembled.

He stood and slipped his arm around her. They settled on the side of her bed; his foot tangled in a lacy bed-skirt. She leaned her head against his shoulder. "We'll get to the bottom of this," he promised.

She hadn't told him everything. "I contacted USNCB."

His pushed her back, his eyes wide. "You mean Interpol?"

She nodded. "Their website posts international crimes. I believe these pearls are the ones stolen from the Tahiti Pearl Museum seven months ago in one of the most daring daylight robberies ever. It happened during an annual festival. Three armed men in grass skirts and Tahitian face paint stormed the museum and overpowered the guards. They forced the guards to turn off the security cameras and alarms. Then they laser-torched into the case, lifted the pearls and disappeared into the festival crowds."

"Good grief."

"I can't go to the sheriff now" she lamented, "it'll appear I'm hiding something."

"Well, aren't you?"

The door slammed downstairs. Maizie.

Emmaline shot Byrd a warning look. "I'm keeping Maizie in the dark. You know how she is. Tells everything she knows."

Maizie called from the hall. "Mr. LeDeux is here. He wants to see you, Miss Emmaline."

CHAPTER 7

Emmaline smoothed her hair with her hand. "What can he want?" Etienne LeDeux, a prominent landowner with an overzealous ego, wasn't her favorite person. "You coming?"

"Wouldn't miss it," Byrd said.

The moment they entered the library Byrd remembered Etienne LeDeux. The short intense man in his sixties stood in the middle of the room. Mr. LeDeux glared first at Emmaline, then Byrd.

"I want to speak to you alone," Etienne snapped to Emmaline.

Drawing up to her five feet, nine inches, Emmaline looked down on Etienne. "Byrd has my full confidence. Whatever you have to say, he may hear."

Shrugging, Etienne began. "It's about Marcel Beaudion. He's gone too far this time. He's trying to kill me."

"Kill you!" Emmaline exclaimed. The two men, rivals for years, with adjoining property, had feuded for as long as she could remember. Even though they had no affection for each other, still Etienne's announcement carried their grudge to the extreme.

"Yeah," Etienne said, "and, with my own gun."

Emmaline shot a quick glance at Byrd before she turned back to Etienne. "Why come to me? "You should contact the sheriff."

"I talked to him," Etienne said. He threw up both hands in Gallic disgust. "That pantywaist ignored me. You, Emmaline Beard, you can get things done in this town." Etienne's eyes narrowed; his expression tightened. "Marcel stole my gun. He shoots at me when I'm in the back pastures with my racehorses.

The shots are too close for accidents. They aren't meant to spook the horses, either. They're meant for me."

Emmaline shook her head. "I can't believe Marcel is shooting at you. Besides, those woods between you two are practically impenetrable. Anyone could be back there. Remember the Black Path brings in all sorts of weird people." Not to mention the protest march.

Byrd listened closely. He'd been away from the area long enough to know little of current grudges. However, he remembered Beaudion and LeDeux had never been on friendly terms. Both men bred thoroughbred racehorses. They competed in races. And he recalled the Black Path, a lonely, isolated stretch of woodland trail.

Etienne gave a snort - like a feral pig's grunt. "Marcel isn't stupid. You think he'd let me see him taking pot shots at me. I dug some bullets from a tree - two of 'em. I gave the shells to the sheriff to send to the crime lab to test. Came back same caliber and same case markings as my stolen pistol." Etienne appeared rigid enough to snap.

"What do you expect Emmaline to do?" Byrd asked.

Etienne wheeled to Byrd. "When I want your advice, I'll ask for it." The man was breathing hard, his face a mask of rage. Turning, he wagged his index finger at Emmaline. "You stop this horse race. You stop it or you'll be sorry."

"How -"

Etienne interrupted. "Two years ago, Marcel brought in that doped-up horse and got disqualified. Some anonymous person wrote to the newspaper trying to stop the races. Marcel blamed me. He's crazy. Why would I want to stop what I support? He's jealous, that's what. Jealous because my horses are better than his. Better bloodlines. Marcel knows my horse is this year's favorite and he wants me dead."

"That's preposterous," Emmaline sputtered. "You can't be serious -"

Etienne interrupted again, edging closer to her. "There'll be no race this year. If there is, someone might get killed." Pivoting, he stormed from the room.

Emmaline stood in shocked silence. "What an idiot."

"No," he disagreed. "What a time bomb."

CHAPTER 8

Following morning: 10:30 a.m.

Emmaline waited most of the morning for Helen to show up. Pride wouldn't allow her to call Etienne's house and ask for the psychic. Not after Etienne's venomous visit the evening before. She went into the library and turned on the television. Dante Washington's protest march flashed on the national news.

A famous anchor's voice announced. "Ville Nouvelle, Louisiana, a backwater community across the Mississippi River from Baton Rouge, finds itself embroiled in a protest march against the federal government. The federals have considered locating a nuclear waste storage facility near the area. Ville Nouvelle isn't the only prospective site -" Emmaline switched off the television.

Maizie burst into the room. "You ain't gonna believe this."

"Believe what?" Had loose-cannon Etienne LeDeux returned?

Maizie, fit to burst at the seams, continued. "A lady I ain't never seen before is here. I put her in the drawing room."

Emmaline frowned. Theatrical paraphernalia filled the drawing room, even spilling over into the dining room. Hardly the place for a stranger,

"Who -"

Maizie rushed on, ignoring Emmaline's question. "I didn't want to send her in here 'til I could tell you first. Says she's Josephine Powell." Maizie took a ragged breath. "Ain't she the dead girl's grandmother?"

Emmaline launched to her feet. "You know she is. My soul, her granddaughter is dead. Where's Byrd?"

"He ain't here."

Emmaline hurried to the drawing room. She hadn't seen Josephine Powell in over twenty years. Yet, she'd have known the woman sitting on one of the blue wing chairs anywhere—the angular face, the abnormally long neck, the masses of bushy, dark auburn hair now streaked with gray. Her first thought, did Josephine know about Carol's murder?

Sensing Emmaline's presence in the doorway, Josephine turned her regal head and looked up. She stood, moving slowly toward Emmaline. "Dear, dear Emmaline, how long has it been?" The scattered expression in Josephine's dark eyes marked her as troubled, despite her stylish white, silk blouse, tailored black pants and large diamond studs in her ears.

Josephine grasped Emmaline's hand, then crushed Emmaline in an embrace. "Emmaline, you haven't changed one bit. You look as young as the last time I saw you—what—over twenty years ago."

"At least twenty years—maybe longer," Emmaline agreed, leading Josephine to the sofa, wondering if she must tell this fragile woman about her granddaughter's death. Hopefully, she already knew, and that dreadful news prompted this visit. "I'm surprised to see you," Emmaline began. That was the truth.

Before she had a chance to say more, Josephine spoke up. "You're wondering why I'm here. I can't blame you. You know I've always regarded you as a dear friend."

"Of course." Safe ground so far.

Josephine's tone shifted. "I ... uh... haven't been well lately. Some heart problems. Nothing major. I needed a short vacation. I had Earl. Earl is my handyman and chauffer. I no longer drive. He drove me to Hot Springs for a few days. Change of scenery, you know."

Emmaline nodded.

"Anyway," continued Josephine. "I gave my housekeeper a few weeks off. She checks my house when I'm away. She phoned Earl and told him that Charlie, my son, arrived at the house a few days ago. Kim, my housekeeper, wasn't certain exactly what day Charlie got there. He'd had some bad luck, something about his boat being in New Orleans needing repairs. And, something about Carol, my granddaughter."

Josephine shook her head, perplexed. "Kim never gets anything straight. I didn't trust Earl's version of their conversation, either, so I called Kim. Got the same information she gave Earl, except Charlie had gone. She said he mentioned Ville Nouvelle. I have no idea why he'd mention Ville Nouvelle. That's why I had Earl drive me here on the way home from Hot Springs." She paused a moment, then asked abruptly. "Have you seen or heard from Charlie or Carol?

"Josephine, brace yourself. I have terrible news." Josephine's thick brows drew together. Heavy anxiousness emanated from the tense woman.

Emmaline took a deep breath, then exhaled slowly. Tell her straight out. The only way. Show the pearls to her—the only way. "Carol is dead. She's in the morgue here awaiting official identification."

Josephine screamed, a guttural sound, coming from deep within her rigid body. She slumped forward in a dead faint, drool pooling down her chin.

"Maizie," Emmaline shouted. "Maizie!"

CHAPTER 9

Emmaline and Maizie struggled propelling Josephine upstairs. Their effort resembled trying to herd a running-of-the-bulls participant up a flight of stairs with Emmaline, in front pulling, and Maizie shoving the woman from the rear.

Once they got her in bed, the woman fell asleep. She resembled a drowned corpse lying back against the pillows, her grayish auburn hair fanned out like gray seaweed around her abnormally white face.

Emmaline suspected Josephine was on heavy medication.

A door opened and closed downstairs. Emmaline went to investigate and discovered a middle-aged man in the kitchen claiming to be Josephine's chauffer. He dressed the part. A navy-blue, uniform-type, pants and shirt. A hat with a stiff bill. He asked to see Josephine. Emmaline led him upstairs, briefing him along the way about Carol's death and Josephine's violent reaction.

"She needs her medicine, then-" he said, stopping mid-flight. "It's in the car."

Earl left and returned a few minutes later with a black leather bag that folded in on itself. He unfolded the bag, revealing numerous zippered compartments. "Ms. Powell is really particular about her medications."

"This way." Emmaline led him into the bedroom. Josephine had wakened. She sat up in bed, sipping a cola. Maizie hovered nearby. Earl approached the bed with the bag. "Ma'am -"

Josephine grabbed the bag like a lifeline, unzipped a couple of the compartments and took out several pill bottles. She shook three or four pills into her hands.

"That'll be all, Earl," she said.

He turned toward the door. Emmaline noted the man's lined and weary face. Working for Josephine apparently took a heavy toll. Maizie tip-toed away, too.

Emmaline sat down on the side of the bed. "I'll stay a while with you, if you like," she said soothingly, smoothing the light blanket about the woman's body.

"That'll be nice." Shakily, Josephine angled the cola onto the bedside table. "You must think I'm insane."

"Of course not. You've had a terrible, terrible shock. Try to rest, and we'll talk about everything later." She pressed Josephine's hand. "I'm here for you." It was the right thing to say, for Josephine smiled and grew drowsy almost at once. Whatever drug combination she'd taken produced a powerful, knock-out punch.

Emmaline pulled a chair to the bedside and waited until Josephine lapsed into deeper sleep. At the first soft snore, she crept across the room, closed the drapes, then slipped out, closing the door softly behind her.

Down in the kitchen, she found Byrd sitting at the kitchen table with coffee and a plate of Maizie's beignets. "You're never here when I need you," she said, both relieved he'd returned and annoyed he'd left the house without telling her.

He gestured overhead, powdered sugar on his fingers. "What's with her showing up here?"

Emmaline poured herself a cup of coffee, settling across from him. "It's a long story." She repeated what Josephine had told her. "Josephine was in Arkansas and returning home when she learned her son, Charlie, was in New Orleans, possibly on his way to Ville Nouvelle. Anyway, Charlie mentioned the South Seas boat trouble scenario to Josephine's chauffer. Josephine wondered if Charlie and Carol were here. That's why she stopped here. To learn if I'd heard from Charlie or Carol. She had no idea about Carol's murder. Oh, Byrd, I had to break the news. Josephine collapsed."

"Wow. How sad for you. Backs up the story the fiancé told you," he commented thoughtfully.

"It does, in a way…" her voice trailed. Gary West hadn't impressed her favorably. Perhaps a forerunner of trouble to follow (Helen would agree with that). Now, with Carol dead, and Josephine in Ville Nouvelle, Emmaline feared sinister intent brought these people she barely knew into her life.

* * *

Later that evening, Josephine woke from her sleep more in control of her emotions and as prepared as possible for the sad duties that followed— identifying the girl in the morgue. If the young woman was really Carol, then Josephine must arrange her granddaughter's services and burial. Before the trip to the morgue the next morning, the three of them sat in the library, Josephine, Byrd and herself. Emmaline trusted the moment to mention the pearls.

Anything to distract Josephine from the sorrow at hand. She had moved the pearls earlier to a desk in the library. She intended to put them in the library safe. Her father had no less than three safes in the house. Praying Josephine's stable mood continued, Emmaline said, "there's something I must show you." She got the package and handed it to Josephine. "Carol left this with me for you and no one else."

"What is it?"

"Open the box."

Josephine opened the box, drew the pearls out and stared at them in perplexed fascination. She looked up at Emmaline and Byrd. "Pinctada Margaritifera," she whispered reverently, taking the strand of black pearls and pressing them against her throat. "Priceless. But I don't understand."

"Pinctada Margaritifera?" questioned Byrd, a quick glance at Emmaline.

"The black-lip oyster, the species responsible for these rare pearls," explained Josephine. She angled a puzzled expression at Emmaline. "Why would my granddaughter leave these with you? "More importantly, how could my granddaughter own such pearls?" Her gaze dropped again to the pearls. She stared at them a long moment. "My Clarke grandmother owned valuable South

Sea pearls. Hers were as large as pigeon eggs. However, these excel hers in beauty, and I'm sure in value."

"They're stolen," Emmaline announced abruptly. "Stolen from the Tahiti Pearl Museum."

Josephine's eyes widened. She paled. Her hands shook. "Stolen? If they're stolen, they must be returned," she cried over-loud. "One thing, I know for certain, my granddaughter is no thief."

"They will be returned," Emmaline assured quickly. "I didn't turn them over to the sheriff because the box was wrapped with no address. I thought Carol left something personal for you. Uh… I never dreamed anything like this. Now, it's awkward and frightening - to give them to the police, I mean. It appears I've withheld evidence on purpose."

"Well, haven't you?" Josephine said quietly.

How dare she make such a statement, Emmaline thought, keeping her irritation in check. "I'll contact the sheriff first thing in the morning,"

Josephine crossed her arms over her body. A gleam of fervent hope spread across her face. "You don't know the girl in your morgue is my Carol. You haven't seen Carol since she was a small child. You couldn't identify her."

"Of course, I couldn't."

"Where's Charlie?" Josephine began, her voice rising. "Kim said he was coming here." She clasped her face in her hands. "This is horrible." Her lips trembled. She dropped the pearls. Quickly, Emmaline retrieved them and slipped them into the box.

"… and Charlie," Josephine continued, on the verge of hysteria. "He's a rolling stone. He and Carol live in Marina Del Ray, California. He's seldom home. I never know where to reach him. Last I heard a few weeks ago, he was in Colorado, wanting me to send money. He always wants money." Josephine looked down at her hands. "Where are the pearls?"

"Here." Emmaline held up the box.

"A great deal of mythology and religion surrounds pearls," the distraught woman said. "Charlie and Carol have chartered their boat to the Polynesian

76

Islands many times. "But they aren't thieves." Her eyes narrowed; her heavy brows met above her prominent nose. "How Carol could've gotten these pearls is a mystery. But, stolen, never -"

"Sheriff Smith will tell us what to do," interrupted Emmaline firmly. "In the morning, we'll go to the morgue first, and then to his office."

* * *

9:00 a.m. Following morning

Josephine appeared stable the following morning as they left Beard House for the Ville Nouvelle morgue.

Byrd drove his Navigator. The nuclear dump protesters were out in full force, blocking the streets. "Is the morgue still the old building on Dock Street?" he asked, threading the vehicle through a gang of protesters milling in front of the parish courthouse. "They could get out of the street," he groused.

"We have a new morgue," Emmaline said. "The new morgue is past the courthouse. You can't miss it. Thanks to our current governor. One who honored his campaign promise. He wasn't all about duck hunting."

Byrd swerved the Navigator to avoid hitting a woman, carrying a sign larger than she was, who stepped in front of the vehicle. "If I hit one of these protesters, I should sue Dante Washington."

Josephine sat expressionless.

Emmaline prayed the woman had taken her fortifying medications before leaving the house. Still, the heavy silence from Josephine unnerved Emmaline. She talked relentlessly to offset the gloomy mood inside the SUV.

"The new morgue has only one technician, Mac Parsley. He has cerebral palsy. He comes across as off-the-wall; however, he's terribly intelligent - and competent." Emmaline laughed nervously. "He seems pleased working with the dead. Well, I don't mean pleased exactly - " What did she mean? Best to drop this conversation.

Mac met them at the morgue door. "Oh, hi Miss Beard. The sheriff said y'all would be coming." Mac led them to the back of the facility and into a semi-dark room housing stainless steel drawers on the eastern side. He punched on lights. The long tubes of ceiling fluorescent bulbs put the sun to shame. "Our pretty girl is in here," he said, pulling out a drawer. It slid on silent tracks. "Take all the time you want."

Josephine rushed to the drawer, took a quick look. "Carol, oh Carol. Her face is smashed. Carol!" she screamed, grasping her throat, slumping against Byrd. He steadied her. Mac hurried with a bottle of water. "Happens all the time."

Josephine recovered and peered at the dead girl again. "Would you turn her head to the right?"

Mac obliged.

Josephine began crying softly. "I prayed it was a mistake—a horrible mistake," she whispered to Emmaline. "See her little round birthmark below her ear. This is my Carol."

Emmaline slipped a tissue to Josephine. "We should leave now. We know it's Carol."

* * *

Back in the Navigator, the trip to the sheriff's office seemed unbearable with Josephine's distraught condition. The woman huddled against the back seat, Emmaline by her side. "We'll take you to the house. It's not necessary for you to see the sheriff."

"No." Josephine ran her tongue over her lips like a lizard. "First, we should have the pearls appraised before we turn them over to the sheriff."

Disagreeing, Emmaline frowned. "I don't think so. These pearls are evidence. We should leave appraisals to the police authorities."

Josephine reached for the box. Emmaline clutched it tighter.

"These were my granddaughter's property," asserted Josephine. "Now they belong to me. She only entrusted them to you because I wasn't at home. I'm the one who should decide what to do with them."

"You told me Carol never owned such pearls," Emmaline reminded her. The unbalanced woman had no idea what she was saying.

"You don't know for sure they're stolen," blurted Josephine. "You could be lying."

"But she isn't lying," interjected Byrd, taking charge of the situation. "She and I both know they're stolen. They must go to the police immediately."

Josephine stiffened. Emmaline reached for the woman's hand. Josephine pulled away. "Don't be upset," Emmaline said reasonably. "Sheriff Smith will know what to do." She didn't mention Interpol to Josephine. Best to get her home. Let Maizie and Earl deal with her.

Josephine knit her fingers together, knuckles white. "Pearls possess suggestive powers," she whispered. "Papeete!" A lock of unruly hair trailed from her chignon. "I'm certain these pearls are Polynesian."

Byrd half-turned his head to the backseat. "You mean Papeete, as in Tahiti?"

"Of course, I mean Tahiti. My husband, James, and I visited Tahiti many times. It's lovely there. So unspoiled. We visited the pearl museum often. Can you imagine a museum dedicated to pearls?"

Emmaline couldn't imagine such a place, and judging from Byrd's troubled expression, neither could he.

* * *

They reached a section of Dock Street where the protest marchers thinned. Byrd drove faster.

Josephine called suddenly. "I've changed my mind. Take me to Emmaline's house. I have nothing to say to a sheriff."

Delayed emotion, Emmaline surmised, relieved the woman chose to go home. Apparently, viewing her granddaughter's body had affected Josephine more after the fact than during the ordeal.

The short drive to Beard House took less than fifteen minutes. With relief, they left Josephine to Maizie and Earl's care.

Byrd drove to the sheriff's office. Kimberley Neel, Sheriff Smith's secretary, greeted them as they entered the outer office. "Hi Emmaline," gushed the petite, shapely brunette, "great to see you. How's the play coming?"

"Some snags," Emmaline admitted, "but under control." Which amounted to one of the biggest lies ever to pass her lips.

Kimberley gestured to Smith's office door. "You can go on in."

The sheriff frowned when Emmaline and Byrd entered. "What now?" He nodded to two chairs in front of his desk.

Emmaline perched on the edge of the chair nearest Smith's desk. Byrd took a metal fold-up chair near the door.

"How can I help you?"

Emmaline opened her handbag and took out the box containing the pearls. Extracting the pearls from the box, she laid them on the sheriff's desk. "I don't know where to begin. Carol Powell gave these to me before she was killed."

Smith gazed at the pearls; glistening midnight black while at the same time flashing iridescent rainbow colors in the bright arc of sunlight filtering through the window. Smith fingered them like so many worthless pebbles. "You think these things are real," he said at last.

"They *are* real," Emmaline said. "I'm convinced they are the reason someone murdered Carol Powell."

"We don't know the girl in the morgue is Carol Powell," replied Sheriff Smith.

Byrd spoke up. "We do now. We drove the grandmother to the morgue. She identified her granddaughter."

"News to me," Smith huffed, toying with the pearls using the tip of a pencil, like someone playing with a spider, or some other unpleasant insect. He looked up. "I'll run these through the computers—see if anyone is missing pearls. Could take a while."

"I can save you the trouble," boasted Emmaline. "Check Interpol. These are real, all right. They're at least twenty millimeters or larger. Perfect South Sea pearls. They were stolen from the Papeete, Tahiti Pearl Museum."

"Really," he drawled. "And, you say Carol Powell gave them to you? Why didn't you turn them in as evidence?"

Emmaline bristled. "I was in shock finding the girl's body. I forgot about them. You remember I told you I was in Carol's presence only a few minutes. She handed me a package for her grandmother. I had no idea what was inside the package. I simply followed her instructions. How did I know she'd be murdered the next day?"

"That same night," corrected Smith.

Emmaline ignored Smith's insinuations. "How can I be sure the pearls are safe here?"

Sheriff Smith's glance carried enough voltage to sear Formica. Unceremoniously, he lifted the pearls and dropped them into a brown envelope. "Kimberley," he yelled, ignoring Emmaline's beet-red face as his blunt fingers sealed the envelope. Finally, he secured the envelope with a rubber-band as Kimberley undulated in, her red miniskirt doing double time.

"Log this package," he instructed. "Unidentified female, LeFevre House."

Emmaline spoke up. "Not unidentified. The dead girl is Carol Powell. Josephine Powell, the girl's grandmother identified her."

Smith glared at Emmaline. "She should come in and make a statement to us."

"She was too upset after leaving the morgue. She's in fragile mental health. She'll come in as soon as she can,"

"Where is she now?"

"We drove her to my house."

"Yes," Byrd affirmed. "She was way too upset."

Smith raised an eyebrow. Emmaline suspected the sheriff was peeved she'd not officially named him as the Ripper in the theatrical. Let him stew. At least, for the moment.

"Those things looked like gum-machine rejects to me," he said to Emmaline, referring to the pearls Kimberley carried to the evidence room. "I'll humor you, though, and keep them under lock and key. Now, the main problem. Why'd you sit on them if they're such hot evidence? I know you told me all this shocked, I forgot, etc., excuses." He smiled. Not really a smile, but lips clearing teeth. "Especially, since you're insisting they're so valuable."

"I opened them the night after Carol gave them to me. Until then, I thought she'd left some trinket for her grandmother." She shrugged. "The package wasn't addressed to anyone."

"Why didn't you bring it in after you saw what you claim is stolen pearls?" Smith asked nastily. "Or the day after that, or the day after that?" He pulled a folder from his desk drawer and made a few jots. "Now, if you two don't mind, I have work to do."

"But...," spluttered Emmaline.

Smith looked up. "If I want to talk to you further about your memory lapse declaring evidence, "I'll be in touch."

Byrd stood. Emmaline followed suit.

"Good day," Smith said.

"Good day to you," Emmaline huffed.

Leaving, she glared at the sheriff's office red-brick exterior as if the façade had done her a dirty deed. "Of all the nerve," she vented, "calling those pearls gum-machine rejects."

Byrd opened the Navigator door for her.

"And how dare he threaten me," she said further. "Nastily jesting about my memory lapse. Who does he think he is?"

"He has a job to do," Byrd said. "You should be grateful he let you off with a sarcastic comment."

She shrunk deeper against the leather passenger's seat, sulking.

He slid into main street traffic. Suddenly, he slammed the brakes and narrowly missed tail-ending a motorhome the size of a small motel. "Blasted road-hog!"

Emmaline craned forward. "That's Pastor Lemuel's RV. I've heard Dante Washington's Los Angeles wife is staying in it. She hasn't been seen around town." Emmaline pointed to barricades on both sides of the street. "As much as I admire Dante, this nuclear protest march has made driving here impossible."

CHAPTER 10

They arrived at Beard House to find a squad car blocking the driveway. Helen Condor's rental stood parked in front of the police cruiser. Emmaline turned to Byrd. "What on earth?"

"Don't get overly excited," he said, raising an eyebrow. "Probably a routine reason a deputy dropped by."

She sprang from the SUV and charged through the kitchen door. Maizie met her. Saucer towered behind the petite housekeeper. "I had to call 'em," Maizie jabbered to Emmaline. "They was killing each other. Them's the craziest two women I've ever seen."

Did Maizie refer to Helen and Josephine sitting across from one another at the kitchen table?

"Nothing to worry about, Miss Emmaline." Saucer hitched up his sagging service belt loaded with every law-enforcement accessory known to mankind. "The situation is under control. Neither of them wants to press charges."

"Press charges for what?"

Helen rose, easing in front of the deputy. "We've never been out of control," she said patiently to Emmaline. "Maizie got overly excited, that's all."

"Over excited my hind-foot," jawed Maizie. "You two was going at it and I ain't no referee." Maizie clamped her arms over her upper body and stared Helen down.

Saucer's radio squawked and buzzed, adding to the tension. "If that's all, ladies, I'm out of here."

"Certainly, it's all," Helen said. "Thank you for coming." She took Emmaline's arm and gestured toward the library.

"Just a minute." Josephine lurched up, mopping her tear-stained, face with a tissue. Long streams of black mascara trailed from each eye. "I can't take anything more today." The woman stumbled toward the stairs.

Byrd, in gallant mode, rushed, taking Josephine's arm. He escorted her upstairs. Minutes later, he joined the two ladies in the library.

Helen, amazingly serene, was speaking. "... as I said, the situation got out of hand before I knew it."

"Exactly what happened?" Byrd asked.

Helen gave an exasperated shrug. "A misunderstanding, as I was telling Emmaline. It had to do with money. I've held several séances for Josephine in the past. Four or five at least. She neglected paying for the last two. I asked her for payment. She went into a tirade. We're related, you know, third or fourth cousins."

Byrd laughed. "Everyone from Ville Nouvelle is related. This place is like the incubator of the world."

"You and I aren't related," Emmaline reminded him.

"Anyway," Helen continued. "Josephine believes I'm filthy rich and it pissed her off I'd dare ask for money. I'm a working woman. I have bills same as the rest of the world."

Emmaline believed Helen was wealthy. Still, a service performed was a service owed. Order the goods - pay up. "Why would you hold other séances after a patron, even a distant cousin patron, neglected to pay you?"

"Who knows why we make questionable decisions. In the past, she always paid, even if it took a while. I thought she'd forgotten." Helen frowned. "The two séances she hasn't paid for occurred the same day. We contacted her husband, James. Josephine, delirious to continue contact with him, demanded I pursue his spirit. Plainly put, she was beside herself. I allowed her to talk me into a second session against my better judgment. I missed my flight that day because of her. That cost extra money. Why shouldn't I ask for payment?" insisted Helen.

"Did you have any luck with the husband the second time?" Byrd asked.

"You mean did Mr. Powell reappear?"

"Exactly."

"He made his presence known, but briefly."

"And, there was no check in the mail," observed Emmaline.

"Precisely. When Josephine flew in my face and grabbed my arms just now, I knew she'd crossed a boundary. That's when Maizie called the authorities."

Helen's explanation of the altercation between herself and Josephine seemed plausible. Unfortunate, Helen chose this day to confront Josephine. The trip to the morgue left the woman unhinged.

"We'd just come from the morgue," Emmaline explained, "Josephine identified her granddaughter's body. She held herself together better than I believed she could."

Helen scowled thoughtfully. "That's what she was rambling about. I couldn't understand a word of her gibberish." With a helpless sweep of her hands, Helen continued. "I'm sorry I upset her. I'll make it up to her. I could press charges, you know. Josephine pounded my arms with her fists. That's assault under the law," Helen said.

"I'm glad you didn't." Emmaline, relieved, suggested. "Let's have coffee and forget the ugly incident." Helen and Byrd nodded agreement.

The heightened tension followed them, though. Their attempts at conversation came across stilted and unnatural. Emmaline solved the problem. She pulled out copies of the Ripper theatrical and gave one to Helen and one to Byrd. "Read this and tell me what you think."

They read silently, the only sound in the room, the loud ticking of the grandfather clock in the corner. Byrd spoke first. "Hey, this is pretty good."

"I'm not certain about the last murder scene," Helen began hesitantly. "It seems busy, stilted. "The Ripper was in a murderous frenzy by this time. He is insane, you know…"

Emmaline took out her blue pencil. "Exactly, what's questionable?"

"Too much dialogue. Too much narrative from your off-scene narrator Too much of both. Better to use the audience's imagination. You know visuals, darker lighting—spookier—silhouettes. Yes, silhouettes. The murder occurring in shadows behind a dimly lit screen; powerful. Engages the audience's fears. Ramps up their imaginations. Leave out the dialogue and the off-scene narrator telling everything."

Helen's suggestions pleased Emmaline. "I see what you mean." Helen's ideas - the reason she'd asked Helen's help in the first place.

Byrd stood, depositing his copy of the play on the coffee table. "I like it. I'll leave you two to hash out the fine points. If you ladies will excuse me." He closed the door with a thud.

Helen tossed her copy of the play alongside Byrd's. "I need to go, too. Etienne is expecting me for dinner. I promised I'd make a salad. Julie is coming."

Julie, Etienne LeDeux's only child, lived in Baton Rouge. Helen hesitated a moment before stating a startling proposal. "I've had some stirrings about the Powell murder. I want to channel Carol Powell's killer in the location where the murder happened. Would you care to join me?"

"Really. I'm excited beyond words!"

CHAPTER 11

New Orleans

C harlie Powell hung around New Orleans a couple of days spending time at the marina, inspecting the Zephyr. She looked bad. Peeling paint. Debris aboard. Even garbage stuffed in the cabins. Carol would never abandon ship and leave their precious boat in such deplorable condition. He did most of his inspections on the QT since the marina manager dogged him for slip-fees each time they met.

Puzzled, he kept driving past his mother's house. She lived in the historic Garden District where neighborhood watch signs dotted most lawns. Her car had never returned. Her goofy housekeeper didn't make sense. The Oriental woman, not staying at the house full-time, came by periodically to check on the property. He called his mother's chauffer's cell phone dozens of times. No answer. *Aha,* he thought. His mother's modus operandi; get new cells phones with new numbers—mainly to throw him off.

He desperately needed money to get the boat out of hock. He needed money to have her repaired before he could sail her back to Marina Del Ray. Someone had done a sloppy job on the engine.

Biggest question of all—where was Carol? She didn't answer her cellular. Where was Gary West, Carol's fiancé? The marina manager described the fiancé jerk as the person who had brought the boat in. Alone, the manager said. No woman with him.

Charlie's arms ached. His shoulders ached. He'd ridden the Harley from the coast. Took his time. A pleasure ride. Sure, it was a Hog. Still, riding it was no featherbed. Too, he was getting no younger.

He rode to Biloxi, Mississippi to visit an old friend. They kicked around the casinos. One night the friend made a remark that troubled Charlie. Left him feeling cold, like a touch of the heebie-jeebies crawling up his back.

"You got a crazy state," the friend had said.

"How so?" Charlie asked without interest. He was too worried about his problems, too stressed about sponging off the friend to even be in reality.

"Unidentified dead people turning up all the time."

"Happens everywhere," Charlie said. "You mean Louisiana or California?" He needed to get out of the casino and back to New Orleans. Maybe his mother had returned.

"Louisiana," the guy said, "seven unidentified dead people this month alone." He chuckled like it was some sort of joke. "Three in New Orleans. Two in Baton Rouge, and two in some place called Ville Nouvelle." The guy brayed like a jackass. "I remember the Ville Nouvelle dead ones because the girl was pretty; blond girl. Had her picture on TV."

"Who was the other one?" Charlie asked idly

"Some Black dude. Young guy. Both of them musta been kill-and-dump cases. Nobody knew them."

The garish casino lights and the loud conversations around him grated on Charlie's nerves. Too, the comment, *pretty blond girl,* triggered anxiety; an unidentified blond girl. Tremors chased through his veins.

Charlie cut out that night. Rode back by his mom's house. No sign of activity. He rode around a while, then filled the gas-tank in Metairie, and headed out for Ville Nouvelle. His mother grew up in Ville Nouvelle. He knew the place well.

CHAPTER 12

Beard House

After the psychic left, Emmaline worked on the play changes Helen suggested. Byrd had gone for a walk. A stress headache coming on, she shoved the manuscript aside. The front door opened and closed. Byrd came into the library. "You still at it?"

"Not any longer."

"How's Josephine?"

"She's awake. Maizie took coffee to her."

"What's on for this afternoon?" He didn't sound overly interested.

She held her breath should he announce he was returning to Houston. "The most exciting thing. Helen is going to LeFevre House to try and contact Carol's killer."

"I thought the police had the place roped off."

"We can use the Black Path. Full view of the gallery from there. You remember the Black Path?"

"Yeah. I grew up here."

The Black Path, a long, meandering trail had existed in Ville Nouvelle since time immemorial, was originally an old Indian trail. Later, Spanish conquistadors marched along it through the impenetrable forests and swamps. Massive trees grew on either side of the rutted, one-lane path. Most landowners erected fences along their property to prevent walkers and hikers from trespassing private land. Of late, the younger generation abused the beautiful area with motorcycles and four-wheelers. And with their after-hours trysts.

"I'm going with you," Byrd announced. She couldn't have been happier.

As they entered Camellia Lane, Emmaline saw the crime tape had been removed. "Would you look. The crime-scene tape is gone. The sheriff hasn't said a word."

"It sure is," he said. "And there's a car."

"That's Etienne's jeep." With access to the premises, Helen had parked on the LeFevre House back drive. She emerged from the Jeep and hurried toward them.

"It's cold and windy," she said, gazing at the sky with a frown.

"Will it stop your visions?" Emmaline asked.

"I don't know." She answered vaguely. "Now, where exactly did you find the young woman's body?"

"There." Emmaline pointed to the concrete turnaround near the back gallery. "Her head and shoulders were on the concrete . . . her torso and legs, pretty much under the upper gallery. When I looked over the railing all I saw was her head and arms. You can't imagine my shock."

Helen started walking toward the house. The wind picked up her magenta cape, swirling it around her body. "We can't talk," she called back to them.

Byrd smirked at the dramatics.

Helen stopped a few yards from the back gallery. They trailed a distance behind her. "Visual cues come to me." She lifted her black-glove encased hands for emphasis. "I may speak aloud. Don't answer me or prompt me. These impressions come quickly, like darting birds or sped-up black and white movie frames. At other times, much slower. Sometimes clear images - often vague suggestions, like a dream not quite remembered. I can't explain my gift or control it." She put her fingers to her lips in the no-talking prompt. Helen pulled her black scarf about her hair.

Apparently, the visions started immediately, for Helen began moaning at once. "Oh, no," she cried. "She's running. Running for her life. Shards of electricity are sparking along the fence. Her handbag. Her handbag's chain strap. She can't scream. She's out of breath. She's running too fast."

The psychic stopped talking abruptly. She stood, staring long moments at the back of the mansion. Finally, she turned to Emmaline. "That's all."

"Who's she running from?" Emmaline forget Helen's instructions about questions.

"I don't know." Helen frowned, her brows a drawn ridge above her eyes. "I will say this. Evil pursued her. Evil murdered her." Helen turned. "Perhaps another day." She started toward the parked vehicles.

Emmaline hated to leave the scene of such psychic activity. "Come to the house for dinner?"

"I can't," Helen said. "Remember, we're expecting Julie at Etienne's."

Emmaline masked her irritation. She'd invited Helen to Ville Nouvelle to help with the play, not spend most of her time with her relatives. Hardly fair.

"Wait!" Helen screamed.

Byrd jumped.

Her eyes closed, her cape flowing in the wind, Helen lifted her head. "He's tall, powerfully built. An aristocrat. Of the peers. It's evening. The streetlamps are lit. He's walking toward his carriage. A lackey of half-wit appearance sits on the carriage box - waiting. Always waiting. The gentleman approaches. His cape is fitted with pockets on the inside containing knives - surgeons' gleaming instruments. He's fond of knives. They fascinate him. He wanted to study medicine. Such was forbidden for his class. He kills and dissects small animals. Always with knives. His curiosity never sated about what lies inside the animals, the organs sustaining life.

"Bloodlust drives him. He cannot see enough of the blood. He revels in it. He digs his fingers in it, his hands. He smears it across his face.

He's in the coach. He goes to the Whitechapel area. Nameless, secret and unidentified, he commits unmentionable atrocities." Helen stopped. She stared into space blankly.

"Can you believe it?" Emmaline whispered to Byrd. "She's seeing Jack-the-Ripper."

"What happened to him?" responded Byrd in an under-breath.

"Never caught," Emmaline said, watching Helen, who slowly oriented herself to the real world. She continued to Byrd. "He toyed with the police, sending letters and even parts of the dead women's organs."

Helen came toward them. "I saw the Ripper," she said. "I saw his end. I'm certain he had a stroke that left him unable to walk or speak. He remained the rest of his life, babbling and insane, unable to communicate. Violence never left him, though, merely his body no longer supported his madness. We may as well leave."

They walked on toward the vehicles.

"You're wondering why I'm spending so much time with Etienne," Helen said to Emmaline. "Etienne isn't my cousin. He's my mother's youngest brother. I refer to him as a cousin because we're near the same age. Mother had a death premonition about him. She fears he's about to die. She hurt him in the past and wants his forgiveness. She's frantic he'll die with them estranged. She doesn't want to face God with this on her conscience. They spoke on the telephone the other night for the first time in over thirty years."

"Is Etienne in bad health?" Emmaline never thought of the robust man as near death.

Helen shook her head. "Not that I'm aware. He assured me he recently received a clean bill of health." She paused. "He's frightfully worried though. He thinks Marcel Beaudion is trying to kill him. I didn't believe him at first, but I've heard the gunshots, too. When he first started hearing the shooting, Uncle Etienne took some of the shell casings to Sheriff Smith to test. They came from Etienne's stolen gun. I want to help him. Do you know anything about Mr. Beaudion's threats?"

"Only that Etienne told me the same thing, you're telling me," Emmaline said. "I thought it was a foolish notion and I told him so."

"I hope you're right." Helen climbed into the Jeep. "We'll get together about the play. Soon."

* * *

Following evening

The evening after they visited LeFevre House, the theatrical preparations had moved forward at Emmaline's place. Emmaline had spent the day supervising the boys from Pastor Lemuel's Boys Ranch. Frowning, she sat on the landing watching Jeremy Worms work on the lightning panel. He'd discovered a problem. Below them onstage, Esther bossed Chad and Scott, who weren't placing scenery panels where she wanted them.

Helen arrived and climbed the stairs, joining Emmaline. "This is a regular beehive."

Chad Ludlum stumbled across the stage carrying a huge lamplight. "I told you to watch your step," Esther yelled. The thickset, young man nodded sheepishly.

"What a taskmaster," Helen remarked.

"She's that and more," agreed Emmaline. "She gets the job done, though."

Scott Mason, the thin red-haired boy, laughed. "Really, Scott," scolded Esther. "Get busy."

"I'd best get down there and do my part," Helen said, standing and hurrying downstairs. Emmaline smiled at the psychic's backside. Helen had kept her word. She'd arrived at Beard House ready to help with the play.

"Ma'am," Jeremy said, coming up behind Emmaline, swishing a lock of hair from his eyes. "I found the problem. He had a narrow, intense face. A disagreeable face in many ways, like he knew what you were thinking and thought you a fool. He wasn't a talkative boy. Emmaline suspected much went on in his brain. Much she didn't want to know.

"Couple of bulbs burned out, Miss Beard. And, a short in an auxiliary board."

"Is it something you can take care of?" she asked anxiously. God forbid they'd need an electrician.

"Yes ma'am. Sure." He had such a cultured voice.

Jeremy sauntered downstairs, a rack of bulbs under his arm, and a rope of cords over his shoulder. You'd never believe he once had a drug problem, Emmaline thought. She knew he was from a proud family. It did her heart good to know she was instrumental in centering Jeremy's life on solid values. She felt herself a proud mother figure - like an eagle, nurturing a wayward eaglet.

She stared at her professional stage below. Her one expensive indulgence. She'd majored in theatre at LSU and had planned to go to New York to study at the Actors Studio founded by the famous Elia Kazan. Tuition at the school was free; however, a prospective student must audition for acceptance. Emmaline auditioned. She waited for the invitation. The invitation never came. She checked back, checked back, and checked back. Finally told she'd failed the audition; she sank into depression. Her father offered his counterproposal to the stupid Elia Kazan. He'd build her the best damn theater this side of the Mississippi River, no matter what it cost. And he did. Her flamboyant Papa - there'd never be another like him.

She was smiling to herself when Esther's bossy voice brought her to the present.

"Chad, I've told you twenty times to move those trees more to the left." The sulky boy lifted one of the huge potted palms, tottering to his left. "Over here?"

"Yes."

"That's it for tonight," barked Esther.

Emmaline walked downstairs. Helen stood in the hall pulling on her coat. Emmaline smiled at her. "Any new impressions about Carol's killer?"

"Some," Helen admitted. "Nothing definite." She said nothing more.

"Small law enforcement departments like our sheriff and his deputies are often forced to call in outside help," Emmaline said, "If we tell the sheriff what you saw in your visions, I believe it could help the sheriff's investigation."

"No, no." Helen frowned, alarmed. "You can't mention anything I experienced to the authorities. Those were impressions, suggestions—vapory insights—nothing the police can use. My visions are random, disjointed, and to the untrained, unreasonable."

Helen had aided authorities in the past on unsolved murder cases. "You've helped the police before, haven't you?"

"Yes," admitted the psychic. "Often a victim's family wants my input. Especially if the case goes cold. The police, not so much."

"Oh."

Sensing Emmaline's disappointment, Helen turned to her. "I must have your word about discretion where the police are concerned."

Emmaline promised reluctantly.

Helen continued. "I confess I have had further impressions about Carol's killer. Frightening impressions. I can tell you this much. This killer is desperate. Cunning and desperate. This person is angry. An aura of great evil and darkness surrounds this person. These revelations are personally frightening to me." Helen tried to explain. "You may not be aware, but when I receive supernatural messages—when I channel a person—especially a dangerous person, sometimes this person becomes aware of being channeled, and in return channels me. The power of evil is greater than we realize. I could become the next victim." Helen added her last statement in an under-breath of fear.

"You don't know how my gift troubles me," she added ruefully. "How many foolish people contact me for lotto numbers, times of their death or the death of a family member. World events—I've even been offered astounding sums of money for election results before the elections take place."

CHAPTER 13

Marcel Beaudion started the shooting the day before. A zinging bullet barely missed Etienne's head as he walked in the woods near the back of his property. Should he go to Sheriff Smith again? What good would it do?

An idea came to him early this morning when he forgot and left the skillet on the range with the fire under it. The scent of scorched grease filled the house. He'd put the fire out -no problem. It sparked an idea. The perfect revenge. Etienne didn't believe in murder; however, he believed in revenge.

With malice aforethought, he struck out with a five-gallon can of gasoline and matches. He set fire to Marcel's best pasture. The fire spread quickly; leaping into the woods behind the pastures. No real danger, he thought, the Ville Nouvelle Volunteer Fire Department would arrive in time to save what few houses lay in range. He knew the inept Fire Department would never arrive in time to save Marcel's barns, stored with expensive alfalfa hay for the man's racehorses.

Blaring sirens announced the fire department's arrival. Etienne watched, bunched along with other neighbors.

A few hours later, the excitement over, the fire contained, he decided the afternoon excellent for a walk. He needed to work off nervous energy. He chuckled to himself as he set out on the Black Path.

The late sun warmed him as he walked along the path. He smelled cinders and ash on the breeze and chuckled to himself. He shucked his windbreaker and looped it around his waist. Spanish moss draped from the trees like coarse gray beards. Moss had a peculiar smell - an earthy scent - like dried nuts. He smiled. Long ago, his Grand'Mere stuffed her mattresses with dried Spanish moss. She dried the moss on wooden racks in the yard. Once dried to perfection, she stuffed it into mattress ticking and sewed up the sides. When piled on the bedframes, the moss mattresses almost reached the ceiling. As a boy, he'd jump into the middle of the sweet-smelling moss bed, giggling while his body sank and settled. No sleep was ever as sweet as the sleep on those beds.

Already he was breathing hard. He must exercise more. Still, the walk exhilarated him. Dusk threatened. He should have brought a flashlight.

The fire in Marcel's pastures had brought as much excitement as Dante Washington's protest march against the nuclear business. Excitement without the traffic snarls, he thought. Why Sheriff Smith allowed the marchers permission, Etienne had no idea.

Smith was a vain turkey, in his opinion. Put more thought into acting in one of Emmaline Beard's plays than sheriffing. He shrugged. They had it going for them - the tall, handsome types.

Ahead, the path sloped downward, taking a sharp turn to the right, close behind LeFevre House where that girl had been murdered. Sad thing, the dead girl. Young and beautiful, he'd heard.

The dead girl had connections to the wealthy Clarke family. New Orleans people. He'd heard of Josephine Clarke Powell, who'd once lived in Ville Nouvelle. She was the girl's grandmother, and she was in town. Tall woman, he remembered, with bushy, auburn hair, a straight nose and an overbite. She'd be in her sixties now. We're all getting old, he thought.

The path took his attention. A verge of ancient trees and underbrush crowded the path - narrowed it. In this section of deep forest, tree branches laced overhead, sunlight filtering through the leaf-canopy playing patterns on the path. Now it was gathering dark. The path didn't fill him with joy. Not with twilight coming on. He shouldn't have walked this far, suddenly not relishing walking home in the dark.

No problem. He'd eat a bite at Sally's Seafood and get a ride home.

He'd found a box of old family photographs Helen's mother would treasure. He'd spoken to his sister on the telephone the first time in years and years. She'd apologized for an infraction she'd committed against him. That's what she called her lie—an infraction. A lie that deprived him of the girl he'd loved.

100

He forgave her - half-heartedly - knowing it pleased Helen. Niece Helen was a famous person. Wouldn't do to get on her bad side, not with her creepy powers. She might put a bad mojo on him.

Almost to LeFevre House, the thick underbrush on his left rustled. The sound startled him. He wheeled around, jumpy because of the fire. He laughed at his foolishness. Imagine being spooked by some harmless woodland creature.

"What?" he gasped. Someone draped in black clothing with a deep hood stepped in front of him, blocking the path. He blinked. "Wha-. . . what do you want?"

"You deserve a screwdriver in the eye for burning property that isn't yours."

"Wha . . . get outta my way. Who are you . . . "?

"Just call me the executioner."

CHAPTER 14

Beard House

Josephine returned to New Orleans. Carol Powell's murder slipped from front page news to a short paragraph on the second page. Irritably, Emmaline rustled the newspaper closed. What was Sheriff Smith doing? State had sent detectives to Ville Nouvelle. They had not questioned Emmaline. Did they believe she'd stolen the pearls and were waiting to arrest her? Byrd was no help with his endless platitudes. She visualized herself in a Tahiti prison.

Byrd invited her to Sally's Seafood for dinner. That cheered her up. The two of them eating dinner, overlooking the Mississippi River. She thought of it as a date and actually simpered once or twice as they ate their meal.

After dinner, they returned to the house. Maizie brought coffee to the library. "When I finish loading the dishwasher, I'm locking up and going to my apartment."

"Have a good rest. I'll see you in the morning."

Maizie turned to leave. "Oh yeah," she said. "Miss Helen telephoned. She said she was going to Miss Esther's tonight. They're having a meeting about the Ripper play."

"That's good news." Emmaline, pleased Helen was finally taking the play seriously."

Byrd sipped his coffee. "Good thing you put the play off until after the horserace."

"I guess so. Everything is backwards this year. "Emmaline tucked her long legs beneath her on the sofa. Byrd had researched Carol Powell's background and discovered nothing new. They'd reached a stalemate along with the authorities.

"I've assigned parts in the play," she said flicking at imaginary lint on her gray slacks.

"Finally."

"Yes. Finally."

"Any surprise castings?"

"Only one surprise," she said, "since you refuse to act."

"Emmaline, don't go there. Have I ever acted in one of your plays?"

"You have not," she said irritably.

"Who's the surprise actor?"

"Etienne. I talked to him the other night. He agreed to play the pub keeper who chases the ripper down an alley."

Byrd helped himself to a second cup of coffee and another slice of lemon tart. Maizie popped around the door wearing bright orange rubber gloves.

"I thought you were gone."

Maizie answered Emmaline, "Got started throwing away leftover food out of the fridge. Sheriff Smith came to the back door. You want me to send him in here?"

"Go ahead. What can he want?" Emmaline asked Byrd.

Byrd stood as Smith came into the room. "Sheriff," he acknowledged, extending his hand.

Smith ignored the polite gesture, strode to the center of the room, professional and unfriendly. He wasn't fishing for more on-stage time, as he usually did. "Where were you two today and this evening?"

Emmaline pushed aside a stack of books on the sofa. "Won't you sit down?" She switched on the green-shaded reading lamp. Smith took the chair at the reading table instead of joining her on the sofa. He pulled out a notebook.

"Where you two were today," he repeated.

"Here, mostly," Emmaline said after a quick glance at Byrd. "Then, Byrd took me to dinner at Sally's Seafood. Why?"

"Where's Miss Condor?"

"She went to Esther's. Why?"

"There's been another murder."

CHAPTER 15

"Who was murdered?" Emmaline demanded, clasping her hands together, her knuckles white.

"Etienne LeDeux." The sheriff's voice carried a threat.

"Marcel finally did it," she gasped, fighting for breath.

Smith's brows arched; his right eye twitched. "What're you talking about?"

Byrd dropped a pen. It rattled across the old cypress floor like a runaway marble.

Emmaline controlled her shock and said plainly. "Everyone in Ville Nouvelle knows Marcel stole Etienne's gun and has been shooting at Etienne for weeks."

"What proof do you have?" demanded the sheriff.

"Why . . . Etienne told Byrd and me Marcel was shooting at him." She gestured around the library. "He told us in this very room."

"Doesn't prove a thing except a third party stole his gun."

The sheriff's demeanor alarmed Emmaline. She glanced to Byrd. He sat quietly, listening.

Emmaline added, "Helen Condor has heard the shots, too. It's no secret bad blood has existed between those two men for years."

"How did Etienne die?" Byrd asked.

"Blunt force trauma to the head and face," said the sheriff. No one spoke for several long minutes. The silence was frightening. "If Marcel didn't kill him, who did?"

The sheriff stood and glared at her. "You know I can't discuss police business. I'll be in touch." He tipped his hat. "Emmaline, Byrd."

Once Sheriff Smith left, Emmaline grabbed her cell phone. "Ignore me, will he?" she said to Byrd as she punched in numbers.

"Who're you calling?"

"Ssh. Kimberley."

Kimberley, Smith's secretary, answered with a cheery hello.

"Etienne LeDeux," announced Emmaline. "How did he die? Is that right? He didn't deserve that. Uh huh . . . does his daughter, Julie, know? Uh huh. Thanks Kimberley. Owe you one."

"What? Byrd demanded.

"Some out of town joggers discovered the body shortly after dark on the Black Path. Bludgeoned to death. Blunt blows to the front of his head and the back. The coroner has the body. No official cause of death until the ME gives his report. Awful. I'm not to divulge any of this."

* * *

The next morning, Emmaline telephoned Etienne's home to speak to his daughter, if she'd arrived from Baton Rouge. Helen could be there, as well. She got no answer. She called Helen's cell phone. No answer. "Where do you think they are?"

"No idea," Byrd said.

She paced the library floor. "I can't sit here with these horrible murders happening under our nose."

"I thought those kids were coming over to work on the set. Esther, too."

"They can do that without me." She stopped pacing. She plunged onto the sofa, pulling a pillow over her body as if for protection. "I can't pull this play off. Not after what Helen said about killers having the power to channel the person channeling them."

"Don't worry."

"Easy to say."

"How about we take a drive. Sometimes getting out of the house gives a person a different perspective."

"I don't buy that, but what have I got to lose." She didn't want to interact with Pastor Lemuel's boys, or Esther, for that matter. A ride couldn't hurt.

Byrd took the Navigator. Emmaline leaned against the passenger side door, her head in her hands. They rode in silence. Byrd negotiated a turn from Palmetto Lane onto South Dock Street. "Would you look at this crowd. Dante has literally stopped traffic."

A flatbed truck with blasting loudspeakers, protesting everything nuclear, sat parked in the middle of the street. Traffic had come to a standstill. A couple of deputies moved to the flatbed, talking to the driver. "What a real mess," Emmaline groused.

"Those deputies will get things moving."

In the meantime, we sit, she thought.

"Not that we're going anywhere in particular."

"Yes, Pollyanna."

Byrd laughed at that jab. After a twenty-minute wait, the crowd blocking the street began to thin. Byrd inched the Navigator forward.

"Stop," Emmaline shrieked. "There's that guy."

Byrd punched the brakes. "What guy?"

"Carol's fiancé. The man who came to the house."

"You sure?"

"Pull over. I'm getting out."

"Pull over where? I can't park in the middle of the street."

"Why not? Everyone else is." She bailed out of the SUV and ran along South Dock Street, the man's blond ponytail bobbing ahead in the crowd. At the courthouse corner, she lost blondie. No. No, there he was, stopping at a hot dog vendor. Emmaline pushed ahead and tapped the man on the shoulder. "I need to talk to you."

He turned around slowly, mustard packets in one hand, hot dog in his other hand. "Sure, lady, great protest, huh? Want a hot dog?"

"- I'm sorry," she apologized. "I thought you were someone else."

"No problem, lady." Hot dog blondie grinned.

"Wrong guy," she said, crawling back into the SUV.

CHAPTER 16

The sun threaded through the ancient pines, pin oaks and sweet gums, tracing a shadowy path along the forest floor. The day had warmed, turning humid and muggy. Jeremy, Scott and Chad trudged through underbrush.

"I don't like it back here," Chad said, his face shiny and pale, dripping moisture. "Pastor Lemuel don't want us this far from the ranch." Panic bled though his voice, his tone carrying a wavering hopeful plea. Maybe the other two would come to their senses and turn back. Besides, they'd miss lunch. Once the ranch served meals, the kitchen closed until the next meal.

"You scared, Stuffy?" taunted Jeremy Worms. He'd renamed the thickset blond boy, Stuffy. A name Chad hated.

Chad's feet hurt in his cheap tennis shoes. His chubby legs chafed in his too large jeans. His mom sent stuff from the thrift store where she worked. "These things are good as new," she'd say. "It's a sin to waste good clothes when people in poorer countries don't have anything."

"No, I ain't scared," bluffed Chad to Jeremy. "I'm hungry and my feet hurt." He wanted to say, how we gonna find our way back? He didn't. You didn't cross Jeremy. You didn't push him too far, either.

Jeremy patted his jacket pocket. "I want to know who's hiding in that motorhome back here."

"It's none of our business," Chad dared to say. What did Jeremy have in his pocket?

"Maybe not yours, crybaby," said Scott, the redhead. "Me and Jeremy want to know."

"I mean to make it my business," boasted Jeremy, glaring at Chad over his shoulder. "You with me?"

"Sure." Chad knew you agreed with Jeremy Worms or else.

"Okay, Stuffy, you wait here while we give the motorhome people a welcome." Jeremy pulled a small caliber gun from his jacket."

Chad's eyes rounded. His breath caught. "Is . . . is . . . that a gun?"

"No, Hawkeye, it's a bow and arrow," guffawed Jeremy.

The next turn in the path brought the motorhome into full view. It stood approximately twenty yards ahead in a small clearing—curtains drawn, lights out.

"Well, well, well, looks like nobody is home," Jeremy whispered. "You two with me."

"Yeah," Scott said. "Let's do it."

"Do what?" Chad bleated. "Whatcha goin' to do?" He never was in the know, and most of the time, he liked it that way. Now, it seemed dangerous not to know Jeremy's plan. Now that Jeremy had a gun.

"Hide and watch," Jeremy gloated. He pulled a plastic bag of black powder from his pocket, sprinted forward, circling the RV, leaving a trail of black powder all around the outside of the vehicle. Jeremy stooped, lit a match to the powder. The powder flared up into a flame, then fizzled out.

"Crap," Jeremy muttered, "thought it'd burn." He struck match after match until red flames shot up along the gunpowder trail—a dangerous circle of death and destruction all around the fancy motorhome.

"Run, you idiots, you wanna get caught?" he whooped.

* * *

Byrd returned from a jog. He found Maizie in the kitchen, putting seafood sandwiches together.

"Is that crab delight?"

"Sure is. Don't be askin' my secret recipe, I ain't tellin'."

"Wouldn't help. Vi ruins every dish she prepares."

Maizie placed the last sandwich on the platter, wiped her hands down her apron. She covered the platter with clear plastic wrap and placed it in the fridge. "What you need is a wife, Mr. Byrd. A woman handy in the kitchen, you love to eat so much."

"You think?"

Maizie lifted a blue-enamel saucepan from the stove and moved to the sink to mix her sweet tea. Byrd loved Maizie's sweet tea, not too sweet, just right.

A sudden ear-splitting explosion shook the house, rattling the windows. Maizie dropped the saucepan, splashing hot tea over her feet. "They done blowed this place up with them atomic bombs!"

Rushing to the older woman, Byrd helped her onto a chair. Grabbing ice from the fridge, he rolled it in a dishtowel and applied the cold towel to Maizie's feet.

Maizie found her voice. "Did somebody bomb the house?"

"No," he said grimly. "Too far away."

Emmaline burst into the kitchen. "Did y'all hear that blast? Sounded like an oil refinery exploded." She grabbed her cell phone, punching in a number. "Kimberley," she shouted. "Are we being bombed?"

Emmaline listened to the other side of the conversation. "I am calm," she said into the phone, rolling her eyes at Byrd. "Uh . . . huh . . . "I see." She punched off. "The sheriff's department hasn't a clue what happened. There's a fire north of town out by the Boy's Ranch. What happened to Maizie's feet?"

"Accident with hot tea. Help me get her upstairs." They spent the next half hour settling Maizie in one of the guest bedrooms and determining her feet

113

weren't as badly scalded as Byrd previously believed. Emmaline insisted on Maizie's sister driving Maizie to the ER to be on the safe side.

Once Maizie and her sister left, Maizie protesting at the top of her lungs she was fine, Emmaline switched on the tiny black and white kitchen television. A news bulletin scrolled across the bottom of the screen. *An apparent explosion on the north side of Ville Nouvelle has occurred. Stay away from the area.*

"North side of Ville Nouvelle?" questioned Emmaline. "How vague is that. Kimberley said whatever happened was out the boy's ranch way."

"Covers a lot of territory," Byrd offered. "You could call Pastor Lemuel."

"I have a better idea," she said, grasping her arms with her long fingernails.

"I'm afraid to ask."

She wasn't listening; she was punching numbers into the kitchen telephone. "Kimberley," it's me again. Any more information? Is that right?" Emmaline, her intent gaze on Byrd, nodded in time to the conversation on the other end of the line. She disconnected. "A motorhome Dante Washington is using exploded out in the woods behind Pastor Lemuel's Boy's Ranch."

"Anyone hurt?" asked Byrd

"We're going out there. Now," she yelled. Get your keys."

Minutes later, Emmaline jumped into Byrd's Navigator. She looked down. *Good grief.* She still wore her fuzzy pink house shoes.

"Exactly where to," he asked.

"Drive north along the river and then double back. I know a pipeline road that leads to the woods behind the ranch property. The motorhome was parked out that way, according to Kimberley."

Byrd, his expression grim, followed her directions along backroads that were no more than pig trails. He had to hand it to Emmaline. She knew her backwoods. At least she thought she did. They made three wrong turns before she hit the correct road, used by oil rig attendants.

"One out of three isn't bad," she said, springing out of the Navigator the moment he cut the engine. They started walking.

"Ouch!" Emmaline screeched. "I forgot about thorns."

"Watch where you step."

They plunged through the thickets until the scent of smoldering metal and melting plastic filled the air. Ahead, in a little clearing, stood the smoking remains of the once majestic RV—a twisted skeleton resembling some giant metal beast.

The Ville Nouvelle Volunteer Fire Department worked the scene. Sheriff Smith and Deputy Saucer Fontenot stood to one side. Emmaline darted across the singed and pocked earth toward the sheriff. Byrd followed. Smith caught sight of them and held up his hand. "What the h -? No nearer," he yelled.

Ignoring the sheriff, Emmaline dashed forward, leaves and twigs adhering to the fuzzy house shoes.

"Is Dante all right?" she cried, halting in the sheriff's personal space. In fact, nose to nose.

"I said, stay back," he ordered. "This is a crime scene."

"Is Dante okay?"

The sheriff shot both of them a malevolent glare. "This is official business," he spat through clenched teeth. "Both of you, get out of here. You're interfering with an investigation." Pivoting, Smith strode forward to meet an ambulance wailing up the country road.

"Good heavens," Emmaline shouted after him. "You can at least tell us if Dante is dead." The unanswered plea bounced off Smith's retreating backside.

"Three murders," Emmaline yelled, competing with the wailing siren. "No one is safe in Ville Nouvelle."

EMTs spilled out of the ambulance and hurried to a makeshift blanket tent a few yards from the RV remains. They lifted someone onto a gurney and pushed the gurney into the back of the ambulance. Byrd nor Emmaline never had a chance to see the injured - or dead - person.

115

"Let's go." Byrd grasped Emmaline's arm, steering her toward the path they'd accessed to the property. Wrenching free, she hissed. "No. Follow me."

"Where?"

"Duck low," she whispered, hunching toward a thick patch of woods on the other side of the RV. "Are you coming?"

"What choice have I? Remember your flimsy shoes."

The ambulance roared away, siren screeching. The heavier underbrush in this section of woods concealed their approach. Smith stood so close, Byrd could reach out and touch him. The smoking RV clogged his sinuses. Emmaline was right. They could see and hear everything here. The sheriff's department photographer arrived. The blaze was now contained, except for sooty embers. Firemen began rewinding hoses. Smith, his boot clad foot propped on a singed stump, asked one of the firemen, "What do you think happened?"

The fireman took off his helmet and mopped his red face. "Not sure at this point. Once the fire marshals investigate, we'll know officially." The man stooped down, gesturing along the ground. "Don't quote me. I'd say arson, but that's a guess. I smelled some type of accelerant, and there's a suspicious burn path around the motorhome. Could be a freak accident. Civilians take every chance in the book."

"That wouldn't explain the explosion," Smith countered.

"If the RV had a full gas tank, you can count on an explosion. Hazmat's coming in case of toxic chemicals."

Nudging Emmaline, Byrd motioned for them to leave. She gave him a baleful look but followed. They took their circuitous path back to the Navigator.

Inside the vehicle, she collapsed on Byrd's shoulder, "Poor Dante, is he . . . do you think he's . . . dead?" She choked on the word *dead*.

"We don't know," he said. A sick feeling rocked his gut. He gave Emmaline a tender look. Now, every friend seemed more precious than ever. "Don't jump to conclusions. Who says he was even in the RV?"

"Someone left in that ambulance." Tears trickled down her face. "Why would anyone want to kill Dante?"

Byrd thought of several reasons—the nuclear protest march that garnered national and international attention—even Dante's presence in his hometown could bring out the crazies. Career enviers. The list could go on and on.

Emmaline wiped the corners of her eyes. She leaned against Byrd's shoulder. "What's happening in Ville Nouvelle? I don't understand. First, Carol is murdered, then Etienne, and now Dante."

* * *

Later in the day, the news channels flashed the explosion reports. The anchor, a pasty-faced man with a mustache, announced, "An RV occupied by Dante Washington and his wife, Shemika Washington, exploded and burned this morning. Whether foul play or accidental, is uncertain at this point. The motorhome and site are under investigation. Mr. Dante Washington suffered no injuries; however, Mrs. Washington, alone in the RV at the time of the explosion, suffered burns. She was transported to a Baton Rouge hospital. No official word on her condition. Stay tuned for further updates."

"Mrs. Washington," Emmaline said.

CHAPTER 17

Ville Nouvelle Downs

Byrd agreed that Emmaline made the correct decision delaying the Jack the Ripper theatrical until after the horserace. With the two unsolved murders in Ville Nouvelle, the mysterious RV fire and Dante Washington's exodus to the West Coast with his burn-victim wife, the edge seemed taken from the notorious play. Too, there had been little time to rehearse. Helen proved small help after her uncle's murder.

The day of the horse race dawned with its usual fanfare. Locals turned out by the droves.

Marching bands from two high schools paraded; horses from surrounding parishes followed the bands along the crowded streets. Food vendors filled a city block.

Byrd, driving the Navigator, threaded the way through bumper-to-bumper traffic to the racetrack grounds. Emmaline, beside him, chattered non-stop. Seizing a narrow parking spot, he inched the Navigator in. He and Emmaline alighted.

"Nobody puts on a show like Ville Nouvelle."

He grinned, enjoying her good mood. Festivity filled the air. Bands played, flags waved, and crowds milled as they made their way to the grandstand. A long line waited at the betting window. "Ready to put your money where your mouth is?" he bantered to Emmaline.

"Byrd, you're ridiculous. Of course, I'm placing my money on Julie LeDeux." She lowered her voice to a whisper. "Though, I can't imagine her racing her father's horse, with Etienne barely cold in his grave."

"There's Julie now." Byrd waved to the tall young woman in tight jeans, a red and black silk shirt and a big black hat. She came toward them.

Julie caught Emmaline's hand. "I'm glad you're here."

"Julie!" Emmaline exclaimed, grabbing the young woman in a bear hug. They'd never been particularly close, but death changes things.

Tears glistened in the corners of Julie's eyes as they drew apart. "I was determined I wouldn't cry."

"Cry all you want, sweetheart," Emmaline said soothingly. "I know your father is proud of you at this moment."

"I know it, too. Cousin Helen contacted him. He's in a better place. I'm riding for him today. He was an honest man who loved his horses and spent his life caring for his stables. I... I won't let a cowardly killer destroy his spirit. Nor mine."

"Of course, you won't, dear," agreed Emmaline.

Julie sighed. She lowered her voice. "Sheriff Smith thinks the killer could show up here today. I pray he's right, and I pray he catches the monster."

The line at the betting window thinned. Emmaline spotted Esther Marshall. "Excuse me, Julie, I want to tell Esther something."

"Likely how to bet," observed Byrd, smiling at Julie. "Tell me," he said to Julie, "how does the race work?"

Warming to the subject, she smiled genuinely. "Today is The Grand Championship Sweepstakes. The races are divided into three sets. It's an elimination process. The first race is stallions competing against stallions, then geldings against geldings, and finally mares against mares. The winners against each other. The Ville Nouvelle Grand Champion Sweepstakes winner is decided by the overall winner from the first and second place winners in the four divisions. That way, every entrant has a chance to win. My father's horse, Daddy's Demon, will break from the sixth hole in the stallion race. You know how it is with stallions. There can be, uh... problems."

"It's a good idea to separate stallions," Emmaline said, returning, pocketing more betting stubs.

Julie turned to Byrd. "Emmaline is right. As I was saying, Daddy's Demon, my dad's stallion was in the stretch last year when a mare got his attention. He went on to Louisiana Downs in Shreveport. He didn't win." Julie pulled her broad-brimmed hat lower, hiding her deep blue eye shadow, and the equally dark blue circles beneath her eyes.

"Who's the strongest contender this year?" Byrd asked.

"On The Agenda," Julie said quietly. "He's out of Lafayette."

The band struck up loud Cajun music.

"Luck ride with you," Byrd and Emmaline called as Julie walked away.

They found a seat in the grandstand. The announcer's voice boomed. "Welcome to Ville Nouvelle Downs and the spring races. To all contenders— may you run la bride sur le cou."

"What did he say?" asked Byrd.

Emmaline laughed. "French for *you run with free rein.*"

The first event started. Burro races with clowns astride their backs. Following the burros, the P.A. system blared the stallion race competitors' names. Each contestant rode to the center of the ring, performing a showy turnaround in front of the grandstand. Julie was the last contestant called. "Miss Julie LeDeux, riding *Daddy's Demon*. Miss Julie LeDeux."

Applause thundered. Demon pranced into the arena, head high, colors flying. He never broke gallop and gallantly lived up to his fiery name. The crowd cheered louder. Julie doffed her hat and waved.

Side riders steered the stallions into lineup for the stallion race. The gate opened. A flag dropped. The horses were off with *Daddy's Demon* in the lead. He took the win with ease; Byrd and Emmaline cheered wildly. "That girl is some horsewoman," enthused Byrd.

"Look," Emmaline yelled, punching Byrd in the ribs. "There by the concession stand. The ponytail guy, Gary West." She bolted from the grandstand and sprinted into the crowd.

"Wait," called Byrd. "He could be dangerous."

He followed her, stepping gingerly through the rows of grandstand patrons. "Excuse me. Pardon me." Once on the walkway, he charged toward the busy concession stands, the last place he'd spotted her. Only, she'd moved out of sight. Where was she? He let out an exasperated sigh. The crowd had swallowed Emmaline as well as the mysterious ponytail guy.

Sheriff Smith came toward him, holding a hotdog in a mustard soaked napkin. "In a hurry?" he drawled.

Byrd explained. "Emmaline saw that guy again, Carol Powell's fiancé, near the concession stand."

"I don't see either of them," Smith said. At that moment, Emmaline appeared. "I lost him."

"Was he ever here in the first place," commented Smith snidely.

CHAPTER 18

L ate that evening, Byrd and Emmaline sat in the library watching the evening news. "What a day," she groused, planting her feet on the coffee table. Etienne LeDeux's murder flashed across the screen in gory detail.

"Yes," the local anchor continued. "The victim's body was discovered on the Black Path, the well-used walking trail near the back entrance to LeFevre House. The house where another unsolved gruesome murder occurred just weeks ago. Miss Emmaline Beard discovered the first victim's body. That victim, Carol Powell, had former ties to Ville Nouvelle. It appears -"

Emmaline switched off the television. "Sickening, the way they gloat about LeFevre House being the scene of two murders."

"Don't worry about it."

"I do worry. The house tour is part of my bread and butter." Emmaline sat up straighter. "I have a surprise."

"Oh?"

"You remember Smith mentioned we could see Carol Powell's autopsy report? Kimberley hinted she has something for me."

"I don't think the sheriff meant it."

"The report is at Kimberley's place. I can borrow it temporarily." Emmaline pushed up from the sofa. She pulled a light sweater around her shoulders. "Going with me or staying here?"

He opted to join her.

Byrd started the Navigator, and Emmaline climbed into the passenger seat. The night greeted them, velvety soft, with millions of stars overhead.

"Kimberley lives south of town in one of the new condos." She gave directions. They approached the condos, erected on former farmland, each identical building graceless and seemingly out of place. Not a single tree stood in sight. Identical gaslights on each manicured lawn shed muted illumination.

"The last one," she said, pointing ahead.

Byrd drove to the building, parked and switched off the engine.

"Wait here." She let herself out and dashed into the darkness. The night seemed to swallow her. A few minutes later, she scrambled in beside him clutching a brown, legal-size envelope. "Pull up there." She gestured to a streetlight out of sight of the condos. She tore the envelope open.

"You should wait until we get to the house."

With an exasperated look, she agreed. "Okay. Drive a few blocks farther and park under a streetlight." He drove a short distance and pulled in to a convenience store parking lot. She promptly switched on the dashboard map light and began flipping pages, speedreading. The fine hairs on the back of her head tingled. "I can't believe this. What was Kimberley thinking? She made a mistake."

"What're you talking about?"

"This isn't Carol Powell's autopsy report. It's a preliminary homicide report on Etienne LeDeux's murder." She passed the report to Byrd.

He scanned the report. "Wow! You're implicated, huh?"

"Looks that way. They found the murder weapon—a ball-peen hammer from one of the LeFevre House sheds."

He read aloud. "Miss Emmaline Beard, owner of LeFevre House and owner of the ball-peen hammer used to bash in Etienne LeDeux's face and skull, has not been reached for comment." A sketch of Etienne's full body, with wounds flagged, filled another page.

"I don't own LeFevre House. Only the land it sits on. As for the hammer, it's random property." She continued. "LeFevre House is a community project. I'm not the only person with access or keys."

"That may be," he ceded, "but you're the main key holder. I doubt Esther has keys."

"Why should she?"

"Or Tom."

"Tom has keys. He's maintenance."

"Just saying."

She pushed the report into the envelope. "Drive back to Kimberley's. I've seen enough. She can return this pack of lies tomorrow."

CHAPTER 19

The following day, Emmaline tried to focus on the theatrical. Esther arrived early along with the boys from the Boys Ranch. Even Helen showed up despite Etienne's recent death. Keeping busy soothed Emmaline's nerves. The murder weapon information rattled her. She expected a visit from Sheriff Smith. She even pushed Dante Washington's RV explosion from her mind.

Her attention this day, the set - how the scenery panels should be painted and placed. She noticed Jeremy Worms seemed exceptionally subdued as he clumped up and down the stairs adjusting the lightning system. "Jeremy," she said, "didn't the RV explosion frighten you boys? "It happened near your dormitories."

"It was awesome," he mumbled. "Sounded like one of those oil refineries blowing up."

"That's what I thought at first," she said.

Jeremy turned back to adjusting the light panel. At last satisfied with the lights, he tested the main spotlights.

"Great job," she said and meant it. The boy was a genius.

Helen took a break from the stage below. She climbed the stairs and joined Emmaline. "You're doing a fantastic job, both you and Esther. I credit you for an outstanding professional performance."

"Thanks." Emmaline needed reassurance.

Helen's hands trembled. An almost imperceptible shudder passed over the psychic. "I must tell you something."

Emmaline braced herself. "What?"

Helen continued. "You recall I told you channeling involves spirits taking over my mind and body ... impressions come... the visions may be past events... present events, or future events."

Emmaline nodded as if she understood the woman's dark gift.

"Etienne," Helen whispered, a sob in her voice. "Etienne's killer is a human jackal, clever, watching, and waiting for opportunities. This murderer is no butcher like the ripper, whose maniacal, sexual frenzies drove him to further atrocities. Etienne's killer is more ordinary."

"Ordinary?" questioned Emmaline. What killer is ordinary?

"I've reached this person."

"Go on."

"This person has no conscience."

"You know who it is?" Emmaline said excitedly.

"Not an actual identity," Helen admitted. "I explained to you. Once I'm drawn into the visions, they seek me. I can't escape them. I can't say anything more. Too dangerous."

* * *

That evening, Byrd dove Emmaline to Sally's Seafood for dinner. She welcomed the outing.

They arrived at the popular eatery at prime time, the place filled with jovial customers, their conversations bouncing off the walls. Byrd looked his best, sitting across from her in a pale lavender shirt with a white tie. Both colors enhanced his red hair. She'd always been partial to gingers.

"You nervous about the play?"

"Not really," she said. "Not after I assigned roles. Everyone seems okay with my choices." She hesitated. "Helen told me something eerie today." Helen's latest revelation left her disturbed. On the other hand, perhaps Helen's fears were nothing more than the psychic's overwrought nerves reacting over Etienne's murder.

She repeated Helen's story about Etienne's murderer. "It upset me. I think Gary West killed Carol. I don't know who killed Etienne or why. And I'm producing a play about what - murders. One of the most infamous killers in history. Who was never caught," she added macabrely, "What if I set the stage for the real murders here?"

"You don't really believe that. Don't tell me you're buying into Helen Condor's psychic claptrap? You knew the ripper play was gruesome going in," he said with a chuckle.

"I may or may not put total credence in Helen's abilities." She paused, careful to choose her words, careful he understood. "I admit Helen is onto something I don't understand. She is totally sincere. She is frightened by her visions. I didn't know there would be two murders when I planned the play. I pray I haven't summoned two killers unwittingly."

"I buy that."

"I'm certain I saw Gary West at the horse race."

"You think you saw him. Number one, why would Gary West remain in town if he killed Carol? "Number two, you were mistaken about seeing him before."

"I think he would stay here to get the pearls. You're right, though, I could be mistaken. I'm big enough to admit it."

"And you chose the ripper theme to be sensational. Sell more tickets," he said as their food arrived.

He fell to eating his seafood salad. She couldn't let the subject drop. "Carol Powell was murdered at my ancestors' home. Etienne was bludgeoned to death with an antique hammer from a shed at the same house. I'm involved whether I choose to be or not."

"Are you ascribing both murders to the same killer? Don't forget Etienne claimed Marcel was shooting at him. The spent bullets from Etienne's gun put truth to Etienne's claims his neighbor stole his gun."

She shifted uncomfortably. "Makes me wonder," she said uncertainly. "I know Marcel and Etienne shared bad blood. Still, Marcel a killer. I just can't picture it."

"Stranger things have happened."

"True. Their feud goes back years over property lines and mineral rights. The old courthouse burned, destroying legalities. Each party claimed what they believed. There was no legal proof."

Pausing, she added, "I don't know how to explain this. but as time went on…. their feud seemed something expected of them. Marcel, the over-the-top, blowhard loudmouth, and Etienne the introverted victim type, made a person expect bad things to happen. Does that make sense?"

"Maybe. I say the introverted victim type has a saturation point. The point where he or she has had enough and fights back."

"Meaning Etienne set fire to Marcel's fields."

"Circumstantial evidence proved that."

"The gas can and the guy at the convenience store?"

"Exactly. Etienne lost the fight. He's dead. Marcel killed him."

Too simple, she thought. Gary West killed Carol Powell. He wanted the pearls. Marcel killed Etienne for setting the fire. Perfect motives. In her mind, the pieces didn't fit.

"Is the play shaping up?" Byrd asked, changing the subject.

"Yes. Esther and Helen drove down to New Orleans to buy masks. Saucer plays several roles as a passerby. Saucer is as big a ham as the sheriff. Can you believe he insists on wearing different face masks to appear different in each scene? Do you know the price of those life-like masks?" She rolled her eyes.

Byrd chuckled. They finished their meal in silence. "You ready to go?"

At Beard House, Byrd went to the library to make phone calls, Emmaline to the kitchen to brew coffee. She joined him in the library with the coffee and fresh lemon tarts.

Byrd leaned back. "You've assigned parts. Any surprise castings?"

Still admiring his lavender shirt in the soft lamplight, she smiled. "Only one surprise, since you refuse to act in my plays." Byrd grimaced. "I've asked Marcel to play the pub keeper who chases the ripper. The part I offered to Etienne."

Byrd almost dropped his cup of coffee. "You think that's smart? Half the town believes Marcel killed Etienne."

"I'm running out of actors."

CHAPTER 20

No suspects in the two murder cases disturbed Byrd. With Emmaline distracted with her play and worried about lost revenue from the cancelled antebellum house tour, he'd spent time thinking about the murders. The three elements necessary in solving any murder - motive, means and opportunity intrigued him. In Carol Powell's case, motive, the stolen pearls, means, strangled and beaten with a heavy object, opportunity, Gary West waylaid her. Etienne LeDeux's murder, more complex. Motive, unknown. Means, ball peen hammer. Opportunity, Etienne alone on the Black Path.

Byrd did not believe Marcel Beaudion killed Etienne. Far too simple. Much too obvious. He believed Etienne set fire to Marcel's fields. In some unknown way, Mr. LeDeux's murder and Carol Powell's murder were related. They occurred in the same small town within a short time of each other. A connection existed.

Carol Powell's murder originated in Tahiti. She obtained the stolen pearls there. She fled to the states with them. She gave them to Emmaline to pass on to Josephine. Why Josephine? Did Carol trust the troubled woman's ability to return the pearls to their rightful owner? Carol died to set the theft aright. In Byrd's opinion, she died a hero, forfeiting her life to return the pearls to the pearl museum.

Emmaline poured second cups of coffee. Byrd thought as he added his four teaspoons of sugar - he couldn't stay in Ville Nouvelle forever. He had a business to run. Thus far, their feeble murder investigation had stalled. He had devised a daring plan and chose not to reveal his plan to her.

* * *

It was time, Byrd thought, to put his plan into action. The following afternoon, he drove to Baton Rouge Metropolitan Airport on Jackie Cochran Drive, parked, hurried inside, secured his ticket and waited until his flight to Papeete, Tahiti. Emmaline wouldn't understand his urgency to visit Polynesia. Not only would she not understand, she'd forbid him going.

Relieved to escape the distractions in Ville Nouvelle, he was free to concentrate on Carol's murder. In Byrd's opinion, the answer lay in Papeete.

He'd puzzled long about the scattered story the fiancé told Emmaline about a South Seas sail that went bad. He'd made copious notes on the hypothetical timeline when the couple sailed from Marina Del Ray and both arrived in Ville Nouvelle. Josephine Powell corroborated the fiancé's story, confirming her son and granddaughter owned a boat, the Zephyr. Too, he'd always fancied a trip to Polynesia for personal reasons.

He boarded the plane at half-past four p.m., before Baton Rouge's heaviest evening commuters hit the freeways. He settled in for the short hop to the DFW airport. From Dallas, he'd fly to LAX. From Los Angeles to Polynesia. All in all, an approximately seventeen hour and thirty-minute flight if everything went well.

Everything went well. He arrived in Papeete shortly after five a.m. the following morning. A westerly breeze ruffled his hair as he hailed a cab. There was only one taxi, and the native driver appeared not to have slept in weeks. Byrd had booked luxury accommodations, this being off season for tourists. He hadn't had time to shop for bargain rooms.

"Welcome M'sieur. Ça va [how are you]? Casino?"

"Non casino." Byrd sprang upstairs. He chuckled to himself. How Emmaline would envy him if she could see him now. A great deal of competition existed in their sleuthing. After a shower, a short nap and breakfast, he dressed in light-weight cotton trousers and a matching shirt with deep pockets. He chose sandals with thick socks since he planned a walk along the beach after taking care of business. Sharp volcanic rocks, and even bits of coral shards, hid in the black sand. Slathered with mosquito repellent (he was aware of Dengue Fever), he started walking toward police headquarters. The French Police Headquarters was in a government building a short distance from his hotel. He passed the Parc Bougainville, the famous local park, with its swaying palm trees, lily pad covered lagoons, and beautiful tropical plants - scenery he'd dreamed about.

The government building resembled an elaborate modern A-frame type structure with a wide red brick walkway leading to the glass main door. Byrd thought it a friendly building more resembling a tourist center he'd once visited, rather than a government property. Unfortunately, he was too early. The door was locked.

He crossed the road, which faced the Pacific. He sat down to wait on one of the huge volcanic boulders facing the sea. As the sun rose higher, he stared in wonder at the blue ocean and blue sky, both the identical azure shade. There appeared no division between heaven and sea - like an encircling blue womb. Shelly, his deceased fiancée, filled his thoughts. "Shelly, darling," he whispered, "I'm here. Here where we planned to celebrate our honeymoon. You see me, you hear me, I know you do. I love you forever." He blew a kiss into the sea breeze.

A man walked past. "Good morning." He had an Australian accent. He appeared none too prosperous, but not seedy. About thirtyish, Byrd guessed. Tanned, his face weathered by the sun, the stranger stopped. "You visiting?" the man asked.

"Yes and no. Some business, some pleasure. You?"

The stranger laughed, joining Byrd on a nearby boulder. "I'm an island hopper. Odd jobs here and there. Amateur tourist guide when needed. Save big bucks for those interested in a look at the real attractions."

"I might be interested. Not this morning. I have business with the Gendarmerie."

"Oh, the Gendarmerie. I wish you luck, my friend, if you've come afoul of the law."

"No, no, nothing like that. I need information." Byrd thought a moment. "Are there many like you - island hoppers - who work odd jobs and the like?"

"Too many, and not all of them reputable. If you know what I mean."

"Did you happen to see a boat here some months back? The Zephyr."

The man looked out to sea; his expression quickly different. Byrd sensed the stranger weighed how much to share. "I saw the Zephyr. Why do you ask?"

"A friend's granddaughter sailed here on the Zephyr. There was engine trouble. She flew to the United States. Her companion stayed here for repairs to the boat. We need to contact him. His name is Gary West."

"I've seen the Zephyr here on occasions in the past. Her skipper, Charlie Powell, is well known in Tahiti." The man spoke guardedly. "I met Gary Powell who was manning the Zephyr, the voyage you speak of. He and a man by the name of Filipino, that's not right. Sounded like that. West needed parts for the boat. Takes time to get things shipped out here. I haven't seen him in months. You... uh... know if the girl made it to the United States." The man stood, jingling coins in his pockets.

"She did." Byrd did not share Carol Powell's cruel fate.

Suddenly eager to be off, the stranger handed a card to Byrd. "Call me if you decide to take a *real* tour of the islands." He walked away quickly. Byrd wondered if he fled further questions. Turning the card, it read: *Bradley O'Connor, Tours and more*. Plus, a phone number.

CHAPTER 21

"**G**ood morning, M'sieur. How may I help you?" The officer, with a mahogany complexion and handsome island features, spoke English with a French accident.

"I'm Bertram Jeffcoat, Sir. From the United States. I wish to speak to a detective about a crime that was committed here in Papeete."

"What crime M'sieur?"

"It's of a confidential nature. If I could speak with a detective."

"Oui M'sieur." The gendarme's smile not so bright, nor his tone so friendly, motioned to a chair before departing through a door to the left of the room. He returned a few minutes later. "Step this way, M'sieur."

Byrd followed him to a spacious office housing an enormous teakwood desk before a wall of dark-tinted glass, the sea visible beyond the glass. An older officer, darker of skin with sharp eyes, looked up. "Allo. I am Gendarme Inspector, Jacques Gagne. State your business." Gendarme Inspector Gagne did not stand. He indicated a tan leather chair before the desk. Byrd sat uneasily, the ceiling fan overhead droning silently, sweeping the fronds of a massive potted palm.

"My cadet says you wish to report a crime," Gendarme Gagne said crisply. "We take crime seriously here in Papeete especially crimes against our visitors."

"I haven't a crime to report," Byrd said, leaning forward. "I need information about a crime committed in Papeete some months ago. I'm Bertram Jeffcoat from the United States. A young woman, Carol Powell, was murdered in our country. She flew from Papeete. Her fiancé, Gary West, remained here because their boat needed repairs. Eventually, Mr. West sailed the Zephyr, Miss Powell's yacht, to New Orleans, Louisiana."

The gendarme, listening intently, missed nothing. "Continue M'sieur," he said when Byrd paused.

Byrd drew a packet of photographs from his shirt pocket and placed them before the gendarme. "The girl in the picture is Carol Powell. She was brutally murdered in Ville Nouvelle, a small town upriver from New Orleans. Before her death, Gary West came to Ville Nouvelle looking for her. No one was aware she'd arrived in town. Later, she contacted a family friend."

"This fiancé - this man - he was questioned about her murder."

"No. His whereabouts are unknown."

The officer spread his hands. "I do not see how I can help you, M'sieur. Many people visit Papeete, especially the yachts, the boats."

"There's more." Byrd drew a picture of the pearls from his pocket. "Ms. Powell gave these pearls to her friend in Ville Nouvelle for safe keeping."

The gendarme's eyes narrowed; his mouth tightened beneath his impressive mustache.

Byrd continued. "The United States police, those in Louisiana, the FBI, even Interpol, identified these as the pearls stolen from the pearl museum here in Papeete. Our police are in contact with the authorities here."

The officer held up his hand. "If you will be so kind as to wait. I will speak to an associate." Inspector Gagne took the photographs and left the room.

Twenty minutes or more later, which seemed hours to Byrd, Gagne returned, accompanied by two gendarmes. "M'sieur Bertram Jeffcoat, I am placing you under arrest for complicity in the robbery of pearls from the Tahiti Pearl Museum."

CHAPTER 22

Ville Nouvelle

"Surely he's in Houston," bemoaned Emmaline to Maizie after Byrd had not returned to Ville Nouvelle for forty-eight hours.

What could've happened? She tried to mask her concern. However, she knew Maizie wasn't fooled. No one in Ville Nouvelle had seen him or heard from him. Emmaline debated telephoning Vi, Byrd's sister. Vi put the direst spin on anything out of the ordinary concerning her only sibling.

Emmaline called his lab and spoke to Byrd's secretary. Betty hadn't heard from him, either. "Nothing to worry about," Betty advised Emmaline. "You know how he is. Off here and there without so much as a goodbye."

Which was true. Betty urged Emmaline not to upset Vi. Betty had her own issues with Violet Causey. Emmaline assured the secretary she wouldn't contact Vi.

Betty's lack of concern did little to ease Emmaline's worries. Something had happened to Byrd. She felt trouble in her bones. With the two recent murders in Ville Nouvelle, she imagined Byrd lying somewhere, his lifeless body awaiting discovery. On the other hand, if he'd left Ville Nouvelle to pursue a clue he didn't want to share, she'd never forgive him. She knew he believed both murders were committed by the same killer.

* * *

Byrd's disappearance occupied Emmaline's thoughts all morning. What alarming thing could happen next? Oh no! Sheriff Smith's squad car stopped at the house. She braced herself, certain the lawman came to tell her he'd found Byrd's body. Or, more questions about the death hammer.

Maizie escorted the sheriff to the library. Emmaline held her breath.

"Good morning, Miss Emmaline."

"Good morning, sheriff."

She exhaled—apparently no dire news. The sheriff appeared in a good mood.

"Is my costume ready?" he asked. He continued, "I'm not appearing before the audience in some ill-fitting piece of crap."

"You're wearing a cloak," Emmaline managed. "Mrs. McAffee is making final alterations. (Mrs. McAffee, the local Mardi Gras costume coordinator, created all of Emmaline's theatrical costumes). Fit shouldn't be that big a deal in a cloak, she thought. No one more vain than the handsome sheriff. However, needing her leading man in a mellow mood, she promised, "I'll let you know the minute your costume is ready." She smiled magnanimously. "Will you have coffee with me?"

"I haven't time. Where's Byrd?"

She wished she knew the answer to that question herself. "He's... uh... away a few days. He comes and goes. Most of the time neglecting to tell me his plans."

"He works in Houston, right?"

She answered the sheriff truthfully. "Yes. He's a chemist with a private lab. He's into research, adhesives, you know, glue and the like."

"Be sure and let me know when the costumes arrive."

"Oh, I will. I will." Not one to miss an opportunity, she said, "Uh, is Marcel Beaudion your main suspect in Etienne's murder?"

Smith stopped on his way to the door, frowned. "Hearsay," he said. "That's how baseless gossip gets started."

CHAPTER 23

New Orleans

Josephine Powell's telephone rang. Charlie Powell eased his mother's bedroom door closed. "Hello."

"Sheriff Smith from Ville Nouvelle. May I speak to Mrs. Powell."

"Oh, hi Sheriff. This is Charlie Powell, her son. My mother isn't available to talk. She's asleep. "Something I can help you with?" Charlie spoke pleasantly, grateful for the distance between Ville Nouvelle and New Orleans. Kept the lawman out of their faces.

"It's about Gary West. Have either of you seen him or heard from him?"

"No, we haven't." He answered too quickly. Modulating his voice to sound helpful, Charlie said, "We've wondered about him, too." He laughed a little too loud. "I spoke to one of his friends on the coast - the guy who operates Gary's store - whenever Gary is out of town."

"I need the friend's name and contact number."

Charlie supplied the information. Josephine mumbled in the background. He jumped. *What was she doing up?* "If there's any way we can help further, let us know." He ended the call. Josephine stood behind him; her hands splayed on the doorjamb to steady herself.

"My mother is taking Carol's death hard," he said into the dead line.

"Who is that? What are you keeping from me now? Was that the FBI again?"

"Mom, Sheriff Smith called. Goodbye." Charlie replaced the phone in its cradle. "He's looking for Gary West."

Josephine whimpered, leaned forward, and lost her balance, her long fingers clutching the door like a maimed crab.

He rushed to her. "Mom, you've had your meds. You're too wobbly. Where's your walker?"

"In the storeroom where it needs to be. Earl put it there."

"Why would you go and do that?" He led her back to bed. "You don't want to fall again," he said gently, helping her into bed, closing the bedroom door behind him. She'd be asleep soon.

Earl gave Charlie the creeps. Rather, his mother's dependence on the chauffer. Revolting, the amount of money Josephine tipped the man. Charlie spied her checkbook before she confiscated it and locked it in her bedroom safe. Hundreds of dollars. Over five hundred dollars to drive Josephine to Hot Springs.

"Bring the phone," she shrieked from behind the closed bedroom door.

He obliged, brought the phone and plugged it into the wall jack.

"I'm calling Helen Condor."

"Now? You should rest first." She settled back and closed her eyes. He knew why she wanted to contact the psychic nut. Josephine believed Helen could reach Carol in the other world. Carol would reveal her killer's identity. They'd gone over this a dozen times.

"Asleep, Mom?" She didn't answer. He tucked the light blanket around her feet. Slipped the phone from her hand to the bedside table. He won this small battle. He needed absolute power-of-attorney to take care of her finances and health decisions. He doubted there'd be a red cent left of the Clarke fortune with Josephine in charge.

It wasn't all about money with him. He couldn't grieve for his only child for his mom's hysterical state. Nor with the enabling Earl hovering. Nor could he leave Josephine. She was too vulnerable.

Where was Gary West? He'd never liked or trusted West from the first time Carol brought him home. He didn't mention it to Sheriff Smith or the FBI, but he'd called in a private investigator to check if West had returned to California. So far, nothing. Something weird was going on - he knew it.

The authorities claimed three men pulled off the Tahiti pearl theft. Carol had the pearls in her possession. She would never steal anything. Had Gary West given them to her, or planted them on her, unbeknownst to Carol? Carol had feared she was being followed, according to Emmaline Beard's information about the girl's state of mind. Followed by whom?

Why give the pearls to such an unlikely person as Emmaline Beard? He wouldn't give the nosy woman the time of day.

West had arrived in Ville Nouvelle before Carol. Had he waited to kill her? Or, was West dead, as well? Three men committed the robbery. Was West one of the threesome? What a mess. Girls never listened to their old man about lovers.

CHAPTER 24

Ville Nouvelle

After Sheriff Smith left Beard House badgering her about his costume, Emmaline drove out to Marcel Beaudion's property. She drove over a bumpy cattle guard to the pastures. When the road ended, she alighted, the scent of burned grass assaulting her sinuses. Devastation everywhere—burned fence posts, charred wire, and ash-stubbled fields. None of Marcel's famous racehorses were in sight. Uneasy, she began snapping pictures with her cell phone. She walked to the stand of pine trees along the far edge of the once green pasture. Noticing a heap of charred debris, she nudged the pile with her sneaker toe. She unearthed a partially burned tent, blackened cook pots, remains of some type of leather bags, charred blankets, and smaller items. This area was once someone's campsite—a protest marcher, a homeless person, or a murderer? She couldn't leave fast enough.

On the drive home, an atavistic impression troubled her. Some primitive sense of great danger, plus the need for self-preservation. What? Had she seen something important and didn't recognize it? Grateful for the photos on her cell phone, she'd replay them once she got home to jar her recall.

** *

When she arrived at Beard House, there was no time to replay cell phone photos or even think about the troublesome sensation she'd experienced at Marcel's fields.

Esther Marshall and Pastor Lemuel's boys greeted her. The boys had completed the Ripper scenery and were setting it up onstage. The stage Emmaline's father had indulgently installed, years before, to appease his daughter.

Esther, her new henna job harsh and metallic, propped her hands on her hips and gestured to the stage. "What do you think?"

Impressed, Emmaline clapped her hands. "Perfect. It's perfect."

Maizie motioned for Emmaline. "Sheriff Smith called. He wants you to come by his office."

"Go to his office." She frowned. "Like I'm some flitting free spirit. Did he mention his costume?"

"I think this is police business," Maizie said. "I ain't envying you, even if the sheriff is easy to look at."

"Good grief, woman. You're old enough to be the sheriff's grandmother."

"I ain't dead yet. And, I know good-looking when I see it."

Emmaline grabbed her purse and keys. At the sheriff's office, Kimberley ushered her in to see Smith.

"Miss Emmaline," he said formally. "We have a few questions." He buzzed for Saucer. The rotund deputy ambled in, his pants riding dangerously low beneath his belly.

What a chameleon, she thought, eyeing the sheriff. Smith, pleasant one minute, and the next, playing the heavy lawman. "What's this about?" she asked sullenly.

Saucer leaned forward, the chair squeaking beneath his girth. "We have some questions about the hammer found alongside Mr. LeDeux's body. It was identified as being from LeFevre House."

Ridiculous, she thought. They'd already identified the hammer as LeFevre House property. They knew it was the murder weapon. "Is this a trick question?" she asked the sheriff, ignoring Saucer. Before he answered, she couldn't help herself, she started venting. "Are you suggesting I lifted the hammer from a shed I have access to, and beat Etienne dead with it? Then I tossed it along the Black Path for y'all to find?"

Smith's eyes narrowed. "How do you account for the hammer being on the Black Path?"

146

Her armpits dampening in the inadequate air-conditioning, she shrugged. "I told you, I can't account for the hammer one way or the other." Her blurted answer sounded shrill, high-pitched, and frantic. Now, she couldn't care less. "There are tools in all the sheds. I can't identify every tool." She remembered this hammer though. It was very old, very heavy, very crude. It had belonged to the LeFevre House forge at least a hundred years before when the property was a working plantation. "Others besides myself have access to the sheds."

"Who exactly has access or keys?"

"Let me think . . . I told you, there's Tom, the maintenance man. He has keys to all the outbuildings. Then, Esther Marshall. From time to time she'll need props or costumes stored in some of the sheds."

Saucer busily scratched notes.

"Is that everyone?" The sheriff spoke business-like. "It's important to be specific."

"The historical society have keys. Who exactly, I haven't a clue? I have complicated ownership of the property."

The sheriff continued. "You're saying yourself, Tom, Ms. Marshall, and others of the historical society had keys to the tool shed at LeFevre House. Anyone else?"

"No one I'm aware of." She paused a moment, the damp feeling prominent. "Wait. There's Alvin Jamerson, the historical society president. He has keys. He loans them to others when there's a need. There's a lot of upkeep at LeFevre House; most of the work is done by volunteers. Oh, I almost forgot. I gave keys to Pastor Lemuel from the Boy's Ranch. He has keys to Beard House, too. His boys are working on the theatrical scenery."

Smith smiled for the first time.

"I can't be everywhere at once," she said.

"Certainly not," agreed Smith.

If the sheriff believed she had anything to do with either of the unfortunate murders, he was as dense as a stump.

Saucer, thumping his black ballpoint pen against his notebook, spoke up. "About Miss Powell's death. Are you sure she didn't hint where she got those pearls?"

"No, she didn't. I told you. We had no extended conversation. It happened quickly. I was totally taken by surprise when she pushed the package into my hands. It was sometime later before I opened the package." Emmaline turned to the sheriff. "I'd no idea the package contained pearls." Smith stared at her. "Have you heard from Josephine Powell since she returned to New Orleans?"

The sheriff's question caught Emmaline off guard. The last person she wished to hear from was hysterical Josephine Powell. "Not since the funeral. Byrd and I attended Carol's services. Josephine's son, Charlie, is with her."

"Have you seen Carol Powell's fiancé, Gary West, again? You told us you've seen him at least twice in the area. I think both times were mistaken identities."

"No. I haven't seen him again."

He'd called her to his office for this. A total waste of time.

CHAPTER 25

The next few days, the upcoming theatrical occupied Emmaline. Opening night wasn't far away. She had little time to think about the murders or worry about Byrd's absence. Even Helen put aside her grief over Etienne's death and pitched in with the Ripper production. Tonight was the first dress rehearsal.

* * *

6:00 p.m.

Emmaline made her way to the second-floor landing from her upstairs sitting room to find Chad Ludlum fumbling with the lighting panel. Esther stood beside the nervous youth.

"Where's Jeremy?"

Chad colored and stared at Emmaline. "He's gone."

"Gone? What do you mean, gone?"

"I mean he ain't at the ranch anymore," gulped the teen.

Esther removed a pencil from between her tight lips. "You didn't know?"

"What are you talking about? Of course, I don't know Jeremy isn't at the Boy's Ranch." How dare Esther keep important information from her?

"He's with his parents," Esther said. "The kid's been gone at least a week."

The week Emmeline had spent obsessing about the two murders and not the theatrical.

Esther sloughed off Emmaline's hostile stare. It was obvious the Worms boy could be replaced, in Esther's opinion. Esther turned to go downstairs.

"Who'll work the lights? We're on crunch time with opening night," Emmaline flung at her assistant. Esther ignored her. She kept climbing downstairs. Back onstage, Esther collared the girl portraying one of the ripper's victims "I told you to lift your skirt saucily," Esther barked. You're a whore, remember."

Emmaline had enough. She stormed to the library, slamming the door behind her. She punched in a call to Pastor Lemuel. "What's this I hear about Jeremy Worms going home? When can you have him back? He's vital to the theatrical."

"My dear Miss Beard. Jeremy is gone. He asked to leave. He's grateful for our help at the ranch, he realizes the mistakes he's made in the past and is ready to be an obedient son. His parents are thrilled. They are creating an impressive endowment for the ranch. Isn't that wonderful?"

She'd never noticed before - the oiliness in the pastor's voice. "An endowment," she said grumpily.

"Tsk, tsk, tsk, Miss Beard. I know you aren't truly a cynic. Jeremy's rehabilitation is wonderful. The endowment is secondary to a changed life."

How dare Pastor Lemuel placate her. "I must have him back for opening night. He's crucial working the lights. Jeremy knows that. I'll speak to his parents," she said desperately. "You talk to them, as well." Surely, Pastor Lemuel realized her donations to the Boy's Ranch were important, too.

"That's impossible, Miss Beard. The family are on an extended vacation in Switzerland. Mr. Worms's sister lives there. After the vacation, Jeremy is staying on with his aunt and will enroll in a private Swiss school. A splendid opportunity for him."

Emmaline ended the call forcibly. *Splendid opportunity, indeed!*

* * *

It seemed rehearsal went on forever. What a day she'd had. She needed a change of scenery. Emmaline decided to eat dinner out at Sally's Seafood. The popular eatery was crowded when she arrived. Disappointed her favorite table before the huge windows was occupied, she followed the waitress to a booth near the kitchen door. She sat facing the front of the restaurant. Two women occupied the booth behind her.

Loud young women. So much for a relaxing meal - what with the two animated chatterboxes and the kitchen noise.

"He's a hottie," shrilled the woman seated directly behind Emmaline.

"Go on," urged her companion. "Details."

"Get your own X-rated life and leave mine to your imagination."

"Bummer. All I've met on Match-Ups dot.com are seventy-year old has-beens."

"You always got your customers."

"Don't even go there."

Both women erupted into hysterical belly-laughs, loud enough to peel paint.

Emmaline scribbled *Match-Ups.com* on her napkin. At the moment she'd welcome a seventy-year old has-been for company. Maybe competition would shake Byrd awake long enough to realize she was a woman and not a pal.

"He's a blond surfer with a divine ponytail. That's all I'm saying," said the taller woman as they scrambled up to leave.

"Surfer in Ville Nouvelle? I'm not believing it," put in the shorter woman. "More like an out-of-work shrimper from Venice or Happy Jack."

Surfer! Blond ponytail! Emmaline grabbed her handbag and followed the twosome. She bumped into her waitress bringing her entrée. "Here's your food."

"Pack it to go. Beard is the name. I'll be back later for it."

She rushed outside the restaurant in time to see the women board an older beige Toyota. Emmaline cranked her Deville and followed the Toyota; thankful the nuclear protesters had trickled to fewer than a dozen die-hards, leaving the streets more accessible.

The Toyota pulled up at Ville Nouvelle's Rest-Awhile Inn. Both women exited the vehicle. Emmaline charged across the parking lot. "Wait a minute."

"What do you want?" demanded the tall shrill one. The woman, approximately late thirties, long dark hair, wore a leopard-print blouse with matching shoes and garish makeup. Her short, blond friend propped her hands on her ample hips and glared at Emmaline.

"I'm Emmaline Beard," Emmaline said, making her name sound as if she was the queen of the universe. "I overheard you talking about a surfer. I think that's my friend, Gary West. I need to see him. It's very important."

"Why?" The tall brunette again.

"A private matter. He'll understand."

"Your hottie likes them mature," giggled the short woman to her companion.

"Eavesdropping ain't cool," sulked the brunette. The two women marched off and entered the motel.

Emmaline stood in the parking lot. Exasperated but not defeated, she jumped into her Deville and drove around the block, stopping across from the Rest Awhile Inn behind a closed carwash. She called Kimberley on her cell. "I need information on two women staying at the Rest Awhile Inn."

"Do you know the time?" complained Kimberley.

"I'm perfectly aware of the time," lied Emmaline. She never understood how to set the console clock at time changes. Daylight Savings time sucked anyway.

"I'm home. I can't do office business."

"Kimberley, you're wasting time. Call the motel night manager. Tell him it's Sheriff's Department business."

"But it isn't," persisted Kimberley. "If Sheriff Smith gets wind of this -"

"I'll deal with the sheriff. Get back to me ASAP. I'm behind the car wash across the street from the motel."

What seemed an eternity later - actually ten minutes - Kimberley called. "They're Dolores Favor and Misty Shores. Sounds like a couple of B string strippers."

Strippers, she knew it. "Thanks -" Emmaline barely got *thanks* out before Dolores and Misty exited the motel and climbed into the Toyota. They hadn't brought luggage. Emmaline prayed they weren't leaving town.

Emmaline followed the Toyota. The Toyota turned onto a levee road leading to a string of questionable joints, Ville Nouvelle's answer to Bourbon Street. They pulled into the barely lit parking lot of a bar called *Say It Ain't So*, patronized by offshore workers.

"Luck, you're a lady," squealed Emmaline when the ponytail guy emerged from a battered pickup truck and ambled toward the Toyota. *Gary West.* Intent on getting the truck's license plate number, Emmaline must first pass Gary leaning in the Toyota's window. In this instance, surprise seemed the better ploy. She stopped behind him. "Hi Gary, great seeing you."

He turned. Oh No. Hot dog Gary. Not the Gary she sought. "I'm sorry. Uh… thought you were someone else."

"If it ain't over-the-hill mama," snapped the brunette. "Wantin' some action? Find your own lover-doll. You followin' us," she demanded, her eyes narrowing. "We ain't done you nothing yet."

The short blonde exited the Toyota and pushed her hip against Emmaline. Emmaline held her ground. She didn't retaliate or step back. 'Yeah, grandma," bantered the blonde. "We ain't done you nothing yet, but that don't mean we ain't gonna do you plenty. What you want with us?"

"Yeah," retorted the brunette, from the Toyota's driver's seat. "Stalking ain't nice, old lady."

Ignoring the two braying jackasses, Emmaline turned to the Gary West look-like. "I'm sorry to disturb you again. You bear a remarkable likeness to my friend. I can't believe he left town without seeing me first."

"What you want this . . . Gary West for? Anything to do with the march?" he asked.

"No," Emmaline said truthfully. "It's a personal matter." She visualized Carol Powell's broken body beneath the old mansion's upper veranda. "Let me give you a card. If you see him, will you give me a call?"

Hot dog Gary grinned. "Sure."

CHAPTER 26

The next morning, she called Byrd's cell phone for the umpteenth time. Still no answer. She sat, drumming her fingers on the sofa arm when the house phone rang. Emmaline almost fainted when she saw the caller ID. *Dante Washington.*

"Hello," she gushed. "What a pleasant surprise. How's your wife?" She couldn't remember Shemika's given name and didn't want to make a mistake.

"Shemika is doing well," he said. "She's out of danger. There'll be more skin grafts later. Doctor wants further healing first."

"I'm so thankful," Emmaline said. Why was Dante calling her? True, as a young teen, he once weeded her flowerbeds. That was years ago when he'd spent time at the boy's ranch.

"You're wondering why I'm calling," Dante said. "Mama has kept me informed about your interest in crime down there."

"I've always loved your mother. She's one of the finest people I know."

"She's that for sure," agreed Dante before continuing. "Since you're a sleuth, there's something you should know."

"What?"

"I've told your sheriff, and I've talked to Pastor Lemuel. The day the RV was torched, Shemika was napping. She swears she heard giggling and hooping voices outside. Sounded like kids. She saw a boy run toward the woods. Then, a fire ring started blazing all around the RV. She panicked, got confused, couldn't remember where the door was. She finally ran out of the motorhome. By then it was engulfed in flames."

"You're saying Shemika can identify someone running from the RV?"

"No. She thought it was a kid. A teen. Coulda been a boy or a girl. The RV was parked on the back of the ranch property. Stands to reason one of the boys could've been back there."

Bingo! thought Emmaline. Made sense Jeremy Worms split to Switzerland. "Did Sheriff Smith agree with your suspicions?"

"Not really. He thinks I was the target. Some of the anti-protesters taking out their frustrations on me."

"And Pastor Lemuel?"

"Negative. You know him. He's overly protective of those boys."

Emmaline sat a long time thinking about Dante's information.

CHAPTER 27

Papeete, Tahiti

A fter a skimpy breakfast of some fiery, curry-type soup over rice, a youngish man identifying himself as Byrd's lawyer entered the cell. The young man smiled broadly. Byrd, in no mood for pleasantries this the morning of the fourth day of his incarceration, scowled.

"Good morning M'sieur. How are you this day?" The man appeared no more than twenty years of age. However, he spoke fluent English. Apparently, the only multi-lingual person in Tahiti.

"This is unheard of!" Byrd thundered at the young man. "This is the fourth day I've been locked up with no counsel, no contact with the outside world. I am no criminal. I have stolen no pearls. I came here for information regarding a murder in Ville Nouvelle - the United States."

"Oui, M'sieur. We are aware. These things take time. How do you say in the United States . . . we are not right down the road?"

"Three going on four days in solitary confinement exceeds any known protocol in the civilized world."

"Oui, M'sieur. It is the difference in the French law and the law of your country. Three days without counsel and visitors is customary and perfectly legal here. Often we receive confessions after the three days." The young man's owlish eyes appeared larger than normal behind his thick, round glasses.

"No confessions coming from me," Byrd huffed. "May I use a telephone?"

"Of course, M'sieur. But they must detain you until the paperwork is completed. Your sheriff of your town has faxed information concerning the pearl theft from our Pearl Museum. Our local police were not informed Interpol is active in the theft. We can only offer our apologies for your inconvenience and see that you receive a grand tour of the islands at our expense."

"No tour," Byrd emphasized haughtily. "A plane ticket to the United States as soon as possible."

"Oui, M'sieur. You may make arrangements with the concierge at your hotel."

Byrd slept the entire flight to Houston—the first sleep he'd had in four days.

* * *

He telephoned Emmaline the moment he arrived in Houston.

"I can't believe you've been in jail this entire time," she sympathized after listening to his story. "If you'd told me where you were going, I'd have seen you released."

"Unfortunately, you couldn't. Three days without counsel and phone privileges is the norm there."

"When are you coming back?"

"To Ville Nouvelle?"

"Of course, Ville Nouvelle."

"Can't possibly get away before Friday afternoon. Why, what's going on? Any new murder leads?"

"I saw the Gary West look alike again. I'm beginning to believe West isn't in the area. Dante telephoned me. He said Shemika heard kids around the RV before the fire."

"How's Dante's wife?"

"She's improving. They're back in LA. The protest march has dwindled to a few hangers-on. The bad news is Jeremy Worms is in Switzerland for good. I'm sure he had a part in setting the RV fire. Chad is trying to work the lights. I can't afford to question him until after the theatrical. Otherwise, I'll be forced to work the lights myself."

"I forgot about opening night. When is the grand event?"

"This Saturday evening. I need you here, Byrd."

"I can't promise," he hedged.

She ended the call more down in the dumps than ever.

CHAPTER 28

After Byrd's phone, call Emmaline had time to herself before Esther and Helen arrived. She remembered the photographs she'd snapped at Marcel's burned pasture. She loaded the snaps onto her laptop. As the pictures scrolled past, she wondered what she'd missed that day in the destroyed meadow. What vague impression teased the perimeters of her brain? Nothing jumped out from the photographs. She replayed the snapshots from the beginning. Nothing. Probably her frustrations and her imagination at play.

She shut down the computer and went to the kitchen. Maizie busily put together a salad for a late lunch. "That looks delicious." Emmaline speared a slice of avocado. "What's this stuff?" She pointed to a huge bag in the center of the kitchen table.

"That's them masks Miss Esther brought for Mr. Saucer. Ain't he gonna be a regular freak?" Maizie laughed pulling first one - and then more - rubber masks from the bag. There were at least a dozen very life-like rubber faces. Some with hair, some with beards, and even a few bald masks. The bald ones had sweeping mustaches.

"She spent a fortune," grumbled Emmaline, budget conscious.

The telephone rang. Kimberley. "Are the costumes ready?" Kimberley asked. She had two roles as the ripper victims.

"Why don't you come over for a bite of lunch? Say in half an hour. You can pick up your costumes and wigs then."

The young woman arrived promptly. They sat down to salad and left-over crawfish etouffee. Maizie had whipped up crème brûlée cheesecake for dessert.

"I may not fit into those gowns after this meal," Kimberley said with a giggle.

"You don't indulge every day," Emmaline assured her, eyeing the younger woman's trim figure.

Kimberley took another bite of cheesecake. "I can't resist Maizie's desserts," the girl said, closing her eyes in pleasure.

Emmaline, more than a little annoyed with Kimberley, and the sheriff's department in general, asked the question foremost on her mind. "Sheriff Smith and you, of course, knew Byrd was locked up in Tahiti."

A dainty portion of the succulent dessert poised on her demi-tasse spoon, Kimberley gulped. "No, no, no," she insisted, eyes wide. "We didn't know. Not until he was released. The FBI and Interpol are working the Tahiti pearl case. Sheriff Smith had no idea. In fact, Interpol has the pearls now. I saw the requisition papers."

Kimberley had never lied to her. If Sheriff Smith knew the extent of details Kimberley passed on to Emmaline, the girl's job could be in jeopardy. "I believe you," Emmaline said. "These murders are making us all crazy with a killer in town and we're no closer learning his identity than the day the crimes were committed." Emmaline paused. "Does the sheriff have any new leads?"

Kimberley looked uncomfortable. "I'm a secretary, not an investigator. I don't know everything at the sheriff's office."

Emmaline suppressed a pithy remark.

Maizie approached the table, plopping down two cups of coffee and a small pitcher of scalding milk for the coffee au lait. "I got a question too," Maizie said, "them noises on the other side of the house. It ain't squirrels and it ain't rats. I'm for nailing them doors shut. And, not only that the other day I found two of them outside doors unlocked. I'm for nailing them shut, too."

"If it makes you feel better, I'll get padlocks," Emmaline said.

Kimberley stood. "Thanks for lunch, Emmaline. You, too, Maizie, you're the best."

CHAPTER 29

L ater that afternoon, Sheriff Rodney Smith couldn't get away for the special rehearsal, but sent Saucer as a stand-in for the sheriff's parts. Beard House became a beehive of activity. Esther and Helen worked through each scene. Emmaline, after hours on the set, made her way up to the landing. Chad bobbed his head in greeting. "I have every confidence in you," she said to the nervous teen.

"Yes ma'am."

The door flew open beside them from the hallway connecting the unused portion of the mansion. A frightening apparition in a black cape, long white hair, and a ludicrous expression on its menacing face rushed toward them. "Get ready to die," shouted the monster.

Emmaline screamed. Chad threw a folding chair at the brute.

"Cut it out!" yelled the creature ripping off its face mask. "It's me, Saucer. Don't you have a sense of humor?"

"This is uncalled for, Saucer," shouted Emmaline, trembling. He apologized profusely. He deserved the huge red bump on his forehead.

Saucer climbed downstairs. Watching him, the unexplainable fear she experienced in Marcel Beaudion's field come about again. The sensation? Of course, someone - watching her. A quick glance down the long dark hallway of the sealed wing of Beard House took her breath. She rushed and closed the door, her heart beating fast.

Beard House had too many unused rooms, too many dark hallways, too many odd staircases and too many entrances. Maizie was right. They should secure the unused portion of the house. Steeling herself, she managed to get through the remainder of rehearsal.

After everyone left, she sat on the side of her bed, her arms crossed tightly over her upper body. She must get control of herself. Instead, her nervous energy intensified. She thought about the half-burned camping equipment someone had pulled from Marcel's pasture fire. Everyone believed Etienne set the fire. A gasoline can had been found in his barn. A local convenience store operator remembered selling gasoline to Etienne.

If Etienne set the fire, had his murder been retaliation? Not by Marcel, she reasoned. Marcel was a big-mouth, blow-hard type, but no killer. A dismal feeling troubled her. She'd missed something in the pasture. Something important. Something she'd seen but blocked. The photographs showed nothing perilous.

With a jolt, she remembered Helen's latest warning. *"I've had a frightening premonition. Trouble is coming. I don't know what, exactly. The message from beyond isn't clear. All I can do is warn you to be careful."*

CHAPTER 30

9:30 p.m.

E mmaline glanced at the bedside clock. Not too late, she thought, to do some snooping. After Saucer frightened her earlier, she realized she must deepen her investigation if she wanted to find the killer. She'd allowed the play, the protest march, Josephine and Charlie Powell, and the attack on Dante's wife to occupy her mentally. Since she had no suspects, her only course of action lay in talking to people who benefited from the victim's death.

Carol's killers surely were the pearl thieves. Since she had no way of learning the thieves' identities, she must concentrate on Etienne's murder. Unlike Sheriff Smith, she did not believe Marcel killed the man. Who, then, benefited from Etienne's death? Simple, Julie LeDeux. Her father's death left Julie a very wealthy young woman. Did she truly believe Julie capable of murdering her father? She didn't know. But there was the financial motive.

Emmaline pulled on the sweater draped over the back of her chair. She slipped outside to the garage. She drove approximately ten yards from Etienne's house and parked in a dark section of road. She believed both Helen and Julie were home, though she'd neglected checking the Beard House bedroom Helen occupied.

She extinguished the car's lights. Helen's rental car was nowhere in sight. Julie's Range Rover stood parked in the circular drive. Few lights gleamed within the rambling Cajun style house. Emmaline walked up the drive. The dim porch light bulb cast shadows across the spacious lawns. She punched the doorbell.

Julie answered the door. She wore an outlandish outfit. Tight pink jeans, a pink rhinestone covered cowboy shirt and matching pink blazer, pink cowboy boots and dramatic makeup. Julie looked surprised. "Miss Emmaline?" she said. "What brings you out here?"

"I want to talk to you. Ask you a few questions."

"I'm about to leave."

"I apologize for popping in like this."

"What do you want to ask me?"

"Where were you the day your father was killed?"

Julie frowned. "I've just lost my father. Why are you asking me this? You have no right. Where I was is none of your business."

"I'm sorry. It's important to know everyone's whereabouts."

"You aren't the police, Emmaline, you have no business questioning me."

"Not answering makes you look bad."

"Everyone knows Marcel Beaudion killed my father. It all started with jealousy over the racehorses. Marcel took shots at my dad for months and months before he killed him."

"Then why hasn't Sheriff Smith arrested Mr. Beaudion?"

"I don't know. I'm calling the sheriff and reporting your impertinence."

"Go ahead. Call him." Emmaline whipped out her cell phone. "Better yet. I'll call him.

"I'll deal with you later." Julie slammed the door in Emmaline's face.

Emmaline rushed down the walkway to her car prepared to wait. Sure enough, a few minutes later the rhinestone cowgirl climbed into her Range Rover and drove away.

Emmaline followed.

Following the Range Rover became tricky since there was little traffic on the isolated country road, making her tail far enough behind to not draw attention. Once Julie reached North Dock Street, traffic increased. The Rover's brake lights flashed. Julie pulled the Rover into a gas station. She eased out, resembling a pink rhinestone Christmas tree, and pumped gas. Before leaving the gas station, Julie punched her Apple watch and held a short conversation with someone.

Back in the vehicle, Julie turned right on Levee Road. The Rover's taillights flashed before making a turn onto the service road leading to Pastor Lemuel's Boy's Ranch.

Emmaline stayed well behind Julie's vehicle. Julie turned onto the long drive to the boy's dormitory buildings - instead of driving on to Pastor Lemuel's private residence. Then she pulled over and stopped.

Emmaline parked behind a stand of shrubs, exited and crept near the Rover. Julie stood near the driver's door. A few minutes later a dark figure slunk alongside the Rover and joined her.

Chad Ludlum.

"What you want to see me for?" Chad said respectfully.

"I'm not trying to get you into trouble," began Julie, "but you must stop riding your motorcycle behind my property. You're agitating the horses. Do you understand?"

"I ain't frightened your horses." Chad's voice rose. "You got the wrong person. That was Jeremy. He ain't here at the school anymore. Anyway, his dad took his motorcycle away weeks ago. Way before Jeremy went to school in Switzerland."

"You're lying. I've heard you, Jeremy, or another of the boys this week."

"Not me or Jeremy, either. You didn't see us," Chad shot back, not so respectfully.

Julie ignored him. "Maybe you don't want Pastor Lemuel knowing you were sneaking on my property. Maybe you killed my father to keep him from going to the authorities."

Chad found some courage. "You're crazy, lady. It wasn't me. I don't have a motorcycle. I never had one. And Jeremy ain't here anymore."

"Keep lying. I'll speak to Pastor Lemuel."

"Go ahead, talk to the pastor. He knows I ain't hiding nothing." Chad's voice shook.

"I think it was you," Julie insisted. "Before Dad died, he said the motorcycle driver was bulked up, like you. That Jeremy kid is scrawny."

"You better leave me alone, lady. I'm gonna tell Pastor you're threatening me." Chad stalked off toward the dormitory.

"This isn't the end of this," Julie called to the boy's backside. She climbed into her vehicle, slammed the door and revved the Rover's engine.

Emmaline ducked lower behind the shrubs in time to avoid the Rover's headlights sweeping the area as Julie turned the vehicle around.

Once Julie's vehicle moved out of sight, Emmaline hurried across the grounds to Pastor Lemuel's house. She punched the doorbell. Within minutes, the porch light switched on and the pastor opened the door. He blinked. "Miss Beard," he said, surprised. "Come in." The pastor wore comfortable lounging slacks and a gray T-shirt. His deck type loafers showed no socks.

Emmaline stepped into the hallway.

"I was in the den reading," Lemuel said. "Would you step back there?"

"I haven't time," Emmaline said. "And, I apologize for disturbing you." She thought quickly; Julie's conversation with Chad gave her an idea. "I want to report a motorcycle disturbing me a few weeks back. I understand Jeremy Worms rode a motorcycle." Emmaline knew the Worms boy came from wealthy parents and enjoyed privileges most of the other boys didn't have. Like having a racy motorcycle for private transportation. Like now being out of the country.

"I'm sorry to hear you were disturbed," Lemuel said sincerely. He smiled kindly. Some would say the personable pastor was a handsome man, Emmaline thought, noting his black hair and mustache, and his fair, almost pink complexion. "When did you see the motorcycle?"

She thought about Dante's RV fire. "A few weeks ago. Very loud and very disruptive. I'm not trying to get any of your boys into trouble. However, I thought you'd like to know. Especially if they're sneaking off campus." She smiled, realizing the late hour. "I apologize for disturbing you this late, but I was out this way."

Lemuel rocked back on his heels. "About what time did you see or hear this motorbike?"

"Late, after nine o'clock, maybe ten o'clock."

"No way was it one of the boys. We have bed check at eight-thirty. Lights out at nine o'clock. I assure you I'll look into the matter, though." Pastor Lemuel gestured down the hall. "Won't you come in and sit down?"

"No," Emmaline demurred. "I've taken too much of your time."

Pastor Lemuel said. "Jeremy's father took the bike away at least a month ago. Jeremy didn't like it, of course. However, his father and I are seeking what's best for the boy. Jeremy is in a Swiss school and doing exceptionally well."

"I'm glad to know Jeremy is doing well." She wished the youth the best, regardless of his sly, cunning personality. "I miss him at the theatrical. I depended on his scene painting and electrical lightning talent."

"I understand Chad Ludlum is helping."

"He is. I'm grateful." Chad, a poor second, but all she had now. "I won't take more of your time. You've been helpful."

"Drop by anytime. We at the ranch appreciate all you do for the boys."

Bulked up, she thought. Julie accused Chad because of his husky appearance. Had Chad Ludlum killed Etienne?

CHAPTER 31

She noticed the motorcycle behind her when she turned onto the long lane leading from the Boy's Ranch to the main road. The bike kept some distance behind. The driver wore a protective helmet. It was too dark to identify the bike's color or the helmet's color. Uneasy, she sped. The bike increased its speed. How many more miles to the main road? Why had she driven out here? Her morbid curiosity. Her heart hammered. Fear balled in her throat. *Calm down.* A coincidence. Motorcycles in Ville Nouvelle, a common sight. She saw the huge tree limb. It lay across the narrow road, its branches level with her windshield. *Think, think!* Her safety classes came to mind. When threatened, cause an accident. Wait. Employ that scenario if a bad guy jumps into the car with you, holds a gun to your head and tells you to drive. Spotting tree limbs in the road, Emmaline seized the split-second - she wheeled the car into a U-turn and met the motorcycle. The bike driver swerved and missed her, missed the tree limbs laying in the road, too. Emmaline lost control of her vehicle, smashing into trees on the side of the road. Woozy, she tried to push her car door open. It refused to budge.

A stunning blow pounded the back of her head. She pitched forward. "Burn my camp, will you, bitch," hissed a voice, or had she imagined it, before everything went black.

CHAPTER 32

Byrd rushed to Ville Nouvelle after learning of the attack on Emmaline. He arrived at Beard House mid-morning, finding her on her bedroom chaise, a chenille coverlet over her long legs. A huge bandage covered the back of her head.

"She had seventeen stitches," declared Maizie.

He assumed as much, judging from the massive bandaging. Too, she kept slipping in and out of consciousness.

Fussing with the coverlet, Maizie added. "She ain't as bad off as she looks. It's the medication."

Emmaline's next lucid moment, Byrd took her hand. "What do you remember?" he asked gently. Surely, she had some recall. Some impression of the person responsible for the attack.

Emmaline blinked. "You came back." Clearly puzzled.

"I came the moment I heard you were attacked," he said, concern threading his voice.

She asked about his Tahiti imprisonment. He gave basic answers, intent instead on questioning her. "You said a voice accused you of burning a camp. Was the speaker a man or a woman?"

Shrugging, her brows drew together. She yawned. "I don't know. Maybe I dreamed the voice -"

He was losing her to the medication.

Maizie pulled Emmaline's coverlet tighter.

"Why did you go to the Boy's Ranch that time of night?" persisted Byrd.

"I wish you'd…" Soft snore.

"She's asleep," announced Maizie, heading toward the door. "She won't nap long. It's time for her protein shake anyway. You want a shake?"

"Why not?" He trailed down to the kitchen.

Maizie pulled the blender out of a cupboard. She gathered ingredients. "I'm scared," she admitted, once the pulsing stopped. "This killer is after Emmaline now. I've been warning her about these unlocked doors on the other side of the house."

"What unlocked doors?"

Maizie explained about the sealed section of the old house, and how of late, certain passageways were found unlocked. "Saucer slipped through there. He had on one of them face masks Miss Esther got for the play. He scared the daylights out of Emmaline. That boy, Chad, too. Chad threw a chair at Saucer. Gave Saucer a bump on his dumb head. A bump he deserved."

Maizie passed him a goblet overflowing with the frothy shake. He sipped the milky concoction slowly. Was the attack on Emmaline a case of Emmaline being in the wrong place at the wrong time, or something more sinister. Had the attacker asked if she'd burned a camp, or had Emmaline imagined it?

Several hours later, Emmaline woke more completely, and motioned him to sit beside her on the chaise. She'd pulled on a robe and made up her face. "Why did you got to Tahiti without telling me?"

He didn't want to talk about his trip, his incarceration, or his final release.

Before he could answer, she shook her finger at him. "You want to solve these murders before me, you old bloodhound."

He grinned. "I wanted to verify Gary West spent time in Tahiti," he said. "He did. Carol Powell arrived with him. They sailed her father's yacht, the Zephyr. The Zephyr developed mechanical problems. West stayed behind to wait for parts and then repairs. Carol booked a flight from Tahiti to New Orleans. West met some cronies while in Papeete. Suspects in the Pearl Museum theft. These men remain at large."

"It makes sense," Emmaline said softly, gazing across the room, "for Carol to bring the pearls with her." She turned to Byrd. "Why give them to me? Why Josephine? Unless -" Realization creased her face.

"Unless," he guessed, "she had no part in the theft."

"Exactly," exclaimed Emmaline, moving to the edge of the chaise. "Gary West followed her. He killed Carol for the pearls.

"I believe you're right," agreed Byrd. "If he's in the area, he's looking for the pearls."

She frowned. "but, why would he kill Etienne?" she said, slumping back, "unless there are two killers."

"I disagree about two killers."

Her brows shot up. "How can you say that," shaking her head vehemently, "what motive would Gary West of Marina Del Ray, California have to kill Etienne? A man he's never seen before in his life."

With no idea of *why,* Byrd felt he knew part of the *how,* or at least a motive for the *how.* "Think about the two murders. What comparable factor shouts out at you?"

"Nothing," she said flatly, crossing her arms over her chest, waiting for his rebuttal. Rebuttal did not come. "Okay," she said. "Name your comparable factors?"

"Violence. These were no ordinary murders. Violence in the extreme in both cases. Carol beaten, her face disfigured. Etienne bludgeoned repeatedly with a heavy hammer. These were passionate killings even vengeful killings."

"But Carol was killed for the pearls?"

"Possibly. Think of West and Carol's relationship. They were an engaged couple. If they were in love and she somehow duped him for the pearls, then left him, imagine his anger and feelings of betrayal."

"I see," Emmaline said slowly. "He'd become a murderous beast."

"Precisely."

A murderer, yes. Would the thieves know Interpol had the pearls? Possibly, they had ways. Which meant Gary West or the other accomplices had no reason to remain in Ville Nouvelle. Byrd couldn't count out the protest march bringing numerous unsavory characters onto the local scene. Many had remained after Dante left town. A few diehard locals, plus various stragglers, kept the protest going.

Had Emmaline become targeted because of the pearls? He didn't a hundred per cent believe the pearls were the reason. Any thinking person, even a thief would suspect she'd turned them over to the authorities, if she ever had them in her possession. What troubled him; Carol Powell's murder with no leads. The same with Etienne LeDeux's murder. Dead ends, both.

CHAPTER 33

Later that afternoon, they sat in the library. Maizie brought early strawberries topped with whipped cream for a snack. Emmaline, her dessert dish aside, thumbed through a selection of books just arrived from her favorite mystery bookstore. "My headaches are gone. I feel great."

"You don't look great."

"Byrd, your bedside manner sucks."

She held up a book with a bright red dust jacket. "This one is set in Switzerland. Which reminds me, I think Jeremy Worms set fire to Dante's RV. And Etienne burned Marcel's fields."

"I think you're right about both Worms and Etienne."

"We need to talk to Chad," she said, laying the books aside. "He knows who set the RV fire."

"You're not serious," he admonished. "Thought you were afraid he'd panic and be unable to work the play lights."

"That's a chance I must take."

"Don't take that chance just yet. No need to add to your stress level." She seemed restless. He wondered if her mood was the result of waning medication. She'd taken quite a blow to her head.

"Another thing," she continued. "You believe one killer committed both murders. I disagree. I doubt Etienne LeDeux ever knew Carol Powell. And the Tahiti pearl theft is as far from Etienne as East from West. Why would Carol's killer beat Etienne to death? Makes no sense."

Byrd had spent three days in solitary confinement puzzling over the same thing. "I admit my theory seems farfetched. It's possible, though," he said doggedly, still harboring his belief only one killer committed both murders. He admitted he saw no linking motive for both cases.

"We must see Josephine," Emmaline said, breaking into his musings.

"Why?"

"Because her son, Charlie, might lead us to Gary West. They knew one another in California."

"You're in no condition to *see* anyone," Byrd reminded her, staring aghast at the bandage on the back of her head. "Remember, the Ripper play opens soon. You're needed here."

"Esther can handle opening night."

"When have you ever delegated opening night to anyone?" He knew her better than she knew herself. "I'm devoting the remainder of the afternoon to golf," he said, suddenly eager to get out of the house and think his own thoughts. "Stay in the house, I'm ordering you."

* * *

Emmaline took Byrd's golf plans as license to form her own. She put in a call to Josephine. "Darling, how are you?"

"Much, much better," Josephine said. "Charlie is taking excellent care of me. I couldn't ask for a better nurse. Though at times, he's too protective. Almost smothering."

"I'm thinking of riding down to see you. Is this a good time?"

"You mean today? This afternoon?"

"Yes."

"Perfect. I'd love to see you. Will you stay the night?"

"Uh, no… I'll drive back." Emmaline fingered the bandage. It would never do for Josephine to see it. She must improvise something.

Emmaline dressed hurriedly. She chose a pale green pants suit and a green velvet cloche hat. The hat cloaked the bandage nicely. An hour and a half to drive down to the city and an hour and a half drive back to Ville Nouvelle. She'd limit her visit to no more than an hour. She should be home no later than eight o'clock. Perfect.

* * *

Josephine's maid had laid out a nice late spread. Gourmet teas, sandwiches and iced cakes. "It's lovely you're doing so well," Emmaline said, wondering where Charlie was. She wanted to question Josephine's son, as well. "It's obvious Charlie is an excellent caregiver."

"Don't give him too much credit. He can be overbearing. He's all I have now that Carol is gone," Josephine said. She looked down at her hands knotted in her lap, then looked up and smiled brightly. "So, you were in New Orleans and decided to call on me."

"Not exactly," said Emmaline, not wanting to mislead Josephine. "I drove down especially to see you. I wondered if you or Charlie have heard anything more from Gary West."

"You could've asked me that over the telephone," Josephine said, a little haughtily. "Or is this visit one of your detecting forays?"

"Guilty." Emmaline laughed, praying to pass off her motive as a joke. Her head felt uncomfortable under the constricting hat. She couldn't dare remove it.

"Whatever the reason, I'm glad to see you. Charlie is quite the taskmaster keeping me at home. I'm fairly rabid for company."

"Where is he?" Emmaline asked, once the subject of Charlie presented itself again.

Josephine glanced at the clock on the mantel. "He's doing his exercises now. He's devoted to calisthenics."

"Do you think he'd take a break to talk to me?" Emmaline, aware of the time, knew she must leave shortly. Especially with her injury and the long drive home.

"I doubt it. He's devoted to certain sets for exact times. It's likely he wouldn't break a set if the house caught fire."

Something other than fire and smoke prompted Charlie to break a set, for he appeared in the doorway, then sauntered into the room. "Refreshments, Mom. Oh, I didn't know we had company. How are you, Miss Beard?"

"Very good, thank you."

Charlie poured a cup of tea, added sugar and lemon, speared two huge cupcakes and straddled a chair without arms. "Nice hat, Miss Beard. You don't see hats much anymore."

"Thank you." Emmaline watched as he placed one cupcake and the cup of tea on a side table. He ate the other in two wolfish bites. A noticeable muffin-top bulged under his tee-shirt. "Visiting New Orleans," he said, blotting frosting from his lips with a napkin.

This cat and mouse had to end. "No, I'm not visiting New Orleans randomly," Emmaline said succinctly. "I came to see both of you. Have you heard from Gary West?"

"Yes and no," Charlie said, after a long draught of tea. "I heard from a California friend that "Gary is on the Coast. He's been back there a long time. Only, he's underground because of Carol's murder. He swears he had nothing to do with her death. Your Sheriff Smith has an all points out for him. He's afraid. Can't blame him."

"If he's innocent, he should come forward and state his case. That's what lawyers are for." Emmaline resisted the growing urge to remove the hat.

"My sentiments exactly," agreed Josephine. She turned to Emmaline. "Has Sheriff Smith any suspects in Carol's murder?"

"It's an active case," Emmaline said. "I'm not privy to the department's inner workings."

"Well, I am," interjected Charlie. "They're dumb as dirt up there. They have nothing, absolutely nothing. Nothing."

Emmaline said. "That's why I feel led to do my part. I don't want Carol's case to go cold or her killer escape justice."

"What about the man that was killed?" asked Charlie. "The one who set fire to his friend's field. Smith solved that one yet?"

"Unfortunately, no." Emmaline met Charlie's impolite gaze. "Both cases are at dead ends."

Charlie stood. His exercise shorts were extremely short, in Emmaline's opinion. "I can't sit here all day. Ran in for a snack. Not done with my routine. Mom." He blew Josephine a kiss. "Drop in anytime, Miss Beard."

Charlie's exodus became Emmaline's perfect exit. She rose. "Josephine, I appreciate you seeing me. "I'm glad you're improving. I really must go."

Josephine didn't protest. In fact, she appeared pleased the visit ended.

CHAPTER 34

That evening, Emmaline, spry, no headaches, no double vision and no need for pain medications, pulled on a half-wiglet from old play props. She peered into her mirror. *A little full,* she mused, rearranging the false hair. She went downstairs to dinner, the added hair atop her head umbrella style, ballooning over the bandage.

Byrd stared at her curiously.

Let him stare. "What?" she demanded. "What are you looking at?"

"You resemble a palm tree." He refrained from adding, a palm tree in a high wind. "Why're you wearing that thing?"

"Glamour," she retorted. "Obviously I failed, in your expert opinion."

"Where were you all day?" he asked.

She observed he choked back a grin. What is it about men, she wondered, besides their warped sense of humor when a woman makes an unusual stab at allure? For punishment, she delayed telling him about her afternoon.

He repeated. "Where were you?"

"I went to see Josephine and Charlie," she confessed, the bombshell in the open. She proceeded with a recap of her conversations with the two, despite Byrd's disbelief. ". . . Charlie assured me Gary West is on the Coast. For some time. Hiding from Sheriff Smith's extradition orders."

"Emmaline, you have a concussion—a gash that could hemorrhage. I can't believe you'd take such a risk."

"I do *not* have a concussion. I have a superficial head wound requiring stitches. The wound is well bandaged. I am in no bleeding danger. Else I wouldn't have gone."

He threw up his hands. "Okay, Teflon woman, what's next on our agenda?"

"I was thinking . . ." She fell silent as Maizie brought in dessert; pecan pie a la mode. Once Maizie left the room, she continued. "I should see Marcel Beaudion. The town believes he killed Etienne. While he isn't my favorite person, the question remains, did he kill Etienne or not?"

Byrd remembered Marcel from growing up in the area—though no judge of the man's current character. "We'll drive out there tomorrow," he said.

"I'm going now," Emmaline said emphatically. "Tonight."

"You're not serious."

For answer, she left the table, went upstairs, removed the wig, and pulled on the green cloche hat. *Attractive,* she decided. *"Palm tree, indeed,"* she jeered into the mirror.

* * *

They rode silently, each in their individual thoughts. Once the few town lights of Ville Nouvelle were past, the road darkened. Fog rolled in off the river. Blinking lights from moored ships pierced the denseness like watching eyes. At Marcel Beaudion's home, lights and loud music swelled from the spacious house. The parking space overflowed with vehicles. More cars were parked in a nearby field.

Byrd angled his SUV alongside a Lincoln. "Some kind of shindig." He turned to Emmaline. "Want to come back tomorrow?"

"Certainly not."

A young brunette met them at the door. A brunette in a costume like cigarette girls in 1940's film noir movies. "Welcome. This way."

The large living area overflowed with people. Emmaline gestured to a dapper man with striking silver hair. "The governor is here."

At that moment, Marcel extricated himself from a boisterous group of guests and came toward them. "Miss Beard. Kind of you to come." If he recognized her and Byrd as party crashers, it didn't show. "Have something to drink. Some hors d`oeuvres, the floor show starts in minutes."

Before he finished speaking, the lights dimmed, jazz belted out over the sound system and a stripper started her routine. Emmaline whispered. "Byrd, that's the woman—the short one—with the Gary look alike—Misty something or other."

Marcel swept away with another group - he didn't look back.

Byrd took her arm. "Let's get out of here."

"Not on your life." She turned toward the buffet table. He followed. "I came to question Marcel and I'm not leaving until I do." She loaded two plates with dips, cheeses, and tiny vegetables. They moved against the wall - inconspicuously, Byrd prayed, munching, Emmaline watching the stripper. He kept his eye on Marcel as the gregarious man worked the room.

Once the stripper's set ended, a DJ shouted. "Let's hear it for Miss Misty Shores."

"More! More!" shouted the crowd.

"Later," the DJ boomed with a hawkish grin. "More dancers later."

Marcel turned up at Emmaline's elbow. "You enjoying the party?" From Marcel's expression, it became obvious the man realized the two of them were *not* on the invitation roster. Byrd was aware Emmaline's political party differed from Mr. Beaudion's.

"You will stay for the speeches," taunted Marcel. "Tonight is the kick-off of our governor's reelection bid. We do what we can for him. Great guy."

Byrd, appalled at the number of key members of Louisiana state government in attendance, grasped Emmaline's arm.

She understood. "We really can't stay." Marcel's visage tightened; his expression darkened. "Before we leave, I have a few questions," adding, "if you don't mind."

"And if I do?"

Mustering boldness, Emmaline gestured around the room. "You don't want to look bad at your own party."

Byrd groaned. Oh, holy crap, no. She didn't say that. She wouldn't make a scene. Blame the head injury.

Marcel took her comment as threatening. "Step this way," he said grimly, steering them into a long hallway away from the festivities. "Okay," he pounced on Emmaline, kid gloves off. "I know about your detective reputation. Do I need my lawyer? I think he's getting a lap dance."

Emmaline went for broke. Why not, Byrd thought. They'd crashed one of the biggest political gatherings in the parish.

"Did you kill Etienne LeDeux?" she asked flatly.

The pompous man seemed to deflate. "You don't really believe I did, do you?"

"My beliefs are immaterial."

"No, I did not kill the man," Marcel said heatedly. "I did not steal his gun; I've never taken pot shots at him. Mr. LeDeux was an excitable, foolish man. Both our families go back generations in this parish. I'm sorry the man was murdered. It is a tragedy." Marcel folded his arms over his impressive chest. "Time for you to leave, Miss Beard. You're out of place here." Marcel added, "The chief of state police is also my guest this evening. The state police are actively investigating both unsolved Ville Nouvelle murders. I could complain to him, that you, an unauthorized citizen, insist on assuming a police role by coming here and harassing me during an important political meeting."

"That won't be necessary." Emmaline took Byrd's arm. He prepared to propel her toward the door. Byrd shuddered. Marcel's one blue and one brown eye had never appeared so sinister. Sheriff Rodney Smith stood watching.

CHAPTER 35

The following morning, Emmaline surveyed herself in her boudoir mirror. Looking older, she thought. She decided her fifties were the decade of total cellular collapse. Everything drooped. What didn't droop dragged. She made an appointment with her dermatologist for Botox injections. Next, her esthetician, to seriously slough off layers of dead skin. Lastly, her Baton Rouge beautician for the works. In the beautician's chair sipping her favorite, Diet Pepsi, she tried to scowl at her image—her face was too tight to frown.

"What happened to you?" asked the beautician, lifting a tress of Emmaline's hair hiding the head wound.

"An accident," Emmaline said. "The stitches are out."

"And you colored your hair yourself?"

"A girl's gotta do what a girl's gotta do." Emmaline pulled a magazine photograph of a famous actress she admired from her handbag. "I want this haircut."

"Well," said the beautician uncertainly, "we'll see what we can do."

After the beauty salon, Emmaline shopped for new outfits to match her sleek copper hair, her unclogged pores, and her absent crow's feet. She chose two outfits. The first, a pale green silk blouse and a pair of moss green leather pants. The second, a bit more daring, a rust-red blouse with a much lower neckline and black skinny jeans. All garments light years from her usual unadventurous wardrobe.

That evening, she invited Kimberley to dinner. She chose a new Thai restaurant that had recently opened down river.

* * *

"I've never seen so many noodle options," observed Kimberley, studying the menu.

Emmaline nodded. "I'll wager, they're all delicious."

"I bet so, too," Kimberley said, sniffing the air. "It smells positively delicious in here." In the end, Kimberley chose the Pad Tai and steamed dumplings. Emmaline, the Thai Calamari and shrimp tacos.

"Sheriff Smith was at Marcel Beaudion's political gathering," Emmaline said once their dinner was served.

"It looks delicious," said Kimberley, drooling over her food. "Uh, what about Sheriff Smith?"

"He was at Marcel's meeting."

"He's a Democrat," Kimberley said. "Why wouldn't he be there?"

Emmaline speared a shrimp.

Kimberley's eyes widened. "Were you there?"

"Byrd and I both."

"Really." Kimberley didn't believe her, which was just as well. "Kickoff for the governor's reelection," Kimberley volunteered.

"More than that," Emmaline suggested darkly. "More to do with the Ville Nouvelle murders."

Let the girl digest that along with the Pad Tai.

"What do you mean?"

Since Kimberley could neither prove nor disprove any happenings at Marcel's, Emmaline began convincingly. "As the sheriff's employee, you do know the State Police Chief and Sheriff Smith were in corners the entire evening. Didn't look good."

Slowly, comprehension dawned on Kimberley. She practically teared. "The State Police are pressuring our poor sheriff. They've sent in two private investigators, undercover people. I think one is a woman. It's all hush, hush. Sheriff Smith is frantic. He's afraid of losing the reelection if state blackballs him. There goes my job, too." The Pad Tai could've congealed for all Kimberley cared.

Emmaline said forcefully. "We don't want state meddling in our parish affairs. Kimberley, tell me everything you know about these new PIs. Everything," she stressed as the waitress refilled their sweet tea.

Kimberley, gray eyes troubled, paused the briefest moment before blurting, "That man who resembles Gary West is Daniel Flippo. He's a friend of West's. He's from California, too, near Marina Del Ray. Mr. Flippo swore he came to town to join Dante Washington's protest march. He participated in the march. The march wasn't the main reason Flippo came here. Interpol contacted us about the two accomplices other than Gary West in the Tahiti pearl theft. This man, Daniel Flippo, wasn't one of them. But he's traveled to Tahiti often. Sheriff Smith thinks he was involved in the pearl theft. Mr. Flippo had solid alibies for both murders."

"What alibies?" asked Emmaline.

"Dante confirmed Mr. Flippo worked one of the flatbed loudspeakers all day and all night the night Carol Powell was murdered."

"And, Etienne?"

Kimberley rolled her eyes. "He was in New Orleans with Dolores Favor and Misty Shores."

CHAPTER 36

The following morning Byrd, dressed in jogging attire, strolled into the library. "Glad to see you're up," Emmaline said to his backside as he dropped into an easy chair.

"Good grief," he gasped. "What happened to you?"

"An improvement, I trust," she said, aware of her revealing red blouse, skinny black jeans, and spiked copper locks.

"Or something," he said, thinking she resembled a Q-tip dipped in red ink. "Why'd you fool with your hair?"

"Really, Byrd!" There were other things on her mind than her recent glamour crisis. "We're getting nowhere solving these murders."

He agreed.

Arching her new perfectly shaped eyebrows, she continued. "State has brought in two private investigators. One may be a woman. Sheriff Smith's job may be on the line if he doesn't solve the Ville Nouvelle murders. We do *not* want a new sheriff," she stressed.

"Who would draw in the ladies at your plays," Byrd said with a smirk.

He had a point. "Too many unrelated incidents are confusing us."

Byrd half listened. He really must return to Houston. He had a lab to run. Betty and Professor Dang, though efficient, needed direction. Their frantic phone calls proved as much.

"We've wasted time talking to Julie, Josephine, Charlie Powell, even focusing on Dante's RV fire, plus Marcel's fire," Emmaline said. "I've concluded none of them had anything to do with the murders. Even -"

Byrd stopped her. "Before you mention it, I believe the attack on you was connected to the murders."

"Care to elaborate?"

At times, Emmaline failed to see the obvious. "Because there's only one killer," he said emphatically. "Strong emotions incited the two murders. Both were violent killings. Physical killings, if you will. You were viciously attacked, too."

She shuddered; grateful for the couple who had stopped to help.

Byrd continued. "I'm convinced your attack was not random. You were followed by the killer on that lonely road. This person is watching you. You are not safe." This, the main reason he stayed on in Ville Nouvelle.

"Which leaves us exactly nowhere," she said, "since we have no idea of this person's identity."

"True," Byrd agreed. He stood, did a few sets of slow stretches before going out to jog.

"Be careful."

Absorbing his warning, she believed Byrd could be right. The house seemed especially lonely and frightening. Her attack leaving Pastor Lemuel's Boys Ranch—she'd initially put down to assault by a stranger. Now, she wasn't certain. The odds of that attack were very unlikely. It was possible she was targeted, followed, and the perpetrator frightened away by the good Samaritans who'd stopped and helped her.

Her memory of the incident—the single piercing headlight blinding her from behind. Limbs lay across the road. She'd swerved to avoid them, made a U-turn. The motorcycle forced her to the side of the road. She lost control, hit some trees. A voice about a camp . . . yes, her burning a camp. Next, the shattering blow to her head. She remembered nothing more. She shuddered, glancing around the old-fashioned room.

Framed maps from every part of the world cluttered the walls, memorabilia from her father and grandfather's travels. The overflowing bookshelves, the tall windows, the comfortable outdated furniture. She shouldn't feel frightened, but she did.

The rambling house had many, many rooms. Sugar was king, in this part of Louisiana, when the mansion was built. Servants glided through the halls. Now, with different economics, most of the house lay closed. The closed section of Beard House troubled her. The disturbed locks. Saucer leaping out upon her and Chad.

She rushed outside and around to the mansion's west side to examine the outside doors. She'd had one door replaced and new locks installed on the others. Was everything intact? Had someone - the killer - forced the locks and let himself inside?

She caught her breath, thrusting shaking fingers behind the overgrown oleander bushes. Releasing her pent breath on a sigh - the door keys still hung in place. How negligent of her. Of course, the keys were left for the repairmen. She checked all the doors. They didn't appear disturbed. Why should they be? She'd conveniently left the keys for anyone. She whisked the keys into her pocket.

* * *

Sheriff Smith and Saucer studied the BOLO (Be On the LookOut) board.

"I don't understand, sir, why Etienne was on the Black Path so late," mumbled Saucer. He stood too close behind the sheriff, his breath warm on Sheriff Smith's neck.

Red pushpins dotted the board. Etienne LeDeux's house, the location of Etienne's body, and the location of Carol Powell's body at LeFevre House.

The sheriff traced his finger along the incident map. Slightly more than two hundred yards separated the place Carol Powell's body was found and the spot of Etienne's dead body. A fortune in stolen pearls motivated the Powell girl's murder. What motivated Etienne's murder? By all accounts, the two had never met. Had no knowledge of one other. Why were they both killed in such proximity to each other?

Smith moved to his desk and sat down, staring at the board deep in thought. No answers came. Turning his attention to the two thick files on his desk, he thumbed through them. Were there similarities linking the two murders? If so, the information eluded him. The Powell girl was killed for the stolen pearls. Interpol now had the pearls. Interpol knew the identity of two of the Tahiti Pearl Museum thieves. They sought the third thief. They wanted Gary West for questioning. West was now hiding in California.

He and Deputy Saucer had investigated LeFevre House numerous times. The house now closed for the tour season with occasional bookings for weddings, garden parties and similar functions.

Smith believed Carol Powell was running for her life and took the chance of leaving the pearls with Emmaline Beard, to pass them on to Josephine Powell. The elder Ms. Powell would know how to deal with the authorities should her granddaughter meet a critical end. Tragically, she had.

Standing on the LeFevre House upper gallery, one could view the section of the Black Path where Mr. LeDeux met his killer. The proximity of the bodies, a mere two hundred yards apart, surely meant the murders were connected. How? By what?

He'd questioned Helen Condor again the day before. Helen reported Etienne in upbeat spirits that day. He'd made a delicious meal. She hadn't felt like eating. She'd gone upstairs. She heard him showering, and later whistling, as he left the house. No, she had no idea why he decided to walk the Black Path late in the afternoon. She knew no reason for his uncharacteristic cheerfulness. Smith believed the dour man showered that afternoon, for otherwise, he would reek of smoke. The successful arson accounted for his glee. It was simple if you thought about it. All well and good, but it must be proven with sound evidence that would hold up in court.

* * *

Smith left his office to question the Rogers couple, who'd stopped to assist Emmaline Beard after her attack. The couple lived downriver in a small working-class hamlet called Point. Both were home this morning. Mr. Rogers worked offshore and was on his fourteen days off from an oil rig. Mrs. Rogers worked part time at a flower shop. Today, her day off.

Mrs. Rogers, a petite blond woman with large blue eyes, invited him in. "Oh, Sheriff Smith. We've been expecting you." She led him into a small living area, neat and immaculately clean. "I'll get Jimmy." She left the room, returning a few minutes later, a dark-complexioned young man with an enormous beer and boudain paunch, following her.

Jimmy Rogers had just stepped from the shower, for his wet black hair lay plastered to his wide head, and he smelled strongly of some manly soap scent. Jimmy shook hands with the sheriff. "We've been expecting you," he said. "Have you found out who beat up the lady?"

"We are working on it. Will you describe what you saw that night."

Jimmy glanced at his wife as if for assurance. "We'd been to the in-laws. They live past that boy's school." He glanced at his wife again. "Tammy's parents. Well, Tammy's mother and her step-dad."

Tammy Rogers nodded.

"I see," Smith said. "Go on."

"It was pretty late. Probably eleven o'clock, I'd say. We saw this motorcycle cut out of the woods and follow the Cadillac ahead of us. Looked like the cycle meant to rear-end the car. The woman veered, looked like she lost control and crashed into some trees. We slowed down…"

"That's right," put in Tammy. She gave Jimmy a grim smile. "I told you to slow down. You never know what kind of people are out - especially late, like that. Some rough bars out that way."

"I see," said Smith. He looked to Jimmy.

Jimmy nodded. "The guy riding the Harley behind the Cadillac, stopped. And bailed through the woods.

"Did you see the motorcycle driver approach the Cadillac?"

195

"Naw, it was too dark, and we were too far behind."

Tammy interrupted excitedly. "The next thing I saw was the Harley blistering through the woods. Jimmy drove up then and we saw the woman slumped over the steering wheel."

Both Rogers fell silent.

"How do you think the attacker was able to land the blow if the woman remined behind the wheel?" asked Smith.

"Her car is a big four-door. The driver's side back door was standing open," recalled Jimmy. "The map light was on."

Yeah," Tammy said. "We saw her real good. I thought she was dead. I never dreamed the lady was Emmaline Beard. She's real famous around here. Has plays at that big house of hers. I've been after Jimmy to get tickets for us, but he never has." Said with a disparaging glance at her husband.

"We had to move a big tree limb out of the road," Jimmy added.

"Yeah, the wind must have blown it down," Tammy said.

Further questions turned up nothing more about Emmaline's attacker other than both Rogers agreed the person was a man. Since it was dark, no color of the motorcycle was verified, other than it was shiny. A troubling question. Why was Emmaline Beard alone so late on a lonely road?

CHAPTER 37

Finally, a break. Two breaks. One, a break Sheriff Smith didn't particularly want, but a break, nevertheless. Sheriff Smith had put out an all points on Jeremy Worms as a person of interest in the Dante Washington RV arson. With the boy in Europe, he doubted the all-points would come to anything. Jeremy's passport flagged. The youth had entered the United States from Canada. Likely, some family member had met Jeremy. Smith wouldn't tip off the Juvies just yet. "Saucer."

"Yes, sir."

"The Worms boy is in the country. Go up to Shreveport. We need surveillance on him and his family, Undercover surveillance."

"Gotcha. I mean, yes sir."

The second break, the discovery of a car along the Mississippi River. Smith ran the tags. The automobile, a rental. The rental had been issued to Carol Powell.

Sheriff Smith got in his car and drove along the river to the secluded road where Carol Powell's rental car had been found.

"Pushed it into the ravine there, sir," said a young deputy with big ears, gesturing to the barely visible back bumper of the car. "Miracle we found it. Looks like they tried to shove it into the river but gave up for the trees and brush."

"Touch anything?"

"No sir."

"Fingerprint guy and photo are on their way out," Smith said, slipping on latex gloves. "A wrecker, too."

He tried to climb down into the ravine. Too steep. He saw the keys in the ignition and the doors unlocked. Nothing to do but wait for the wrecker. Peaceful to watch the busy river and think while he waited.

The rental car posed questions. What had Carol Powell done between approximately eleven o'clock a.m., when she gave the packet of pearls to Emmaline at LeFevre House, and the time of her murder? The coroner had set Carol's death between 10:30 p.m. and 1:00 a.m., charging the rain for the lengthy window of death. The body lay in the rain until the following morning.

Crime scene evidence showed Carol killed at LeFevre House on the upper gallery—her body then thrown to the parking lot below. Reason and logic should have prompted Carol to leave the area immediately after giving the pearls to Emmaline since, obviously, she knew she was being followed. She had an automobile at her disposal. Why would the young woman drive to such an isolated area such as this? Had the killer forced her here?

A mystery, all of it. The protest march was in full swing the day Carol was killed. Strangers flooded the small town. Maybe, the killer spotted Carol and followed her. She lost control of the rental car and plowed into this ravine. Grilling her for hours about the pearls could be the reason for detaining her and killing her later. Maybe Carol lied and said she'd stashed the pearls at the antebellum tour house. The killer took her there.

Or had she managed to escape the killer most of the day and evening? Terrified, she'd fled to the tour house for safety. The killer followed her and killed her. Didn't make sense. Knowing the area, Carol knew where Emmaline lived. Why not go to Beard House?

None of it made sense. Smith gave up his frustrating reasonings when the wrecker arrived, followed by fingerprint and photo deputies.

CHAPTER 38

Emmaline's mind wandered while Byrd jogged. She really should exercise. However, her bad knees, from basketball days, sufficed as her excuse. She should explore the dozens and dozens of low impact exercise options—something trendy in Baton Rouge. Something exotic and mysterious.

Exercise, new hairdos, sexy clothing, none of these things aided in solving the two murders dumped at her backdoor. Literally her backdoor, she thought wryly, Carol Powell murdered at LeFevre House, and Etienne LeDeux nearby. And, now state had two undercover agents in Ville Nouvelle. Who were these agents? She had no idea. Neither did Kimberley. Difficult to identify strangers after Dante's protest march, since many stragglers remained in town. Once experiencing bayou country, many outsiders opted to stay.

She pulled her notebook from the desk drawer. Notations, notations, notations. She scanned the jumbled notes about her trip to New Orleans to question Josephine and Charlie.

Surprise trip to New Orleans: Saw J. and son. J. peculiar as always. C. overly friendly.

Is C. a sterling character? Was he involved in the pearl theft? Is he above harming J. for her

money? Both relieved to see me leave.

She closed the notebook and slipped it back into the drawer.

She thought about Byrd's Tahiti trip. He'd learned both Charlie and Carol had visited the area many times. Was Charlie involved in the Pearl Museum theft? The man Byrd encountered on the Tahiti beach mentioned knowing both Gary West and Charlie Powell. There was a third unnamed conspirator in on the theft. Was that person Charlie Powell? Or was that person Daniel Flippo, the Gary West look-alike guy?

She glanced at her watch. Byrd should return soon. Annoyed that Helen continued spending most of her time at Etienne's place after his death, and even after Julie returned to Baton Rouge, Emmaline knew she must depend on Esther for the burden of the Ripper's play last-minute rehearsals. Chewing the pencil eraser tip, she second-guessed her decision in choosing such a morbid production. How did she know going in that two people would be murdered?

Byrd's booming voice sounded in the kitchen.

She hurried there. "You were gone long enough."

"Sat in the little park awhile." A dish of freshly made beignets sat before him.

"Coffee, Emmaline?" Maizie wielded the coffee pot.

"Yes." She turned to Byrd. "We need to take a trip."

"A trip? Like where?"

"Marina Del Ray. To look up Gary West's friend. The one who minds the trinket shops when Gary is away. He may fill us in about Charlie Powell."

"Charlie Powell? You're not serious."

"Never more so."

Byrd frowned, wiping powdered sugar from his chin. "Out of the question."

"I don't see how you figure -"

Interrupting her, Byrd said, "Charlie Powell? You saw Charlie Powell in New Orleans. He's with his mother. You talked to him. You found out nothing. On the other hand, what do you think about that kid, Jeremy Worms, being back in the states?"

"What," she faltered, "he's in Switzerland, dodging the police."

"Not any longer. I ran into Kimberley in the park. She jogs, too."

She would, Emmaline thought. Petite, couldn't weigh much over one hundred pounds, and pretty to boot. Some girls had all the luck. "Jogging Kimberley told you Jeremy is back?"

"After we visited a short while." Byrd smiled dreamily.

Visited all right. Shapely, pretty Kimberley in skintight jogging attire. What man wouldn't visit? "She told me you'd want to know Jeremy's passport flagged at the Canadian border. Smith is sending Saucer to Shreveport on surveillance. They think Jeremy will eventually show up at home. Kimberley said to keep the info under wraps."

What a lucky break, Emmaline thought, though she'd have a hard time forgiving Smith's secretary for sharing with Byrd and not her. The telephone rang. Esther Marshall.

Byrd pushed back from the table and wandered into the drawing room. Impressed with the stage set up for opening night, he turned when Maizie entered the room carrying a huge silver tray. She proceeded to unlock the largest china cabinet and began stacking valuable china on the tray. "Gotta move all this stuff. Strangers being in here."

"If it's locked -"

"Flimsy little old locks like these ain't stopping nobody," Maizie said sagely while loading the tray. "Them outside locks didn't stop Saucer pouncing."

"I thought Emmaline forgot and left the keys nearby."

"She did. That ain't like her neither. Too much stuff going on."

"Let me get that for you." Byrd moved to lift the heavy tray and carried it down the hall to the old butler pantry, where Maizie locked the valuables away from the prying public.

CHAPTER 39

The early spring Sunday morning dawned unseasonably humid and warm, aided by a favorable gulf stream, as Saucer negotiated a sharp curve near the Worms property. This section of Shreveport boasted old money and large impressive houses located on an acre or more - make that three acres or more - spacious lots. He drove slowly past the Worms house, barely visible at the end of a freshly tarred, winding private drive. Stopping for pictures - impossible, for the narrow, two-lane road featured practically no shoulders. He drove almost a mile before a cross street allowed him to turn around.

Saucer drove slowly, scanning the undeveloped tract of woodland across from the mansion. Fenced with a locked gate, he couldn't park there to observe. He drove around the block and approached the Worms property from the rear. He found an unlocked service gate in a chain link fence. The circular driveway back here held a Mercedes Benz, obviously out all night, due to the fogged windshield and windows.

Perhaps someone arrived too late to bother parking the automobile in the unattached garage. There appeared to be no movement in the house, and the curtains were drawn. Sunday morning sleep-ins.

Abutting the Worms property to the rear stood new construction on a wooded lot. The perfect place to park and watch the Worms house. Which is exactly what he did. He drew his binoculars out and focused them toward the rear entrance of the Worms house. He glanced at his watch and listed the time in his notebook, 7:45 a.m.

He'd picked up a copy of the *Shreveport Times* from a coin operated vending machine. He slid his seat back and unfolded the newspaper. Not much interested him until he came to the Society Section. He stared at the reason Jeremy Worms returned to the states from Switzerland. The upcoming marriage of his sister, Jill Ann Worms. Jill Ann, a young woman with straight blond hair and thin lips, smiled into the camera. He'd bet anything the Mercedes parked at the back entrance shuttled Jeremy home during the wee hours.

Now to get some evidence pictures. He added a lens to his camera and waited. He hadn't long to wait. At 8:30 a.m., a man dressed in a suit emerged from the house and opened the back gate. The man climbed into the Mercedes, started the engine and let the motor idle. A short time later, a well-dressed woman and a younger woman, Saucer presumed to be Jill Ann, came from the house and got into the car. They drove away. Likely to an early church service. No sign of Jeremy, though. They'd hardly sport him around, Saucer thought, certain the youth remained in the house.

Saucer dug into the sack of fast food biscuits and the second cup of coffee he'd snagged earlier—the coffee now somewhat lukewarm but sweet and creamy.

The next two hours, no activity occurred outside the back entrance to the Worms house. Nor had the man and two women returned.

Bingo! At 10:30 a.m., Jeremy emerged from the backdoor dressed in athletic shorts and a long-sleeve T-shirt, a basketball in his hands. He began shooting hoops at a fancy in-ground basketball goal near a hard surface tennis court. *Yipes!* Saucer muttered. There were two tennis courts, the second one with a grass surface like Wimbledon. Saucer snapped picture after picture, laughing out loud at the perfect shots. Smith's *gonna love it,* he almost shouted.

CHAPTER 40

Sunday morning

Emmaline waited for Helen to arrive for brunch. Perusing her planner, she gasped, "My soul, *On Whitechapel Road* opens next Friday evening." Her preoccupation with the murders blinded her to reality. She'd delegated practically everything to Esther Marshall. *Esther is capable,* she reasoned. The woman's brassy personality and pugnacious spirit said it all. Helen's psychic insight, though valuable, weighed less and less, especially after Etienne's murder. She'd invited Helen for brunch.

"You want me to serve in here?" asked Maizie, interrupting her musings.

"Yes, please." Emmaline closed the planner and pulled the tilt-top table to the center of the room. Maizie rolled in the loaded mahogany teacart. Emmaline had no sooner draped a snowy white luncheon cloth across the table when Helen came through the door. "Oh, how absolutely delicious it smells in here."

"Maizie's amazing brunch," said Emmaline, unstacking cups. "Tea or coffee?"

"Coffee, please." Helen settled in the chair Emmaline indicated. "Is that Maizie's famous fruit compote?" asked Helen, smiling appreciatively.

"It is. Along with eggs benedict and orange marmalade coffee cake."

Their plates filled; they ate silently until Helen said, "I know you're worried about opening night. I'm terribly sorry I haven't been more help."

"Who would've dreamed Etienne's murder," sympathized Emmaline gravely. "Too dreadful for words." Secretly, Emmaline thought, even before the murder, Helen had devoted far too much time to a relative she seldom saw.

"I remember the Fanning case," Helen reminisced. "Both you and Byrd were brilliant clearing that up."

Helen referred to David Fanning, the youth who'd disappeared their senior year of high school. Byrd and Emmaline had brought the killer, who'd gone free over twenty years, to justice.

"You'll solve these murders, too," Helen assured her.

Emmaline couldn't suppress a sarcastic snort. "Is that a hunch or is it from the crystal ball?"

"Really Emmaline, you're too funny. I'm not a twenty-four-hour oracle."

"How's Julie?" Emmaline recalled Julie's glittery cowboy outfit the night she popped in to question her. "I didn't know she was a country western fan."

Helen laughed. "You mean her pink rhinestone get-up. She came in third in a Dolly Parton contest in Baton Rouge."

Brunch continued leisurely. They talked of inconsequential things like the old friends they were. Finally, Helen changed the subject to the theatrical. "I made some dialogue changes. I think Esther went overboard with the *methinks* in scene two." She fished the corrected script from her bag.

* * *

Later that afternoon, Chad Ludlum and Esther arrived to rehearse. Helen returned and joined Esther on the set. Chad and Emmaline, on the landing, watched the stage proceedings below. Sheriff Smith arrived next, then Kimberley. Saucer was suspiciously absent.

The curtain went up. Action started. Chad made two mistakes early on, pink lights on a victim rather than blue. Plus, blinding yellow lights in the second murder scene. "Chad are you all right?" Emmaline asked kindly.

"I'm not any good at this, am I?"

"Of course, you are. You simply must think about what you're doing before you push the levers. Properly lighting the stage is crucial."

In the beginning of her theatrical career, Emmaline had hired a professional lightning master, purchased a permanent stand, installed additional power sources, and added moving lights capable of producing the most extraordinary stage effects.

Jeremy Worms had worked the complex system like a pro.

Chad must master the lightning system also. She had no one else. She looked at the sad young man. He appeared acutely distressed. She said softly. "I think I know what's bothering you."

His face went white, tears gathered in the corner of his eyes. He blinked and blinked and blinked. It did not help. He opened his mouth to speak. No words came.

"Sit here." She indicated the folding chair next to the one she occupied. He moved toward her, much in the manner she imagined victims approached the guillotine.

"Yes ma'am," he squeaked breathlessly, his eyes huge, his irises drowned in fear.

"Chad, I suspect you were involved with setting fire to Dante Washington's RV." Before he could reply, she added. "Sheriff Smith is below. We must speak to him at once."

"I know." Barely above a whisper.

The interview between Sheriff Smith and Chad took place in Emmaline's library behind closed doors. When the two emerged, Chad did not wear handcuffs. For that, Emmaline felt grateful. Sheriff Smith spoke. "Chad will not be rehearsing."

Alarmed at her lightning tech being led away, panic gripped her. "Where are you taking him? I need -"

"Miss Beard," interrupted Smith stiffly. "Apply to the university. Any theatrical major will be able to help you."

DEADLY BLACK PEARLS

CHAPTER 41

"I've had Chad arrested for arson," Emmaline lamented to Byrd later that evening. "My single lighting technician. Can anything more go wrong with this production?" She threw up her hands dramatically. "Two murders, two cases of arson, an attack on me?"

"Turning the boy in was best. You said he suffered under a heavy case of nerves."

"I know. Still -" A knock sounded at the library door. "Who is it?"

"Me. Maizie." Maizie opened the door and entered the room. "Some women are here. Said they are actresses. They want to see you, Emmaline."

"Actresses? I know of no actresses."

"Yes, you do," announced Dolores Favors as she and Misty Shores minced into the room. "We are actresses and we heard about your theatrical," continued Dolores. "We'd love parts. Women on the street, Stand ins. Anything?"

"Yeah," piped up Misty.

"How about murder victims?"

"Perfect," they answered in unison.

"At least they're professionals," Emmaline said to Byrd after the two departed, roles assured.

"Professionals at something or other," he alluded. "You fill in the blanks."

"Really Byrd. Don't be such a prude."

* * *

Monday morning

Monday morning, Emmaline telephoned Kimberley. "I'm busy. I'll call you back," said the secretary, disconnecting at once. True to her word, Kimberley returned Emmaline's telephone call within the hour. "What can I do for you?"

"I'm calling about Chad Ludlum. I'm worried about him."

"No need to worry. Pastor Lemuel and the Juvies came last night. Chad told them everything. The Juvies have all three boys. Chad Ludlum, Scott Mason, and Jeremy Worms."

"Jeremy Worms, isn't he in Switzerland?"

"He was. He slipped back to the states for his sister's wedding." Kimberley paused, then added. "It's out of our hands and up to the authorities what happens to the boys."

"They did a dangerous thing, even if it was a prank," said Emmaline.

"Like I said, it's out of our hands here."

"Who're you talking to?" whispered Byrd, sauntering into the library as Emmaline disconnected.

"Kimberley. She said the Juvenile Division have all three boys in custody."

"Well, well, well. Why did Jeremy return to the states?"

"Came for his sister's wedding."

"Stroke of luck. I'd hate to see the other two pay for his involvement."

"So would I," agreed Emmaline. "You want a snack?"

"Be still my heart. What has Maizie concocted?"

"Some leftover crab stuffed mushrooms and a Buche De Noel." Emmaline said over her shoulder as she led the way to the kitchen.

"The Christmas log cake. It isn't even the holidays."

"Maizie says baking the cake keeps her in practice for Christmas." Emmaline switched the kitchen light on and loaded a dessert plate with a generous slice of the log. On a paper plate, she slipped several stuffed mushrooms and set both dishes before Byrd.

"Aren't you having any?"

"Yes. Actually, some of yours." She speared half a mushroom.

The snacks consumed, they trailed back to the library. "Booray?" she asked, pulling out a deck of cards.

"Not in the mood."

She hated his grumpy attitude. "You heard about my cousin, Girard Beard, Papa's ward. He was a devout little soul."

Byrd shrugged.

"Papa sent him to seminary to become a priest. Girard came home only having learned new swear words and how to cheat at Booray. Papa pulled him from seminary. He now works in a casino dealing Blackjack."

"Perfect spot for him."

"Yes," she said with frustration. "If solving these murders were as simple." She spoke staring into space soberly. Rounding on Byrd, she asked. "Where was Carol Powell the eleven and a half hours before she was murdered? The coroner placed the time of death between ten-thirty p.m. and one a.m. She gave the pearls to me at LeFevre House at approximately ten-thirty that morning, maybe closer to eleven. Ten and a half to eleven hours later, she's dead. Where did she go during that time? The authorities found her ditched rental car. Why wreck a rental?"

"Wiped clean of fingerprints, too," Byrd said. "Could've happened shortly after she left LeFevre House. Or anytime." He thought a moment. "Maybe something or someone frightened her. Don't forget the protest march flooding

Ville Nouvelle with strangers. Her killing could've been random, the work of a psychopath."

Emmaline challenged him. "Psychopath doesn't add up. What are the odds? She came here to get rid of those pearls. She had to know they were stolen. I think she feared someone dangerous following her."

"Logical," agreed Byrd. "Hmm, running from Gary West?"

"She -" Emmaline tried to recall the minutiae of her very brief conversation with Carol Powel. Despite concentrating, her brain focused more on her personal discomfort the morning Carol came to LeFevre House. Her ill- fitting costume, her ragged nerves and her shortness of breath.

Her turning the tour over to Esther. She looked at Byrd. "She seemed to be running from everyone. I told her about her fiancé coming to my house looking for her. I think she said *no* quite hysterically. Then, she ran away."

Leaving Esther in charge and not feeling well, she went to the back veranda to catch a breath of fresh air. Away from responsibility and the tourist, her anxiety eased. Then she heard someone running. Running toward the back veranda. More surprised than shocked, a young woman identifying herself as Carol Powell rushed onto the veranda. Carol thrust the package to her. Said to give it to Josephine Powell, Only to Josephine, no one else. As quickly, the girl darted across the lawn and fled out the side gate onto Camellia Lane.

"That could - or could not - indicate fear of him."

"Well," blurted Emmaline succinctly, "She asked no questions about where to find him."

"Her fiancé was in Tahiti before he came here," Byrd said.

"I know. According to him, he was instructed to come here and ask for me if he couldn't locate Carol or Josephine. He mentioned nothing about pearls. He only appeared worried about finding Carol. He never contacted me again. Obviously, he left the area when he couldn't find her."

"He was seen in California later," Byrd said. "Spotted under the radar. The authorities haven't located him. What's he guilty of? Pearl theft. Murder."

"Possibly neither," she speculated. "The man you met on the Tahiti beach knew both Charlie Powell and Gary West. Charlie Powell is sort of a loose cannon despite his family's wealth."

"The beach guy knew the others suspected in the museum theft."

"The answer to Carol's murder must lie in Tahiti," speculated Emmaline.

"I'm not sure," Byrd said, recalling his horrifying experience in jail there. "Gary came here first. Carol arrived with the pearls. Carol was murdered here, not in Tahiti."

"Which leads us to the deadest of dead ends," Emmaline announced. "I don't trust Charlie Powell. It's true he was born into money with every advantage. I know Josephine was never pleased with how he turned out. Spoiled rich kid who constantly took advantage of her."

Byrd nodded gloomily. There were always reasons for actions, the rich being no exception. "How about we play a hand of Booray," he suggested. Get the cards and deal."

CHAPTER 42

Sheriff Smith studied his notes on the Powell murder. Carol Powell arrived at LeFevre House before eleven a.m. the morning of the day she was murdered. How did she know to find Emmaline at the tour house? Had she asked directions from anyone? Where did she go after she left Emmaline? If she feared a killer following her, she'd have remained at the tour house begging help. What about Gary West? He was looking for Carol. Now, from all reports, West had left the area. Had he known of Carol's death before he left town? He was seen in California. He certainly was never seen again in Ville Nouvelle. There were crowds of strangers in town for the protest march. Then, the look-alike Gary, Daniel Flippo. Flippo also from Tahiti. Was there a connection between the two men?

Saucer, at his computer across the room, ran background checks. Smith called to him. "You looked into the Powell girl's car rental?"

"Yeah. Rented at the New Orleans airport. Ran a check on her credit card activity. Ordinary stuff, gasoline, fast food. She bought gasoline at a station downriver before she got to Ville Nouvelle. No card activity after nine-thirty a.m. the day of her murder."

Smith mused. "She fueled before looking up Emmaline. Perhaps she intended spending as little time as possible in Ville Nouvelle."

"Yeah," blurted Saucer, "Dump the pearls. Hit the road."

"Looks that way. Only it didn't happen that way." The sheriff drummed his pen on the desk. "What happened to Carol Powell after she left LeFevre House? With a full gas tank, did she head to the interstate? Obviously not," he speculated, answering his question himself. "Instead, it appears she drove the rental to Little Bayou road and wrecked it? Why?"

"Somebody tore down the Little Bayou road sign," Saucer said. "The deputies found it in the woods. Thought vandals did it."

"I've thought of that," Smith said. He believed the missing road sign was a deadly set-up, and not the work of vandals or teenagers. The Powell girl taking the wrong road—a premeditated act. "Why wait until ten-thirty or eleven that night to murder her," he said, thinking aloud. "She wasn't sexually assaulted. She was beaten with a metal object. Especially about the face. Could have been a chain according to the coroner."

"It don't make sense," Saucer said, "unless it was to teach her a lesson. The beating, I mean."

Smith sat up straighter. "You may have something there." At times, Saucer's mental process amazed him. "That would indicate the killer knew her, followed her, and killed her. There was no sign of a struggle at the car," Smith reminded Saucer. "The beating didn't take place there."

"Maybe she was hurt. That's a really deep ditch."

"A possibility. Again, no sign of blood was found." Smith opened his desk drawer and dropped the pen inside. "Saucer, I want you to go back to the crash site. Take a couple of deputies. Comb the surrounding area within a ten-mile radius in every direction. Don't come back until you find something."

"Yes sir." The deputy rumbled up. "You gonna be at rehearsal tonight?"

"If possible," replied Smith, Emmaline's Jack-the-Ripper play the furthest thing from his mind.

* * *

The Booray game continued until after lunch. Emmaline took the pot. "You weren't paying attention."

"Neither were you," Byrd retorted. "Sheer luck you won."

"True," she agreed. "Coffee?"

"Why not." They trailed out to the kitchen. Maizie had left a fresh pot brewing.

"I really need to get back to Houston," he said, adding his usual four heaping teaspoons of sugar. "Talked to Betty. Sales expo coming up. Big convention. We have a booth."

"A glue booth. Makes sense you'd stick around. Get it. Stick around," she chortled.

"You have a sick sense of humor."

She ran her hand through her spikey red hair and tugged at her blouse, which threatened to go off-shoulder. "Seriously, I need you here." She didn't like his obstinate frown. "If you go, you absolutely must come back for opening night."

"I'll try."

* * *

Beard House grew increasingly lonely after Byrd drove away. The sneaky little chemist had packed his bags earlier. With a quick peck on her forehead, same as one would kiss a loyal dog, he was gone.

Full rehearsal tonight with Esther in charge. Maizie had the buffet canapes prepared. She'd gone to her apartment to binge her favorite soap, a Spanish production, forcing her to read sub-titles and drool over the sexy leading men.

Which left Emmaline at odds. Which she didn't entertain for long. Her walking sneakers on, she drove the back way to Etienne's property. Avoiding the front of the house, she thought she saw Helen's car in the drive.

Parking as out of sight as possible, she slid out and started toward the pasture. Tender shoots of early spring grass pushed through the singed brown stubble as she climbed through the barbed-wire fence and started toward the camp site she'd discovered days before. Soon the field would forget it had ever burned, she thought philosophically, reaching the pine thicket. However, she'd never forget Etienne LeDeux's murder, nor Carol Powell's. Forever imbedded in her memory. The old obscure thought toyed around the farthest perimeters of her brain. Something she'd seen. Seen - but not consciously registered - her first trip out here. Maddening. What had she seen that day?

She prayed no one had cleared the camp site. Great! The clutter lay as it had previously. The remnants of a tent, a charred tarpaulin, scorched pots. Food tins, labels burned off from the fire. She found a stick and poked through the debris. Roly-poly worms balled, playing dead. Centipedes scrambled away.

Rolling up her sleeves, she began to drag the stick through the tarpaulin remains. Byrd should be here. He believed one person committed both murders. Why? Nothing tied the homicides together, other than they both occurred in Ville Nouvelle during Dante Washington's protest march. Likely, a crazed person did the killings then left town. In a movable society like today's, such was possible and, unfortunately, happened more than she liked to think.

She pushed the stick into the tarpaulin and lifted a corner of it. A link of thick metal emerged. A chain.

CHAPTER 43

"**B**ad connection. I can't hear you." Sheriff Smith disconnected. "Sounded like the Beard woman." Kimberley nodded, sorting files.

Saucer burst into the sheriff's inner office mopping his brow and hitching up his ill-fitting trousers. "We found a coupla suspicious things. First, somebody drove a motorcycle to the Powell woman's car, then away from it. The tracks went all the way to the paved road."

"What paved road?"

"Route 47 that goes past Marcel Beaudion's place and on past Mr. LeDeux's."

"What else did you find?"

"The craziest thing. The stake from the Little Bayou road sign. Somebody broke it off and dumped it in the woods."

"Not so crazy," mused the sheriff. "Explains why Carol Powell took the wrong road. With no road sign instead of turning onto Little Bayou Road leading to the bridge over the river, she turned onto that obsolete road. If a motorcycle was chasing her, she easily wound up in the ravine."

"Yeah," Saucer said. "Whoever conked the Beard woman on the head drove a motorcycle."

A deputy stepped to the door. "Miss Beard to see you, Sheriff."

"Send her in." He turned to Kimberley. "That'll be all. Saucer, you stay."

Emmaline entered. Smith noted her out of breath and disheveled. "Did you try to telephone me?"

"I certainly did," she said. "You hung up on me."

"Not intentionally. You were breaking up."

She dropped into the chair in front of his desk. "I found the missing link, literally,"

"Missing link?"

"The murder weapon. A chain. It was in a pile of burned trash in Marcel Beaudion's field."

"You didn't touch it or move it?"

"I'm aware of contaminating a crime scene." She stood. "I'll meet you out there."

* * *

Later that evening, Emmaline put in a call to Byrd. She related the day's findings, the chain, the missing road sign, the motorcycle tracks leading from the Powell girl's rental. "No random accident. Carol was targeted."

He whistled. "Don't do anything foolish. I believe the killer is watching you."

"Why me? I had nothing to do with either Carol or Etienne being murdered."

"Hello, remember the pearls. Etienne told you Marcel was shooting at him. You were attacked. Now, you've unearthed a clue even the authorities missed."

"I am rather good, aren't I?"

Byrd smiled. She was incorrigible. "What's up with these State Police investigators? These undercover detectives."

"I have no idea," she said. Nor has the sheriff mentioned them. Kimberley is in the dark, too."

"Watch your back," he warned.

"I am." She longed for him to return. He boosted her confidence and bravado, not that she lacked either capacity, but Byrd by her side reinforced the skills.

"Otherwise, what's going on?" He said he would try being present for her theatrical opening night.

She hesitated a moment. "Rehearsal, rehearsal, rehearsal." Continuing with a nervous laugh, she said, "Two young men from LSU's performing arts program are working the lights. I got lucky there. It's coming together. You should see the sheriff strut in full costume."

"What about the strippers?"

She chuckled. "Dolores and Misty are pros. They dress up the production. Couldn't have found two better prostitutes if I'd combed brothels."

The call ended. She sighed. The two trips walking across Marcel's field earlier left her exhausted. Later, she'd helped Maizie with the buffet spread for the theatre troupe. Time to rest. Only keyed up and restless, she doubted she could fall asleep.

She stared out the bedroom window. Fast moving clouds blanketed the darkening sky. Spring appeared, pausing on the horizon earlier in the day. Now the lawns wore a dismal, wintry mantle. A study in gray relief, gray branches, gray coils of Spanish moss, and even the massive banks of evergreen shrubs appeared more olive-gray than green. She shuddered. The overgrown shrubs surrounding the old mansion could potentially hide a legion of assailants.

Byrd's warning spiraled a grumble of apprehension. She'd downplayed her vulnerability until she believed such didn't exist.

It jolted her to think the motorcycle attacker was likely the killer. If only she could remember anything significant about the man on the motorcycle. The night was blindingly dark on that lonely road. He wore a black helmet obscuring his face.

Her scalp, sensitive and touchy still from the stitches, reminded her she owed her life to the strangers who'd stopped to help.

I'm home. I'm safe, she thought. I shouldn't worry, should I? The old house included a warren of secret passageways, stairs and false walls where ancestors once stashed pirate's loot to avoid taxations from the three nations ruling Louisiana at different times.

She remembered the secret panel in her adjoining sitting room. Did the mechanism work still? She hurried there, removed the correct brick from the fire surround and pressed the hidden spring. The panel alongside the fireplace creaked open, revealing an indeterminate depth of darkness and a fusty odor. Emmaline stepped inside. She didn't go far. She had no light. She knew the steep passageway stairs led down to the drawing room. Other walkways led to other parts of the house. This passageway could save her life. *What a dumb thought!* She stepped into the sitting room, slid the panel closed and replaced the brick in its notch.

CHAPTER 44

Captain Mark Sessions of the Louisiana State Police Investigative Department contacted Sheriff Smith. The tense meeting did not go well. "You got that, Sheriff." The Captain, tall, fit and graying at the temples, frowned. "The guys at the top want you and your people to pull back. This is bigger than your force. Not only international but Homeland Security."

Smith didn't like being cut off from active duty. The murders happened in his jurisdiction. Solving the murders should be his baby. Now, he could kiss the information loop goodbye, as well. After the meeting, he called Saucer. "Bring my car around. We're taking another look at Beaudion's field."

"Yes sir. The coroner said the chain is the murder weapon," added Saucer.

Smith growled back to the deputy. "The coroner said a chain is *consistent* with the device used to beat Carol Powell." The chain found in Beaudion's field now rested at the crime lab for residue analysis.

The drive to Beaudion's field passed in silence. Smith hated to admit they'd missed the chain in their search of the premises. Smith and Saucer alighted. A BRPD policeman manned the crime scene. Not unusual for the Baton Rouge Police Department to provide backup. The uniform looked at the sheriff's badge, then Saucer's. He motioned them through the yellow tape. After a thorough look, the sheriff noted nothing new. Tipping his hat to the uniform, he and Saucer crossed the pasture to the car.

"Go out the highway. We're looking at the ravine where they found the victim's rental."

"Yes sir."

Nothing new turned up. Dry run. Back at the office, both men studied the BOLO board. Saucer, in the folding chair before the sheriff's desk, tried to cross his chubby legs. Giving up, he leaned sideways like a drooping lumpy statue, elephantine feet clutching the floor.

Sheriff Smith shot the red laser pointer on the chain's photograph. Why would a vagrant carry such an item? Another puzzle, the tent remains. Not just any tent, but an expensive Ripstop Nylon fabric tent with cross-woven fibers. These were manufactured for strength and for any weather extreme, rain or snow.

The 8 X 10 glossy blow-up of Carol Powell, in happier days, rested next to the after-death shots, one taken by the crime scene photographer, and another at the morgue. The pictures haunted the sheriff. "Why destroy such an attractive face?" he mused. "A beautiful girl."

"It wuz a shame," remarked Saucer, his unintelligent manner almost dull.

Smith continued, "destroying her face could indicate the killer knew her. There have been cases where a killer can't look on the face of their victim. It appears the dead person is looking back at them with horror-frozen accusation. Take away the face, take away the person."

"I get you. What do we do next?"

"We're playing a waiting game at this point." Interpol and Homeland Security. Something major was going down.

* * *

Wednesday morning

Mid-week, Emmaline made an appointment at the beauty shop. *Today is Wednesday. Byrd will arrive Friday.* She could hardly wait for Friday. Staring into the beauty shop's all-revealing mirror as the operator spiked her gelled hair into unbelievable heights, she decided to corner Byrd about their relationship. Past time. Her daring coiffure gave her courage. He'd bobbled along out of reach long enough. Time to reel him in. "I want that pair of dangly bronze earrings in your showcase," Emmaline said, pressing a $10.00 tip into the woman's hand.

"You mean those three-inch chandelier earrings?"

"The exact ones."

She left the beauty salon in high spirits. Her gut feeling told her Carol's murder would soon be solved, thanks to her. She'd found the murder weapon. The chain. True, no official confirmation from the crime lab yet, but that was simply a matter of time. She reached to pull out her cell phone and call Helen. Wouldn't hurt to learn what sort of vibes the psychic entertained about her old friend, Emmaline Beard. She'd bet they were bubbly, happy vibes.

Let it rest for the moment, she thought. Why disturb Helen? Helen and Esther were too busy to disrupt with opening night three short evenings away. She enjoyed the freedom of delegating responsibility to Esther and Helen. Should she give up the theatricals after ten years?

Etienne's murder crept into her mind. Her over-the-top happy demeanor darkened. Some devious killer bludgeoned the man to death with a hammer from a LeFevre House utility shed. Attempting to cast guilt on her. It hurt to think she had enemies of that caliber.

Could Etienne's killer have anything to do with Papa Beard, her father. Papa, a forceful man, made enemies right and left. He and Etienne clashed often when both served on the town council. Hypocritical Etienne had publicly criticized Papa for marrying his late-in-life racy brides. Emmaline didn't approve of any of the gold diggers either and made the fact known. It irked her they still were riding the gravy train with their divorce settlements. Maybe farfetched to think Etienne LeDeux's murder had anything to do with Papa. She thought all along Carol Powell's murder had no bearing on Etienne's murder. Byrd believed both murders were the work of the same killer. Byrd could be right.

* * *

She entered the house through the kitchen door.

Maizie ogled Emmaline's hairdo.

"Like it?"

"It shore is high, ain't it."

"If you say so." Emmaline snagged a cup of coffee and two beignets. "I'm going upstairs. When Esther and Helen get here, tell them, uh, I'm planning a trip." Why she said that, she didn't know. Perhaps to do with her romantic daydreams about her and Byrd on a Nile cruise.

"You ain't said nothing about any trip."

"No? Well, excuse me, you're the first to know."

"That red hair dye's done gone to your brain."

Emmaline ran upstairs laughing.

* * *

Wednesday 11:45 p.m.

Freedom from the tedious dress rehearsal. Is this burn-out? Should I continue these theatricals? What if I moved to Houston to be near Byrd? Emmaline pulled her nightgown over her head. She'd outfoxed both Esther and Helen. Even Maizie. She'd slipped out of the house earlier and ordered an oyster po-boy from Sally's Seafood and ate it as she wheeled through town, leaving rehearsals to her two friends, the buffet to Maizie.

She giggled like a schoolgirl, wrapping her arms around her upper body. The filmy silk nightgown may not be warm enough. She threw an extra blanket on her bed and slithered beneath the covers.

CHAPTER 45

3:00 a.m. Thursday morning

S omething pleasant and sweet-smelling choked Emmaline. From deep sleep, she fought smothering material clogging her nose and mouth. A nightmare? No this was happening. She clawed wildly, fighting rough hands shoving her back onto the bed. Struggling to breathe, she wrestled to sit up. A cloth fell from her face. She couldn't see an inch ahead in the dark bedroom. What happened to the nightlight? Forcefully dragged from bed, her knees collapsed, she fell to the floor. Yanked upward, she croaked, "What -?"

"Shut up. You want to live. You move along." *A man. Who?* The man, his back to her, strapped ropes about her upper body, pinning her arms to her side. Ropes tight as tourniquets. He pushed a hood over her head. The hood fabric settled on her shoulders. He shoved her along the hall tethered like an animal. Gasping for breath, dizzy and nauseous, slowly her reasoning surfaced. Chloroform, he'd used chloroform. She struggled to focus. *This isn't right.* He stopped her with a jerk, pushing her aside.

A door creaked. Shoved forward, she stumbled into a narrow passageway. The rough planking beneath her feet seemed familiar. Yes, the secret passageway in the closed section of the house. It had to be. "Where -"

"You're dead, lady, you don't shut up."

Hooded like a hanging victim bound in ropes awaiting execution, she stumbled along. A door opened. He pushed her forward. She fell. Something soft landed at her feet. The door slammed closed. Keys rattled. Next, a heavier sound like chains and padlocks. Huddled against a wall, her toes grappled the maniac's gift. A blanket. Scooting forward, she tried to lift it with her feet. Didn't work. She tried to stand. Too weak. The chloroform. She rolled onto the blanket for its warmth in the unheated room and struggled to a sitting position. She slowly worked the hood off by bracing her head against the wall behind her; she rocked her head back and forth and up and down. She stared into pitch dark. "Who -"

She'd not recognized the voice, though in the deepest recesses of her brain, it registered familiarity.

* * *

6:00 p.m. Thursday evening

Maizie wheeled the squeaky serving cart containing the last covered trays into the dining room. Through the arch to the drawing room, now transformed into a theater, she watched dress rehearsal in progress. Always exciting, the raised stage, the enchanting lights, the voluminous red, black, and gold curtains swishing mysteriously, and the rows and rows of folding chairs. Just like fairyland. Where was Emmaline? Why hadn't she come downstairs?

Maizie laid out cheeses, bleu-cheese stuffed olives, radish roses, and Creole deviled eggs. Next, a huge platter of hot crab balls. Another platter of shrimp tempura.

"Ain't you a honey." Saucer loaded crab balls onto a paper plate.

"Ain't you something, too," grumbled Maizie. He should wait for the others. She wanted to swat his greedy hands, but he was the law.

Face red with worry, Esther barged into the dining room. "Have you heard from her?"

"No, I ain't," Maizie said. She stacked the trays back onto the cart. "Would you mind to help me get them plates off the kitchen table? Emmaline don't like paper plates."

"In a minute," Esther said, "I need to see Helen first." She rushed out.

Sheriff Smith sauntered into the dining room, handsome in his ripper garb, a cape and top hat, he poured a cup of coffee from the urn on the sideboard. "When did you see Emmaline last?"

"Yesterday evening. She'd come home from the beauty shop. Her hair all stiff and pointy." Maizie didn't mention the new earrings hanging nearly to Emmaline's shoulders.

"How did she seem?"

Maizie thought a moment. "Real sassy."

"Sassy, huh."

"Yeah. She didn't eat dinner. After I got through over here, I went out to my apartment to watch television."

"Did she leave the house later?"

"I don't know. Like I said, I watched television 'til late. Fell asleep on the couch."

"Did she seem upset or mysterious? You know, like going off on one of her sleuthing sprees?"

Maizie thought a moment. "Oddest thing. She was real happy. Said she was taking a trip."

"A trip?"

"Uh huh. She said it joking like. But, she musta gone somewhere."

"Her car is here." Smith had checked the garage.

"Somebody coulda come got her," Maizie said vaguely, worry lines beginning to crease her forehead.

"Do you mind going upstairs and check if any clothing is missing. Things she'd take on a trip."

Esther bustled into the dining room on the cusp of the conversation. "How could Emmaline leave tonight? Final dress rehearsal." She fisted her hands. "The height of inconsideration. Anyway, the show must go on," she said in her

229

brisk manner. "Everyone is here." She glanced at the generous spread on the snowy linen. "I'll announce the buffet is ready. We'll eat and then get right to rehearsal. Exciting, isn't it?"

Maizie rolled the cart into the kitchen and started up the stairs.

Smith followed, waited until Maizie was out of sight before putting in a call to Byrd Jeffcoat in Houston. "Sheriff Smith here. Have you heard from Emmaline?" Byrd had not. The moment he disconnected, Maizie clumped down the steep servants' stairs into the kitchen.

"Well, what's missing?"

"Nothing. Least ways nothing I saw. Funniest thing, she mighta took the blanket off her bed. It's gone."

CHAPTER 46

Thursday 7:30 p.m.

Emmaline shuddered in the dark. Her shoulders throbbed from the unnatural strain of her arms tied behind her back. She'd moved her fingers constantly to keep them from going numb. Her wrists chafed from the tight ropes. Likely, her wrists bled from struggling to free herself.

Where was she? She knew her location instinctively in her heart. The priest hole - the narrow windowless chamber in the heart of the older, sealed section of Beard House. Why was she here? Who had she threatened?

With no true idea of time, she wondered if it was now the following morning? Surely, rehearsal was over. Something skittered across the floor. She screamed. Who could hear? A childhood memory of the priest hole played into her imagination. She'd told Papa a lie. She couldn't recall the lie. Time had erased it. Papa warned her, "Lie to me again and I'll put you in the priest hole. When you're very sorry, I'll come for you." He'd laughed. "If the pirates don't get you first. They sneak from their pirogues into the house like ghosts."

Thank goodness there were no pirates today slipping through uncharted swampy bayous from Barataria Bay to elude New Orleans custom officials. No, she thought, resting her head against the rough wall. Pirates looted during the long ago past. Today's threat loomed much more terrifying—a killer or killers. Killers who wanted her out of the way. Wanted her silenced so severely they'd drugged her in the dead of night, kidnapped her and forced her into this hell hole. It had to do with the two murders. Why hadn't they killed her? What did the kidnapper want of her?

CHAPTER 47

Houston, Texas
7:00 p.m.

Byrd threw clothes into a bag, made a quick call next door to Vi. "I'll be out of town a couple days."

"Where are you going?" Leave it to Vi to ask questions. Questions he hadn't time or inclination to answer.

"Promised Emmaline I'd be there for her play's final dress rehearsal."

"It's past seven now. Rehearsal should be long over if you're driving. It's over two hundred and fifty miles to Ville Nouvelle. Are you flying?" She rattled on before he had a chance to reply. "I wouldn't advise flying. It's stormy. You know that Korean airliner crashed. Officials blamed it on a storm."

"I'm aware of the plane crash you refer to, Vi." He rolled his eyes, though Vi wasn't present to see. "I'm driving. The last rehearsal before opening night goes on until all hours."

"What about the glue convention? You said you couldn't come to dinner tomorrow night because you are expected at the expo. You said you didn't want to impose on Professor Dang."

"I know. I squared it with Dang. Gotta run, Vi. Love you." He clicked off before Vi delved into her litany of reasons he shouldn't pursue a life of his own. He wondered for the hundredth time if it was possible to enroll his sister on an online dating site without her knowledge. Just let the prospects start popping up on her computer. He would post a picture of Kim Novak. He'd always thought Kim Novak was a honey.

The CD player droned Willie Nelson's "On the Road again" as Byrd headed to U S 190 W. He hated I-10 traffic and its stream of eighteen wheelers.

Mist shrouded the windshield. Byrd flicked on the windshield wipers. Their quiet clacking annoyed him, made him fear for Emmaline's safety. She'd never take a trip during final rehearsal or opening night. Facing an approximate four-hour drive, he said a prayer for Emmaline's safety. God forbid the killer had murdered her.

CHAPTER 48

Rehearsal

Sheriff Smith swirled the cape and faltered. What lines came next? He never forgot lines.

Esther hissed from the left stage wing. "My pretty, my pretty..." she coached.

He nodded. "Right. My pretty. My pretty pet. Out late, are you, dearie. A wee glass and a ride in my carriage?"

"Cut." Esther again. "Take five. Wardrobe malfunction. Over here, Miss Favor."

Smith hurried to the dining room and fished a bottle of water from the cooler's icy sludge. Esther would take forever adjusting Dolores Favor's sexy costume. Dolores, a well-built woman, proved to have a sharp eye. Smith, trained to observe body language, marked keen caution in the stripper, the way she surveyed her surroundings, and studied her fellow actors. At one point, her Bourbon Street slang slipped. A cultured tone emerged, quickly addressed. Not off the charts for someone wishing to run from their past to take up a new identity in New Orleans' sleazy strip joints.

All the world's a stage. Shakespeare got it right. What do we really know about one another, he mused, especially as we are able to mask true personalities and project false personalities?

Emmaline Beard, he believed he understood. Slightly overbearing, in-your-face mentality, nosy, and at times wistfully vulnerable. This trip did not fit her. In the years he'd lived in Ville Nouvelle, he could recall only one trip the woman took - a Caribbean cruise. A three-day cruise at that. If not a trip, where was she?

She fancied herself a detective. To detect, it stood to reason she'd leave the house. Maizie couldn't recall if Emmaline had left the house. Smith put in a call to the department. "Need information on Emmaline Beard's movements today. Check gas stations, beauty shops, restaurants, the movie." Ville Nouvelle had one movie house. "Get back to me ASAP." He disconnected, wondering if she had run into the Ville Nouvelle murderer.

CHAPTER 49

The Priest Hole

Emmaline choked trying to swallow thick saliva. Her mouth parched, she craved water. How long since she had even a sip of water? Days it seemed, her fantasies running wild. Would she starve to death in this bleak pit of a room? She longed to cry. She refused. Tearful emotions solved nothing.

The kidnapper had left her alive for a reason. If the monster had a reason, he would return. Return at his convenience, not hers. He left a blanket. That proved some humanity. If he planned to kill her, would he consider her physical condition in the cold priest hole? Likely not.

Exhausted, she closed her eyes. Eyes open or closed made no difference in the inky blackness, except with her eyes closed, her imagination visualized light. Blazing lights of every hue like those at her theatricals. Her eyes snapped open. The theatrical. Was dress rehearsal over? Had Maizie declared her missing? She could kick herself for the silly comment, *maybe I'll take a trip.* What a stupid thing to say. Had pragmatic Maizie believed her?

She dozed.

The door rattled. Emmaline's eyes sprang open. A scrim of light appeared at the foot of the door. Her heart raced. She held her breath. The light disappeared the moment the door creaked open. "Who -?" *Let it be Maizie,* she prayed. *Let it be Maizie. Let it be Maizie.*

"Game over." The man's voice. "Where are the pearls? If you lie to stall me, you're dead."

That's what this is about. "I can't talk -" Her throat shut down. "Water -"

A plastic bottle hit her in the stomach. "Please . . . my hands . . . open it."

Without a word, her assailant moved behind her, catlike, and loosened the ropes. Before she could stretch her frozen muscles, he whipped her arms in front of her and clamped tight handcuffs around her wrists. Emmaline's fingers detected the top of the water bottle; she got the cap off and drank deeply. She began to tremble uncontrollably. How could he see her in the dark? Was this a real person or a manifestation of a ghost or spirit? Perhaps the evil spirits of pirates occupied this hole still.

"How can you see me?"

He snorted. "You wonder am I flesh and blood. Scientific data exists that proves the gifted among us see with our brains as well as our eyes. I'm a synesthete." He seemed pleased to claim himself gifted.

His voice lowered dangerously. "The pearls."

"I don't have them." She fumbled screwing the water bottle cap in place. She dared not waste a precious drop. "I turned them over to our Sheriff Smith. They're evidence in Carol Powell's murder."

"You're lying."

"It's the truth. Believe me."

"Once more. Where are the pearls?"

"Sheriff Smith has them."

A blow struck her across the forehead.

CHAPTER 50

9:30 p.m.

Esther wanted a run of the play's final scene when Sheriff Smith's cell phone pinged. "Police business," he said, stepping off stage and into the dining room for privacy. "What you got?" he asked the deputy.

The deputy reported Emmaline's earlier movements of the day. "Sir, she did leave the house later. Got gasoline, ordered food from Sally's Seafood. A neighbor saw her return home about 4:45 p.m."

"No evidence she left after 4:45 p.m.?"

"No, Sir."

"Did this neighbor see a car, a taxi, later at the house?"

"No, Sir. This person, an older lady (the deputy gave the neighbor's name and address to the sheriff) is pretty interested in the goings on at Miss Beard's place. She recognizes whose cars come and go."

Smith punched the phone off, well acquainted with the nosy neighbor scenario. He motioned for Saucer. "An informant confirmed Emmaline arrived home and did not leave afterwards." Which meant to Smith Emmaline Beard must be somewhere in the house. Which meant she purposely hid to avoid rehearsal, or she was unable to attend. Both possibilities seemed farfetched but demanded answers. "How well do you know this house?" he asked Saucer, thinking about the unused wing.

"I know it a little. Why?"

"Go through the house, the unused part, too. Look for forced entry, trap doors, anything out of the ordinary. I'll make excuses for you to Miss Marshall."

"Yes, sir. Gotcha."

Smith returned to rehearsal, dozens of questions swirling through his brain.

CHAPTER 51

Priest Hole

Emmaline lifted her cuffed hands to the blood oozing from the blow to her head. How deep was the gash? She staunched the blood with a corner of the blanket. The total darkness threatened her sanity. She'd read somewhere a person could go insane in long periods of darkness. Thank God the monster had left. The gifted monster capable of seeing in the dark. The monster who threatened to kill her. Where had he gone? To search for the pearls? Perfect opportunity to plunder the house if rehearsal wasn't over and everyone invested in the play.

She tried to think logically. Could she escape this person? The person wanted the pearls. She was targeted because the monster knew Carol passed the pearls to her. Who knew about the stolen pearls? Gary West, his criminal accomplices in Papeete, Josephine Powell, and Charlie Powell. Josephine, though slightly unhinged, was no thief. Charlie, Carol's father, however - Emmaline was not certain about him.

Was Gary West, Carol Powell's fiancé, the monster who abducted her? She tried to recall the sound of West's voice the morning he had appeared at her house. Her memory cloudy, she couldn't remember. She shuddered.

The authorities reported Gary West had left the area for California. Likely, he'd never left Ville Nouvelle. Gary West must be the monster holding her in darkness. But, why wait this long to come for the pearls? It made no sense. The pearl theft had been hush-hush. Only one brief quote in the Courier, the local weekly newspaper. Interpol and Homeland Security had shut down publicity.

Was West the motorcycle riding maniac who'd attacked her that night on the lonely road?

Where had he hidden until now? There were hundreds of places in the swampy wilderness around Ville Nouvelle.

Her head ached. Surely, someone would realize she'd never miss a final dress rehearsal. She regretted delegating much of the theatrical's grunt work to Esther and Helen. She'd done so because of her distraction with the murders. Why had she made those foolish remarks about a trip? Horror rippled through her. West wouldn't find the pearls. The pearls were with the authorities. Would West return and kill her? Sick realization dawned then. Of course, he wouldn't return. No reason to return. The Priest Hole would do its work for him. She was as good as dead, locked away in the pits of the house in this soundproof chamber. She screamed and screamed until her throat and voice betrayed her.

CHAPTER 52

10:30 p.m.

After rehearsal, Helen approached the sheriff. "I don't feel right about Emmaline's absence," she said. "I don't believe she's taken a trip."

Smith wondered if she'd consulted her crystal ball or whatever gadget psychics used. Right now, he could use help, other worldly or not. "Where do you think she is?"

Helen answered immediately. "She isn't far. She's desperate. That's the message I received. That and darkness."

"Darkness?" He gestured toward the window. "You mean like night?"

"No. Not a dark night. A soul darkness." Tears formed in the corners of Helen's eyes. "I can't talk about it any longer. The impressions are desperately oppressive. Like death." She pulled her cloak around her shoulders. "I'm going now. I promised Esther I'd stay at her place tonight. She wants to discuss last minute adjustments to the play. Call me if you hear anything from Emmaline." She fished a business card from her handbag and handed it to the sheriff.

He nodded.

Maizie came into the dining room. She'd pulled off her frilly serving apron and now sported a shapeless old sweater. "I'm going out to my apartment. If you hear anything from Emmaline, let me know. I'm real worried. This ain't like her. She ain't gone on no trip, neither."

"Can you remember anything else she said?"

Maizie's wrinkled forehead creased deeper. "No. I told you everything. It wasn't like she was telling me for sure about a trip. She was laughing, like it was a joke."

"I'll let you know if we hear anything," he promised.

"Yeah. I ain't gonna sleep a wink `til I hear something."

While Saucer searched the house, Sheriff Smith searched the grounds. The area designated as the front yard ran approximately seventy-five yards from the street. Huge azalea bushes surrounded the entire front gallery. Smaller plantings outlined the larger azaleas. The property to the east of the house abutted a side street - the side street where the elderly woman neighbor had observed Emmaline returning home. The Beard House driveway led to the garage off this same side street. A large paved parking area surrounded the garage.

Above the garage, Maizie's apartment. Her apartment was now well lit. The housekeeper had returned home. Smith checked the area behind the garage, mostly given over to overgrown cane. Anything could hide in the thick cane patch.

To the west of the garage, the larger section of lawn ran into several acres. A pool with palm trees, a gazebo, a rose garden, and some sort of outdoor terrace. Farther west, this lawn sloped down toward a natural drainage stream leading to a swampy area with tall trees. Everything seemed in order, though it appeared this western-facing formal lawn and its facilities were seldom used. Neglect hung over it.

He looked back at the sealed part of the old mansion which faced this western lawn. Years past, guests would spill out from the house and enjoy these pleasant acres. Not now, though. Must cost a fortune to keep all this up. All in all, Beard House had enjoyed better days, he thought, turning toward the sealed wing of the house. He checked the main doors. The locks were in place and secured. Some ragged wisteria vines needing trimming hung over one door. *Isn't that odd.* Bending over, he trained his flashlight onto the ground beside the brick walkway. Tracks. Looked for the world like motorcycle tracks—recent motorcycle tracks.

CHAPTER 53

As the sheriff observed the tracks, *someone* approached. Tensing, he slipped behind a massive shrub. A woman! "Stop," he ordered. "Who are you and what do you want?"

She moved forward. "I said to stop. Stop or you'll catch a bullet."

The woman, in his field of vision, surprised him. Dolores Favor. He holstered his gun. "What are you doing out here?"

"I could ask you the same thing," she drawled, propping her hands on her hips. "Ain't you the top dog, pulling guns on people?"

In no mood to play games, he barked, "What are you doing out here?"

"If it's so important to you, I lost a valuable earring. Me and Misty took a walk earlier, you know, looking at how the other one percent lives." She gestured toward the pool, the gazebo and outdoor terrace. "They need to cut the grass if you ask me. Am I being detained, or can I go?"

"You can go."

She turned and said over her shoulder, "if you find a gold earring, it's mine."

He motioned her off. Wondering how she'd arrived, he followed her to the side street. Her older model car stood parked farther down the dark street. Something about Dolores Favor bothered him, and it wasn't her hot body in skimpy hooker's clothing.

"Sheriff Smith. Sheriff Smith, where are you?"

"Saucer, that you?" The out-of-breath deputy plowed into Smith as the sheriff returned to the house.

"You ain't gonna believe this, sheriff. While we was rehearsing, somebody tore up Miss Beard's bedroom. I mean tore it up good."

They rushed upstairs. Saucer had told the truth. An antique armoire lay overturned on the floor, its contents thrown over the room. The bed, its mattress and box springs lay on the floor, the ticking slashed. Curtains pulled down and shredded. Every bureau drawer dumped on the floor. The closet ransacked - Emmaline's clothing ripped and tossed about. The adjoining bathroom and sitting room were in similar destructive disarray. Even the light fixtures were smashed.

"Looks like a maniac had a field day, huh," said Saucer.

"No. It appears someone searched for something, and they didn't find it."

Every upstairs room showed the same wanton damage. Smith put in a call for the crime photographer and fingerprint specialists. He couldn't afford to wait.

The perpetrator had worked earlier, while they were all busy with the rehearsal. That person likely remained in the house somewhere. Anywhere he or she wished to be, he thought, recalling the many unused rooms in the sealed wing. His thoughts zoomed to the motorcycle tracks and the cane patch maze. He radioed headquarters. "Get some deputies to Beard House immediately. Search the premises. Thorough search of the cane growth behind the garage."

Now to wait. If his hunch was right, the prowler's next target: the downstairs. He wouldn't allow the person that luxury.

CHAPTER 54

Priest Hole

A key rasped in the lock. Chains rattled. Emmaline sat up. The monster! He'd come to finish her off.

"Wake up, bitch!"

"I'm awake." She couldn't believe she had a voice after her screaming fit. She felt his hands plundering along the blanket. What was he doing?

"Stand up."

"I'm - I'm trying." Her equilibrium berserk in the darkness, she fell back against the wall.

He flashed light in her face. She screamed in horror. Then realized he'd pulled on the hood he'd forced her to wear earlier. Only now, it had eye slits.

"Your last chance to live. You take me to the pearls. I let you live."

"But -"

"Get moving." He shoved her toward the priest hole door.

"Okay, you win." She'd do anything to get out of this hell hole - say anything - promise anything." If she could get downstairs by some miracle, maybe she could get away from him. If not, she'd rather die there than in this darkness. If only some of the others had stayed on after rehearsal. "I will need to get to my Papa's safe," she said. "He had several. I don't know which one ... my – er - accomplice used. He said -"

"Shut up. No talking."

She led the hooded figure to Papa Beard's bedroom. The room Byrd occupied when in town. It was destroyed. She tried to not show surprise. "I must try to remember the combination." She fumbled with the dial. "Wrong," she whispered. "I always get it wrong."

Hood man pushed an automatic pistol in her side. "Get it right," he warned.

The clock on Papa Beard's bureau pointed to eleven forty-five p.m. Her heart sank. Esther and the others would be gone. Even Maizie, already in her apartment. Her fingers trembled. "I think I have it." She started the combination rotation. She opened the safe. No pearls, of course.

"Somebody in there?"

Emmaline's heart stopped. Sounded like Deputy Fontenot. She longed to cry out. The gun gouged her back, forced her into the closet across the room. Her kidnapper squeezed in with her and closed the door.

Heavy footsteps padded around the bedroom, then left, leaving the door open. Her heart sang. Saucer was in the house. Oh, God, maybe other policemen, too. Maybe Sheriff Smith. She thought fast. She'd take as long with the safes as Hood man's patience held. She led the way to Papa Beard's former office down the hall.

CHAPTER 55

12:30 a.m.

Byrd pulled into the Beard House driveway, cut the lights and noticed the squad car, parked in the dark, beside the garage. What was going on? Lights burned in Maizie's upstairs apartment. Should he alert her? No. Best to go on to the house. See who was there. He eased to the door off the kitchen, fished the key out of his pocket and let himself inside. He reached to switch on the lights, when an iron grip caught his shoulder. "Who are you?"

"Uh," he spluttered, "Byrd. Byrd Jeffcoat. Who are you?"

"Keep it down," Sheriff Smith said. "I'm the sheriff. We can't risk a light. I think the killer is in the house." Heavy treads sounded overhead.

"Who's bungling around upstairs?" Byrd asked.

"Saucer. He'd searching up there. I'm banking on him to flush out the bad guy."

"And Emmaline?"

"Not sure yet."

"That's not good."

"Matter of time," replied Smith.

Minutes later, Saucer clomped downstairs. "Upstairs is clean," he announced to the sheriff, "Nothing going on up there."

"Keep it down," warned the sheriff. "If someone is in the house, best to keep them wondering about our number and location."

"Yeah. Sure, Sir. Who's that beside you?"

"Byrd Jeffcoat," answered Byrd.

"Yeah. You're gonna love the play," whispered Saucer to Byrd. "It's really good. We went through all of it tonight. Do I smell coffee?"

"The urn in the dining room." Smith, exasperation in his voice, warned again, "No talking."

"Oh, yeah," Saucer whispered in a stage whisper that could be heard to the street.

"Sssh," ordered Smith. "Someone is coming downstairs."

"Stay here," Smith said to Saucer. "Guard the backdoor. Let no one leave."

Smith eased into the butler's pantry, Byrd behind him.

Dim sconce lights along the main hall showed two individuals moving toward the library. Byrd squelched a gasp. He thought he saw a headless horseman, but realized it was a man wearing a black hood. Emmaline, her hands cuffed, walked ahead toward the library. Sheriff Smith motioned Byrd to stay back. Byrd eased into the dining room as Smith maneuvered up the hall.

The library door closed behind the hooded man and Emmaline. After a few minutes, Smith eased the library door open. A hail of gunfire erupted.

What happened next happened fast. A man ran from the library, half dragging Emmaline. She was alive, thank God. Without thinking, Byrd grabbed the coffee urn off the buffet table and threw it in the man's face. He screamed and fell. Emmaline ran toward the front door. The man writhed and screamed, rolling on the floor.

Smith switched on the lights and grimaced at the scalded man on the floor. "Thanks Byrd. Thought I was hit, but his fire went wild." He cuffed the man.

Saucer rushed in. "Who was shooting?"

"Call backup and call an ambulance. We have a wounded suspect."

"Gotcha. I mean, yes sir."

CHAPTER 56

Friday 3:00 a.m.

Byrd drove Emmaline to the ER. After a thorough checkup and stitches in the gash on her forehead, the doctor released her. They returned to Beard House. Maizie met them, grabbing Emmaline in a bear hug.

"You really want to stay here the rest of the night after everything that's happened?" he asked her.

"What do you suggest?" she grunted, slumping into a kitchen chair.

"How about Maizie's apartment? You don't want to see your room."

"Yeah," Maizie piped up. "I insist. I have a guest room, you know."

"I'll think about it," promised Emmaline. "Now, I'm starving. I want something to eat."

Maizie went to the fridge and rustled up a plate of crab balls and leftover shrimp from the earlier buffet. She poured a glass of milk.

"Delicious," groaned Emmaline. Food had never tasted so good in her life. Especially now that she had a life. "He planned to kill me," she said.

"Don't talk about it now," Byrd said. "You're still in shock." After she finished eating, he helped her up the stairs to Maizie's apartment. Once she was tucked in bed wearing one of Maizie's granny gowns, he bent over and kissed her on the lips. "I'm glad you're alive," he said and meant it.

* * *

Friday 6:00 p.m.

The standing room only crowd gathered for *On Whitechapel Road*. Alvin Jamerson, the historical society president, officiated as freelance announcer. "Ladies and gentlemen," he began in his authoritative voice, "We're beyond pleased to offer this, the tenth theatrical, presented by Miss Emmaline Beard. Miss Beard's devotion to our community is highly valued. Not only for her cultural contribution, but for good old-fashioned entertainment." Thunderous applause sounded.

Mr. Jamerson waited a few minutes, then held up his hand. "Sit back and enjoy *On Whitechapel Road*. He gestured to the balcony. "Ladies and gentlemen, Miss Emmaline Beard."

Emmaline stood, beaming down at the audience. More applause. She blew a kiss as the lights dimmed, the music started, and the curtains billowed to open. But not before she spotted Jimmy and Tammy Rogers in the audience. She blew a special kiss to them. They knew why.

Two dozen red roses arrived earlier. The card read: *Not as lovely as the ones I weeded, but they'll do. Break a leg. Dante and Shemika Washington.*

Emmaline sighed, one of the roses in her lapel.

Sheriff Smith promised to fill her in about the hooded captor after the performance. She could hardly wait. He was evil she knew that.

Helen eased beside her on the balcony. She squeezed Emmaline's hand. "I'm thankful you're all right. I knew you were in mortal danger. I didn't know exactly how or where. The messages are like that, elusive and mysterious. I want you to know your aura now is sunshine and roses."

"Thank you. Are you staying after the performance?"

"No. It's far past time I left for home. Mother is calling every day. I stayed this long because of Etienne's murder. For Julie, to give her support. Can you believe that man killed Etienne for burning his campsite?"

"Yes, I can believe it," Emmaline said, recalling the horror in the priest room.

"Who was he, really?" asked Helen. 'I know his name, Dan Flippo, but it means nothing."

"I don't know everything. Sheriff Smith plans to tell me all about it. He was Daniel Flippo, the ponytail guy I kept mistaking for Gary West. He was one of the pearl thieves. He entrusted the pearls to West to get them to the states. Carol Powell took them without West knowing. Flippo found out about the switch, followed both Carol and Gary here. He murdered Carol, when she wouldn't tell him where the pearls were. When West learned what happened to Carol, he fled to California. I understand he's in custody there."

"Justice," I suppose," Helen said, "but it will never bring Etienne back. Or Miss Powell."

"No," Emmaline said.

"I must run," whispered Helen, standing, "I have a taxi waiting."

"Goodbye old friend." After a short embrace, Helen slipped away.

CHAPTER 57

After the performance, Emmaline went to her room. Her heart swelled as she surveyed the neat clean bedroom, thanks to Pastor Lemuel's boys. Not strong enough to greet her audience, Sheriff Smith filled in for her. She gave permission for only one person to visit after the performance, Pastor Nairn Lemuel. She heard his knock.

"Come in."

He entered her sitting room and grasped her hand. "I congratulate you on a wonderful play," he said. He smiled sheepishly. "I confess when I first heard the play subject, I was disappointed in your choice."

"I thought you would be," she said.

"However," he continued, "your play depicted evil realistically and brought home warnings to us. We must be vigilant and watchful to combat evil around us. For it's there."

"It is," she agreed.

"Also," he said, "I appreciate your support of my boys for giving them gainful employment. Most of them need the salary. Helping your productions gives them a sense of purpose and the knowledge that even though they've made mistakes in the past, mankind is often ready with a helping hand."

"You're very kind," she said, "and I appreciate the boys' hard work getting my house back in order after the killer ransacked it looking for the pearls."

"I heard about those priceless pearls," he said, "where they as magnificent as rumor says?"

"That and more. They will be returned to the Tahiti Pearl Museum."

"Your roses are beautiful," the pastor said, turning to leave.

"A gift from Dante and his wife. She's recovering nicely."

"For that, I'm grateful. Dante loves his hometown despite his phenomenal success. I'm proud to have had him at the Boy's Ranch. He wanted no charges filed against the boys other than juvenile correction. He offered great help with the nuclear protest march, too."

"The nuclear dump site is off the table?" she asked.

"Yes."

CHAPTER 58

Friday 11:30 p.m.

Once the theatrical crowd departed, Emmaline summoned Byrd. "I feel like going down to the library. This has been a momentous evening, and I don't want to end it alone. Tell the others to join us. Maizie has whipped up some late-night treats.

You're not too tired for this meeting?" he asked.

"Absolutely not. What are friends for?"

She met them in the library, Esther, Sheriff Smith, Saucer, and Kimberley. Maizie's array of sumptuous finger foods, a delight. "I want you to stay, too," she said to Maizie.

Chatter swept around the room about the play's success. In the midst of the small talk, a sense of curiosity remained.

"Sheriff Smith," said Emmaline, "tell us everything that happened. I'm sure we all want to hear the full story."

A chorus of we do, we do, sounded.

Sheriff Smith stood. "First off, I want to divulge a secret. With your permission, may I call in two secret persons?"

Emmaline clapped her hands. "Secret persons? Delightful. Show us these secret persons."

"Ladies," he called.

Dolores Favor and Misty Shores entered the library. "May I present Miss Dolores and Miss Misty, undercover detectives with the Louisiana State Police.

"What?" screeched Emmaline, before she broke out into a horse laugh. "Not really."

"Yes, really," confirmed the twosome.

"You can thank Dolores and Misty for trailing Daniel Flippo here and keeping him under constant surveillance. It was a dangerous job."

Emmaline laughed. "You're not strippers?"

"Not exclusively. We're out of here now our cover is blown," Dolores said.

Once the two women left the room, Sheriff Smith continued. "There isn't much more to tell. Flippo is a hardened criminal with a long record. Gary West got in over his head with the lure of big money. He wasn't one of the original pearl thieves, but he knew about the heist and had met Flippo before. Flippo set him up as a courier. I'm sure Flippo meant to kill Gary, too, once he'd served his purpose."

"That explains Filipino," interrupted Byrd.

"Filipino?" questioned Smith.

"A guy I met on the beach in Papeete. He mentioned one of Gary West's friends. Couldn't recall the guy's name. Said it sounded like Filipino. Filipino. Flippo. Get it?"

They all laughed.

EPILOGUE

That evening, the balmy weather held . . . a good omen for the first *Whitechapel Road* theatrical production. Helen Condor had telephoned earlier and was to meet Emmaline to go over the million last minute details.

"How do I look, Byrd?" Emmaline asked as she prepared to leave the house. She was dressed especially nice for the play in a black dress and striking silver jewelry. She wore an emerald pendant.

"Smashing," he said and meant it.

Smith would cinch his favor with Emmaline as he made his Jack the Ripper debut in the *Whitechapel* play. The man had a great sense which side of his thespian bread needed buttering and when.

Byrd left the house shortly before eight, taking the long way around to avoid the protesters.

Arriving at Jardinière Drive, he squeezed the ATV into a tiny parking spot and hurried the two blocks to the house. He couldn't believe the crowds. What had happened?

He slipped backstage and found Emmaline setting the fuses on smudge pots.

"What's going on? I can't believe the full house."

"Isn't it wonderful? We can thank Dante."

"Dante?"

"Yes. He advertised the theatrical over his sound system all day. I can't believe the turnout. I'll make it up to him some way."

"Is Smith here?" Byrd asked, changing the subject.

"Yes. He's dressing. Why?"

"He telephoned. Linda's coroner's report is in. He's offered for us to take a look."

"How perfectly marvelous," she said.

Byrd slipped into the main hall and took a seat on the back row. He caught a glimpse of Lanky from the Boy's Ranch on the landing, manning the lights. Spectacular lighting, too, he admitted grudgingly. The performance started. For all the press, Lt. Smith's portrayal of the ripper seemed stilted and awkward.

Byrd knew the production ran for three performances, Saturday evening, Sunday afternoon matinee, and Sunday evening. If it became a hit (usually her productions weren't hits) the play ran as many weekends afterwards as enough tickets sold.

He left Emmaline to rest.

www.ingramcontent.com/pod-product-compliance
Lightning Source LLC
Chambersburg PA
CBHW020316200626
46814CB00006BA/2275